SWEET HEARTS

Connie Shelton

SWEET

HEARTS

The Fourth Samantha Sweet Mystery

Connie Shelton

Secret Staircase Books

Sweet Hearts
Published by Secret Staircase Books, an imprint of
Columbine Publishing Group
PO Box 416, Angel Fire, NM 87710

This book is a work of fiction. Names, characters, places and
incidents are either the product of the author's imagination or are
used fictitiously. Any resemblance to actual events or locales or
persons, living or dead, is entirely coincidental.

Book layout and design by Secret Staircase Books
Cover illustration © Myszka Brudnicka
Cover cupcake design © Basheeradesigns

Publisher's Cataloging-in-Publication Data

Shelton, Connie
Sweet hearts / by Connie Shelton.
p. cm.
ISBN 978-1945422195 (paperback)

1. Samantha Sweet (Fictitious character)--Fiction. 2. Taos, New
Mexico—Fiction. 3. Paranormal artifacts—Fiction. 4. Bakery—
Fiction. 5. Women sleuths—Fiction. 6. Valentine stories. I. Title

Samantha Sweet Mystery Series : Book 4.
Shelton, Connie, Samantha Sweet mysteries.

BISAC : FICTION / Mystery & Detective / Cozy.

813/.54

For Dan, always my partner and my inspiration.
Each year gets better and better.

Chapter 1

Cold sunlight glittered on the frosted stalks of dead carnations and gladioli that rested against Iris Cardwell's headstone. Samantha Sweet took a deep breath against the tears that wanted to clog her throat. She reached for Beau's gloved hand. He gave a squeeze.

"It's been a month but I still haven't quite accepted it," she said. Sam's experiences with the healing touch she'd acquired from a local *bruja* worked wonders in some cases but none of her efforts, it seemed, had been quite good enough this time.

"She had good doctors and they tried. That second stroke was just too much." He blinked hard and Sam, noticing, stared at the ground.

Beau pulled her hand upward and kissed her fingers through her purple woolen mitten.

"I should bring some bags out here and clear away the flowers," he said.

"They look sad."

"Mama had a good, long life. She held on for a long time after Dad . . ."

She sniffed and nodded, letting the silence settle into a comfortable one.

Beau blew out a white cloud of warm breath. "Well, darlin', it's Monday morning and I gotta be at my desk pretty soon."

He placed a gentle hand at her back and guided her toward his department cruiser parked at the edge of the small cemetery.

Me, too, Sam thought. Although it was barely daylight, she was already late to open the bakery but she'd been unable to refuse Beau's wish to stop by his mother's gravesite after he'd spent a night of restless dreams. Her own thoughts were filled with plans for their upcoming wedding.

* * *

At Sweet's Sweets, Sam's assistants were busy and the kitchen felt toasty warm and redolent with the spicy smell of apple-cinnamon scones and her nutmeg-laced crumb cake. Sam picked up the design sketches for her wedding cake. The three tiers would be iced in pale ivory buttercream with just a hint of rose, a champagne tone that she would match exactly to her dress. Mauve roses, stargazer lilies, and clusters of sugar daisies would form a thick bouquet on top, then trail down the tiers between swags of traditional bunting and delicate piping.

"It's going to be fantastic, Mom." Her daughter Kelly stared over Sam's shoulder.

"A year ago, I would have never imagined marrying Beau

Cardwell." He, the county sheriff who could be posing for sexy men's cologne ads, and she the pudgy baker who'd met him while on her other job, breaking into a house.

"But you are. And Valentine's Day is the perfect time."

Sam looked back at the sketches. "This is way too much cake for such a small gathering. And I was thinking of doing a groom's cake for Beau, as well. Maybe a law enforcement theme, or, I don't know, perhaps something whimsical with his ranch animals on it."

Kelly smiled, no doubt imagining the two dogs cavorting over the top of a chocolate cake, Beau's favorite. "Well, you've got only a week to decide."

One week. Her stomach fluttered.

Sam scanned the kitchen, trying to fix her mind around the crazy amount of work this Valentine week. Her stainless steel worktable was covered with heart-shaped cakes on turntables, awaiting decorations. She'd become so adept at piping out freeform hearts that she could do them in her sleep. Her assistant, Becky Harper, stood at the far end with a fat pastry bag in hand, looping rose petals onto a waxed paper square on top of a flower nail nearly as quickly as Sam could do it herself. A tray of the finished flowers—red, white and pink—sat on the table, and as Becky filled each one she carried it to the large walk-in fridge so the flowers could properly set up. Sam would need them for replacement cakes and cupcakes, which had been practically flying out of the display cases all week.

"We went to the cemetery this morning," she said in a low voice.

Kelly bit at her lip. "I really miss her, Mom." She had worked for Beau as caregiver to his aging mother until a stroke in December put Iris into the hospital then in a nursing home. Kelly quickly found employment at Puppy Chic, the dog grooming shop next to the bakery, and the hours were reasonable enough that she often went by the home during the holidays and stayed with Iris through the evenings, reading books to a group of the elderly inhabitants. Until that second stroke.

Sam slid her arm around Kelly's shoulders and planted a kiss on the top of her brown curls.

"I better get going," Kelly said. "Riki's got a full house this morning." She gave her mother a quick hug before heading toward the back door.

Meanwhile, Sam had her hands full with wedding plans. The thought of her parents and sister coming from Cottonville, Texas here to Taos, spending time with Beau whom they'd only met once, less than a month ago, and all the little details of the wedding in the parlor at her best friend's bed and breakfast—it was all beginning to make Sam's head hurt.

She set the sketches back on her desk and picked up a pastry bag full of hot pink icing. With a number 32 decorating tip, she began piping a shell border on one of the heart cakes. The squeeze-relax rhythm of the work put Sam into the place she liked best, the world of creating beautiful objects from butter and sugar. Minutes passed and her mind settled. She switched tips and added string work to a couple of the cakes, then retrieved a tray of roses from the fridge and began setting them in place. A few leaves, her neat lettering proclaiming Happy Valentine's Day, and she soon had six cakes ready for the displays out front.

She balanced one cake on each hand and headed for the sales area where a customer was picking up a box of cupcakes she'd just purchased.

"Here, Jen, can you grab one of these?"

Her assistant turned from the register and reached for the cake, sliding the glass door of the case open with her free hand.

"I'd swear that they get prettier all the time," Jen said.

It was a little hard to come up with brand-new ideas when the standard Valentine colors of pink and red, and the standard gifts of roses and chocolates remained favorites with the customers. But she had to admit that she'd been pretty successful at adding little twists; the bright fondant coatings, classic brocade textures and sparkling gold and silver accents had gone over so well with her custom designed cakes that she'd thrown in a few of those details for the stock cakes as well.

"There are more in the back," Sam told Jen. "Give me a hand?"

The only two customers were taking their time about deciding, so Jen excused herself and followed Sam to the kitchen. The minute they walked back into the sales room with the new creations, both patrons spotted what they wanted. One woman took an oval cake covered in red fondant with quilting and gold beads, topped with white frosting carnations and an impressive fondant bow. The other exclaimed over one of the heart-shaped cakes with traditional red roses and ribbons of icing which trailed over the sides. Jen rang up their sales and sent them out with her customary, "Have a magical day!"

Sam stood at the beverage bar, where she poured herself a mug of their signature blend coffee and closed her eyes as she took the first sip.

"Good thing we got the two extra bakers, huh," Jen said, stepping from behind the counter to organize and wipe down the bistro tables that looked like they'd seen several visitors already this morning.

"No kidding. I don't know what I'd be doing right now." Sam sipped at the coffee and willed some extra energy into her limbs. "What I *should* be doing is working on my chocolate techniques. I don't know . . . I'm just not getting the results Bobul did."

"Well, he was really experienced. You can't expect to be that good right away."

"I'd just like to be a hundredth as good. Skilled enough to produce something I could put out for the customers without embarrassment."

When the mysterious European chocolatier had showed up before Christmas, his delectable creations wowed the customers, sending Sam's holiday sales skyward. Then, just as silently as he'd arrived, he'd left on Christmas Eve. Sam had stopped by his rented cabin, but the place was abandoned. Eerily abandoned. She had no idea where he'd gone, but felt sure he wasn't still in Taos. She would have heard about it if his chocolates were being sold anywhere else—it was a small town.

Meanwhile, Sam had spent every Saturday of the past month driving to Santa Fe for classes on chocolate-making techniques. Although she'd managed to turn out a passable Belgian chocolate for dipping strawberries, and she could now mold and unmold shaped pieces without breaking half of them, nothing she'd created so far came even close to the flavor, texture and whatever magical thing that Gustav Bobul had done to turn her clients into raving chocoholics.

A customer walked in, grabbing Jen's attention, and Sam carried her own mug to the kitchen. At her desk, she reached for the bin where she stacked the order forms for all their custom work. She verified that all the pages were in sequence by delivery date, discovering what she already knew—the early part of the week had practically nothing due, but the weekend and Valentine's Day, they'd be slammed.

Twelve proposal cakes and four weddings in addition to her own—what on earth had she been thinking, agreeing to February fourteenth as her wedding day? Beau didn't care; he'd told her that a lunch-hour ceremony in the judge's office would be fine with him. Typically male, he was only thinking of the fact that they would soon be living together, sharing their lives.

Sam wanted that, too. But she also wanted their wedding day to be special. It was her first time at this, his second. His first marriage lasted five years and ended with his model-gorgeous wife deciding that life in this little town would never suit her and figuring out that she would never convert Beau to a city guy. Sam's past included a hot time with the charmer who fathered Kelly, an escape from commitment there, and thirty years of sporadic dating while she raised a kid on her own. No man had ever struck a chord with her the way Beau did; there'd been absolutely no one she could envision committing to for a lifetime. Until now.

She touched the antique garnet ring on her left hand, remembering how Iris had pressed it into Beau's palm Christmas night, insisting that he should give it to Sam to formalize their engagement. The ensuing six weeks had become a flurry of plans and decisions saddened by the sudden absence of Iris. Now—in memory of that sweet older woman—Sam wanted to make their wedding a special day, with her beautiful creamy lace dress, her friends and family near, and the cake of her dreams.

She'd made hundreds of lovely cakes for lovely brides but there was that one fantastic creation, still in her head, that she'd never made for anyone else. It wouldn't be the biggest cake of her career—far from it—but it would be hers. She glanced again at her sketches.

"Ms Sweet?" It was Sandy, one of her temporary bakers. "I just wanted to check this with you? These four layers are to be carrot cake, right?"

The woman phrased every sentence as a question, from *I'd like a job here?* to *I guess I'll go home now?* The first few days of this had annoyed Sam to no end but she finally made up her mind that she couldn't let it get to her. Sandy would only be here this month, and she really did know her way around a commercial bakery.

"That's correct," Sam said. "Hey, thanks. I was just glancing through the orders and it looks like you've checked off quite a few of them."

Although the ideal situation was to bake, decorate and deliver a cake within two days, they simply didn't have the staff or oven space to handle the volume this week. So Sam had decided that they would bake a lot of the layers and put them in the freezer for a few days before decorating. This morning when she'd arrived she noticed that Sandy and Cathy were taking that decision to heart.

Still, most of Sam's work would necessarily fall right at the end. Friday through Monday were going to get absolutely crazy. And Tuesday was her wedding day. Of course, there was one way . . . but it involved calling upon her source of mystical power—dare she call it magic?—something she'd resolved to cut from her life. Something she still hadn't fully revealed to Beau.

"Sam?" Jen poked her head past the curtain that separated the kitchen from the sales area. "A lady who wants a custom cake." She tilted her head toward the front of the shop.

"Be right there." Sam sighed and wondered how she was going to live through the coming week.

Chapter 2

A woman sat at one of the bistro tables, hands folded in front of her. She was about Sam's age, with salt-and-pepper hair in a short, layered style. When she looked up, the lids over her dark brown eyes seemed tired. Deep lines of long-term sadness etched the corners of her mouth. A smile flickered and she introduced herself as Marla Fresques.

"Did Jennifer offer you some coffee?"

"Yes, she did. I don't care for any, thanks." The thin fingers went back into their clasped position.

"What can we make for you?"

Marla's mouth opened and then closed again, as if she had one answer in mind but thought better of it. She took a deep breath.

"I know this is short notice," she said. "But I wonder if I can get a cake by tomorrow afternoon."

As if this week weren't busy enough already. Sam worked her mouth into a smile. "It would depend on what you have in mind." *Please do not let it be another wedding.*

"It's for a small gathering in my home."

"A birthday? A shower?" With hope, Sam envisioned a quick, standard cake.

"I'm sorry I wasn't more specific." Marla stared at her hands for a few seconds. "It's a remembrance. For my son."

"Oh, I'm so sorry." Sam filed away her cute birthday cake ideas.

"Tito, my son . . . He disappeared ten years ago. I believe he is still alive, somewhere. We get together and pray for his safe return, every year on his birthday. It's tomorrow." Marla fixed her with a steady stare. "I know that someday he will come back."

Sam had no idea what to say to that.

"What type of cake did you have in mind?"

Marla's shoulders relaxed. "The white cross is a sign of hope. Red is Tito's favorite color. I want the cake to contain those things . . . but I am not sure in what way."

Sam directed her pen at the order sheet she'd brought out with her. Sketching quickly, she suggested that the cake itself could be in the shape of a cross. It was simple to create but always carried a lot of impact—she tended to get lots of orders for them around Easter.

"Then we can put red flowers in a garland, draping it like so." She sketched some shapes to indicate what she had in mind. "What's your favorite flower?"

Marla gazed upward for a second. "I love daisies. Tito always liked roses."

"Perfect." Sam filled in the rest of the details on her

form. "We can have it ready for pickup around three, if that's good? Or, I can deliver it."

Sam almost bit her lip as soon as the words were out. Where did she think the extra time would come from?

But the look of sheer gratitude on Marla Fresques's face was so touching, Sam knew she would make the time. Whatever this poor woman's story was, the expression in those chocolate eyes was haunting.

She watched the customer get into an older sedan, one that showed the dings and scuffs of many years' use. It was probably the car she'd been driving at the time her son disappeared, and the woman held onto it like a lucky talisman. If she kept the same house and the same car, then the young man would come back. How unwavering, a mother's hope for that kind of reunion. Sam shook off the haunting feelings as Marla pulled away from the curb.

The order called for red velvet cake, and Sam found that the freezer contained a half-sheet of it that wasn't committed to anyone else. According to the tag it was baked yesterday, so it would still be nice and fresh. She pulled it out and made space on the stainless table. Working quickly with a serrated knife, she cut the sheet into pieces and placed them together to form a cross. A coating of white buttercream sealed the raw edges and she placed it into the fridge to set. In the morning, it would be a quick matter to add flowers and borders.

"Becky, hold back five of those large red roses for me," Sam called out to her assistant. "And when you get a chance, could you do about a dozen white daisies, yellow centers?"

"Sure thing. I could use a break from making roses anyway." Becky's skills with the pastry bag had steadily increased since the shop opened and Sam knew she could trust the young woman for good results.

At her desk, she turned to the stack of orders, calculating quantities, and entering an online order for supplies from her wholesaler in Albuquerque. A couple of the proposal cakes required special elements. One was to be in the shape of a ring box with a giant molded-sugar diamond in it. Apparently the groom wasn't too intimidated by the idea that his bride would see this thousand-carat thing right before he presented her with something undoubtedly less sizable.

She rummaged through the bin of plastic molds until she found the one for the 3-D monster diamond solitaire. Another cake, for a bridal shower, needed a glass slipper for the fairytale-romance theme, and she had a mold for that as well. The technique for cooking perfectly crystal-clear liquid sugar was tricky, and Sam knew that if she could get it right in one try, she might as well make both items at the same time.

An absolutely clean pan, clean molds, and pure white sugar were the essential elements. She let herself get lost in the work, setting up the molds, cooking the sugar and checking it with the candy thermometer. Watching the instrument reminded her that she needed more practice on her chocolate techniques. Perhaps she could make time for that a little later in the day, she thought as she carefully poured the clear, molten sugar into the molds.

But that never happened. Shortly after lunch—two pizzas brought in and shared among the crew—Kelly called.

"Mom, help! Riki left on an errand and I have an emergency over here!"

The panic in her voice sounded genuine. Sam dropped

the phone and dashed out the back door. The grooming shop, like Sam's own place, had a back door to the alley and luckily it was unlocked. Sam flung it open to the roar of what sounded like a hundred dogs, all barking at once. In the work area, a dozen wire cages lined the walls. The doors to two of them stood open, and the dogs in three others loudly protested their own captivity. A deep metal sink stood to one side, with a spray hose shooting water toward the ceiling.

"Watch out—the floor's wet!" Kelly scrambled after a sudsy dog with long reddish fur but the animal was far quicker, completely undeterred by the water that pooled over the concrete floor in the work area. As Kelly lost her footing and went down face-first, the dog bolted for the short hall that led to Puppy Chic's small reception area.

Sam headed after the dog, arms out to her sides to keep her balance.

"You okay?" she asked Kelly as she passed the prone figure.

Kelly pulled herself to her knees. "Not if that dog gets away. He belongs to the mayor."

"I got him." Except that the dog was out of sight now. Sam hustled as quickly as she could, following the soapy trail.

From the hallway, she could hear the dog shaking himself vigorously. In the reception room, a medium-sized Sheltie stood, cornered near the glass entry door. A black Lab was giving his best effort to mount her.

"Oh, god," Sam yelled, "stop that! You dogs, get over here!"

Like they were going to mind her commands.

The wet Irish Setter had flung soapsuds all over the

room and now he circled the Sheltie from the other side. Sam reached for him but she might as well have been trying to grab a fish barehanded. None of the dogs had their collars on, but Kelly had grabbed up a leash with a loop in it. She snagged it over the head of the Lab and pulled at him. Toenails screeched across the tile floor and it took all Sam and Kelly could muster to pull him back to the work room.

"That's his crate," Kelly said, indicating one of the ones with the open doors. "Somehow he figured out how to open the latch."

They shoved the Lab inside and slammed the door, double checking the latch.

"We better get that other one—"

A scream came from the front.

Kelly's eyes went wide. Her feet slithered sideways as she headed for the other room.

Sam was right behind her daughter, and they found a woman standing inside the reception area, clutching a wide-eyed Yorkie to her chest.

"What is—?"

"Give us a minute, ma'am, if you could," Sam said.

Kelly had looped the snare over the Setter by now and Sam found another one to use on the Sheltie. She held the smaller dog aside while Kelly basically slid the bigger dog across the floor on his wet feet. They disappeared into the back room.

"Sorry about that," Sam said to the new customer. The sound of a metal crate clanged from the back. "I'll just—" She tilted her head toward the hallway and started pulling the Sheltie with the cinched-in lead.

Kelly passed her in the hall, her brown curls sticking

out at wild angles, her plastic apron askew over her chest. She rolled her eyes as she headed toward the front, and Sam could hear Kelly putting on her best customer service voice as she greeted the stunned woman as if she'd not witnessed anything out of order.

Sam found a crate for the Sheltie, across the room from all the other occupied ones. When she had the little girl securely locked inside, she turned off the spray hose at the sink.

"The lady decided to wait for another day to get the Yorkie groomed," Kelly said as she walked into the room.

"Gosh, I wonder why."

Sam and Kelly both dissolved into giggles.

"What on earth—" Erica Davis-Jones's silhouette showed against the open rear door.

"Oh, gosh, Riki, I am *so* sorry!" Kelly grabbed up a mop that Sam hadn't noticed before. "We had a little mishap . . ." She began mopping at the pool of water.

Sam mouthed an apology to Riki and then headed back to the pastry shop. And she'd thought life as a baker got a little crazy at times.

By that evening, when Kelly walked into the house, the whole incident had taken on tall-tale proportions. Sam had hoped to have quiet time at home to work on her chocolates, but two people had already called to ask about the riot at the dog groomer's place and Jen said it was all the bakery customers could talk about all afternoon.

"Yeah, a few people said they'd heard that dogs were getting away and running all around the plaza," Kelly said. "Riki had her hands full, explaining that her shop really is a safe place to bring your dog."

"Sheesh, I hope that one witness doesn't cause her to lose too much business. It's amazing how much harm an old gossip can do."

"Nah, you know Riki. She was a little peeved with the owner of the Sheltie for bringing the dog when she was in heat. Riki has a rule about that and the woman didn't tell her. But by the time she finishes telling the story in that cute accent of hers, everyone actually gets a good laugh over the whole thing."

Sam handed Kelly a truffle she'd made. "What do you think? Honestly."

Kelly took a bite and let it rest on her tongue. "Well, it's not Bobul's. Sorry, Mom. It's good. Really. Creamy and tasty."

"But I don't know about selling them in the shop," Sam said. "People got used to a pretty high standard when he was there at Christmas. I'm afraid these will disappoint."

Kelly pursed her lips and nodded. "You're right. They're almost there . . . but not quite."

Sam couldn't take the chance of losing customers because they thought the quality had gone downhill. It wasn't worth the risk. She stared at the rack of truffles she'd just finished.

"They'd make nice favors for the wedding," Kelly suggested. "Or I could take some to the nursing home. The old folks love their sweets." '

Sam stared at her. *Who is this girl who's always thinking of others?* Ever since her experience with Beau's invalid mother she'd loved spending time with the elderly. Even if she had to mush up the candy and spoon feed it, Sam knew her daughter would do so, happily.

Kelly went to the refrigerator and pulled out the makings for a sandwich. It had become her routine a couple nights a week, to eat something quick at home and then go spend the evening at the nursing home reading stories and holding withered old hands. When Kelly carried the sandwich into the living room to watch one of her reality shows while she ate, Sam began the kitchen cleanup.

She'd tried everything with this chocolate venture, including handling the mystical carved wooden box—a gift from a purported witch that seemed to give Sam special abilities. Although her chocolate making had definitely improved over her early efforts, something was still missing. She ran hot water into the sink, dunking her pans and bowls beneath the sudsy surface, sending a silent plea out to the universe at large. *What will it take for me to get this chocolate-making right?*

A knock at the back door disrupted her thoughts.

"Hey beautiful," Beau said, stepping in and depositing a grocery bag on the counter. While he slipped his jacket off and hung it on a hook near the door, Sam peeked inside. He'd brought a roasted chicken, salads and rolls from the deli counter at the supermarket. It smelled heavenly, the meaty scent a welcome break from the sugary smells that surrounded her all day.

They indulged in a lingering kiss until Sam became aware of Kelly's presence.

"Sorry, you two," she said, "but I need to get to that door." She picked up the small paper sack into which she'd put some of the truffles, and pulled her hoodie from the wall hook. "Off to see the oldsters. You guys behave while I'm gone."

"It'll be nice when I have you all to myself," Beau said, watching Kelly get into her car and back out.

"Sorry. I should give her a little lecture about lecturing us," Sam said.

"Ah, it's not that much longer. She's a cute kid, and she was so good with Mama." His voice tightened.

Sam turned to the cupboard to get plates, giving him a moment as she bustled around with flatware and napkins.

"You know . . . you can move into my place any day now," Beau said, coming up behind her as she pulled the food cartons from the bag and set them on the kitchen table.

She'd taken a few things out to his big log ranch house, basically an overnight bag and couple of changes of clothes, but the task of really moving there—packing up her kitchen stuff and emptying the garage of more than thirty years clutter . . . the task seemed monumental. Of course, she reminded herself that she didn't really have to move absolutely everything right away. Kelly would continue to live in Sam's house. She'd even talked about buying the little place, rather than having Sam sell it to a stranger. So far, it was more speculation than a real plan, and since their engagement at Christmas Sam had found herself with very few spare minutes to think about it.

Beau's hands ran down her arms and he paused, picking at something that was stuck to the sleeve of her baker's jacket.

"Oh gosh, I didn't even change—" Sam reached for the dried gob of cake batter on the sleeve. "Let me just—"

"I don't mind," Beau said, but she was already on the way to her bedroom.

"Just find a bottle of wine. I think there's white chilling in the fridge or some kind of red in the lower cupboard. I'll be right back."

She kicked aside an empty cardboard carton, stripped off the baker's jacket and tossed it into the hamper, followed by the black slacks that comprised her working wardrobe. She felt remiss in not making more effort to dress nicely for Beau in the evenings. Once she'd moved into his place, she resolved, she would be home for dinner every night and she would be dressed in something that she hadn't worn all day long. A vision of the long drive from her shop out to his house flitted through her mind. No more five-minute commute to her little place. She tamped down the thought while she pulled a silky blouse from the closet and buttoned it.

She had a pair of amber earrings that went perfectly with the blouse, and she reached for the carved wooden box that held her small jewelry collection. She'd come in here when she got home a few hours ago, purposely handling the box, hoping for some of its energy to pass on whatever mystical skill she needed to make the perfect chocolates. The energy was there, but somehow the skill didn't come. She raised the lid of the box again. The dull brown wood began to glow slightly at her touch.

She'd still not found the right moment to tell Beau about its magical powers. When was the right time to tell your fiancé that you may have inherited abilities from a genuine witch? She had told him a little of it, back when Bertha Martinez gave her the box. On one of Beau's cases, she'd seen invisible fingerprints in a strange plant substance. But he'd never quite put together the fact that she also sometimes used the box's powers to boost her energy, to impart a healing touch, to occasionally see auras. Now she had to tell him. Before the wedding.

"Whatcha doing in here? Dinner's getting cold." From the doorway, his voice startled her.

She pulled out the amber earrings and held them up. "Just getting these."

Chapter 3

Sam continued to fret over the secret she'd withheld from Beau, but he filled the time talking about his day and satisfying his hearty appetite with gusto. She picked at a drumstick and nibbled bites of the macaroni salad that she normally loved.

"Beau?" she said as they began clearing the dishes. He put them into the dishwasher while she scooped coffee into the filter basket and started the machine. "Beau, there's something—"

The kitchen phone rang, startling her. As she reached for it, she noticed Beau eyeing the truffles she'd made this afternoon. She pulled a small plate from the cupboard and gestured for him to choose their desserts while she reached for the handset.

It was Delbert Crow, her contracting officer for her

other job. Before Sam had the money to open Sweet's Sweets, when baking at home wasn't providing quite enough income she'd been forced to look for gainful employment. And that had come in the form of a contract to take care of properties where owners were in default on their mortgages. Some special program that involved the Department of Agriculture. Sam wasn't too clear on the details of how it worked, only that her duty was to break into the houses, if necessary, clean them up, maintain the yards, and get the places ready for sale—basically, jump whenever Delbert called.

She tensed at the sound of his voice. This was one week when she *really* didn't need any extra duties. She caught Beau about ready to pop a whole truffle into his mouth.

"Those are pretty rich," she whispered.

"What, Ms Sweet?" Delbert Crow asked.

"Nothing. Just finishing dinner here at home." She'd often wondered if the contracting officer had any sort of a life. He worked out of an office in Albuquerque and called at the most inconvenient times. She'd never met him face-to-face but pictured a curmudgeonly older guy who drew big red X's on a calendar to mark the countdown to his retirement. She forced her mind back to what he was saying.

". . . start the spring cleaning?"

Her brain raced to catch up. Something about the unseasonably warm temperatures they'd enjoyed recently. It happened nearly every February, a few days of such glorious weather that everything—including a lot of the fruit trees—believed it to be the end of winter. Then, unfailingly, wham—another stretch of freezing conditions. Whatever some fat old groundhog back East said didn't matter, the familiar pattern was how New Mexico seasons were destined to play out.

"All my properties are securely winterized, Delbert," she said. "I check on them every couple of weeks, but there's no point in doing any real landscape work or turning the water systems back on until we know we're past the hard freezes."

He grumbled a bit when she reminded him that she would be on her honeymoon until the end of the month. *And don't bother me until then.* But what she said was that she would call him when she returned.

By the time she'd hung up Beau had poured mugs of coffee and carried them into the living room, where the TV set was tuned to college basketball.

"I hope you don't mind," he said. "It's one of the few broadcast Lobo games I've gotten this season." He scooted over to made a space for her and tucked his arm around her shoulders when she sat down.

She nibbled at a truffle and sipped her coffee. No point in insisting that they talk about what might well turn into an awkward subject; she put thoughts of the magical wooden box out of her mind and savored her dessert. Now if she could just figure out how to re-create Gustav Bobul's techniques in chocolate.

* * *

Four-thirty in the morning always came way too early for Sam. Even with months of practice, there was always that moment when she felt tempted to roll over and bag everything until nine. It was the one aspect of opening a pastry shop that she hadn't really taken into account. She slapped at the button on her clock to shut off the obnoxious electronic beep.

Turning on the bedside lamp, she rubbed at her eyes and wondered how Beau would take to the new routine in his life. Being a rancher at heart, he probably wouldn't view the pre-dawn wakening as anything unusual. She groaned her way across the room and slipped into her work attire more from habit than by conscious thought. Twenty-five minutes later she was unlocking the bakery's back door, switching on lights, and turning on the large bake oven that would labor all day without complaint.

Mixing and baking the shop's usual morning offerings had become second nature. Muffins, scones, crumb cakes and turnovers came out of the oven as if they'd put themselves there in the first place. While Sam performed the routine tasks, her mind zipped ahead to the specialty cake orders for the day. Coming up with a variety of different proposal cakes for the town's prospective grooms had proven to be a challenge. More often than not, the guy placing the order had no clue what he wanted, other than to wow the girl into saying yes so he would have an unlimited supply of early morning sex. Most of them simply wanted a fitting accompaniment to the nice meal, which was then going to be followed by a ring and the question.

She sprinkled a cinnamon brown sugar mixture over a coffee cake and glanced at the shelves where her food colors and supplies were organized. One of her customers had dropped a hint about his girlfriend loving the delicate flower, forget-me-nots, and Sam already a picture in her head for that design, coating the cake with chocolate fondant, which would contrast nicely with the pale blue flowers. She put the coffee cakes in the oven and set the timer.

Another man wanted to go very traditional with hearts and flowers. Sam envisioned white fondant with very tiny piped red hearts around the sides and top border—maybe some string work to make the little hearts flow together, then piped red rosebuds surrounding a raised dome where he would place his ring. She pulled cake layers from the freezer and set to work.

The morning drifted by, Sam only dimly aware of the other girls arriving and starting their duties. Sandy and Cathy reviewed the orders and went to work baking the correct number of layers in the correct sizes. Becky oversaw the pastries that came out of the ovens, helping Jen to keep the display cases filled, coming back to her own favorite task of making flowers for the cakes. She brought the red rosebuds, sixteen of the delicate things, out to Sam, who placed them around the base of the hearts-and-flowers cake.

"Okay, this is ready for storage," Sam told Becky, turning to the next order in the stack while her assistant carried the romantic little cake to the fridge.

"It's going to get crowded in there," Becky said when she returned.

"Be sure we set the smaller cakes close together at one side. Once we start assembling wedding cakes, we'll need all the tall spaces we can create." Sam pulled out the next of the order sheets. "At least this cross-shaped one will be gone this afternoon. It takes up a lot of shelf space."

Staring at the smooth white cross with its draping of contrasting red roses and delicate white daisies, Sam wondered again about Marla Fresques and the family so deeply affected by the disappearance of the son. The intense impression of sadness surrounding the woman was understandable but there was something else . . . Bits of Marla's conversation filtered back but Sam couldn't quite pinpoint the sense of mystery surrounding the woman.

The cross cake reminded Sam that once she'd promised to deliver it she'd committed to two others, as well. She would just have to make time for three stops. She turned to the work table again and set about piping trim on four dozen heart-shaped cookies, finishing them just as Cathy set three flavors of cupcakes in front of her. Sam sighed. It was good to be busy.

Busy, right up to the moment that Sandy, carrying a huge mixing bowl of batter, stumbled in front of Sam and drenched her with the gooey vanilla substance.

"Sam? I'm so sorry?" Her blond hair began to work out of its net as the younger woman dropped the bowl and jostled a row of cakes on the cooling rack.

"Slow down, it's okay," Sam said as she grabbed for the rack and steadied it.

"Oh my god? Oh my god?"

Sam reached out, to keep Sandy from losing her balance in the slick spill. "Let's just get this mopped up . . ."

Becky had set down her pastry bag and was already reaching for the trash can and a dust pan. Before Sandy could track the mess any farther around the room, Becky began scooping.

"Cathy, can you take a minute to run us a pail of water?"

Sam let Becky take charge. She wiped her feet on the wet mop that Cathy provided, then went to work on her clothing with paper towels. It wasn't making much difference.

"I'll have to go home and change," she told the crew. "I

can't very well make deliveries like this."

Sandy looked like she wanted to cry. Sam swallowed the impatience in her voice and tried to reassure her that accidents could happen to anyone. While Becky mopped the floor and Cathy washed the mixing bowl, Sam retrieved Marla Fresques's cake from the fridge and loaded it into her van, along with the others.

"I'm not sure how long the deliveries will take, but everyone can just keep working on what you're doing." She breathed deeply of the bright outside air when she got to her vehicle. Sometimes it really was better to put the hectic atmosphere behind her.

After a quick stop at home where she changed into clean black slacks, a vivid saffron top and black wool jacket, Sam pulled out the three order forms and checked the addresses, deciding on her route. One, a torte for a business luncheon, wasn't really due until the following day but Sam reasoned that they would rather get it early than late, and tomorrow's schedule might bring nearly anything. The place was only a few blocks off the plaza, so she headed there first. The second was for a child's birthday party on the north side of town, and leaving there set her on the path toward Marla's home beyond Arroyo Seco.

Passing the turnoff to Beau's place—soon to be her home too—she cruised past bare earth fields lying brown in the February afternoon. Although the sky was brilliant blue, the air felt chilly and the forecast called for increasing humidity and the inevitable reversion to winter weather. Beyond the few buildings comprising Arroyo Seco, the road curved twice and Sam spotted the narrow lane she wanted.

The Fresques house sat amid a cluster of parked cars, a small adobe with a pitched metal roof. Bare-limbed cottonwoods and elms surrounded the place and a small yard with brown grass and mulched flower beds stood out front. A driveway ran beside the house but it was blocked by two vehicles, one being the older sedan Marla Fresques drove yesterday. Four other cars sat along the road, pulled out of the traffic lanes onto the verge of short, tan mountain grasses. Sam slowed, hoping for a parking spot with minimal distance to carry the large cake board, but another vehicle had come up impatiently behind her. She edged her van to the right at the first open spot. The other car passed and pulled in just ahead of hers.

"Oh, that looks good," the woman from the car said, staring.

Sam wasn't sure whether she was referring to the bakery themed artwork on the van or to the cake that Sam was pulling from the back.

"Could you use a hand with that?" the lady's husband asked, stepping forward.

"Sure." Although Sam had loaded the rectangular board into the van alone, it would certainly be easier with some assistance.

The man placed his hands at the right intervals under the board for perfect balance and lifted it easily to his shoulder. In his pressed jeans, western shirt and string tie, he looked the type who was accustomed to managing heavy loads and coming to the aid of women. Sam sent him a polite smile.

"Hard to believe it's ten years now," the woman said conversationally as the three of them walked toward the house. "Poor Marla, just waiting so patiently."

"You've known her since—"

"She was a wreck. Well, she and Tricia both. Can you imagine? Their little girl was still a toddler. Tito supported them well. It was a blow to be left alone like that."

The husband skirted the two cars in the driveway, obviously heading for the back door of the house, so Sam and the wife followed along.

"And then, Tricia dying so young. Cerebral hemorrhage—it was *so* sudden . . . well, little Jolie was very lucky to have her grandma to take her in."

The woman stepped ahead and opened the back door for her husband. He edged sideways to get through the doorway and Sam followed, wanting to be sure there was a secure place to set the cake.

Marla Fresques stood in the kitchen, her sad eyes scanning the room and she perked up when she saw Sam and the cake.

"Oh, Samantha, it is beautiful! Exactly as you described it to me." She gave a quick hug to the woman who'd walked in with Sam, then directed the husband to carry the cake through a swinging door to a dining room.

Sam followed along, helping Marla move a few cups and plates aside to make space at one end of the dining table. Checking it over, she adjusted the angle and quickly wiped a tiny smudge of frosting from the paper-covered board. *There*, she thought. *It looks good.* She turned to Marla to ask about a cake knife, but the hostess was halfway across the room, her attention snagged by someone else. The other couple, too, had blended into the crowd in the adjoining living room.

Sam wandered back toward the kitchen. Surely it couldn't be too hard to rummage around for a knife and cake server without bothering the hostess. She could see to it that the cake was ready to serve and then make a quiet exit out the back.

". . . only a matter of weeks. You know how doctors are about telling you anything, really."

Two women in very similar dark dresses stood at the far side of the room, near a doorway that probably led to a small pantry. Sam sent a little smile their direction but pretended to be so busy that she wasn't noticing their conversation.

"Jolie doesn't know yet," the shorter woman said in a low voice.

Sam spotted a wooden block with knife handles sprouting from it. She pulled a couple of them before finding the one that would work best for the cake.

"When is Marla going to tell her? She can't wait until the last minute."

Doctors? A matter of weeks? Was Marla critically ill?

Chapter 4

Someone else walked into the kitchen just then and the women headed toward the rest of the party. With a cake server and the knife in hand, Sam followed.

"Sam, thank you," Marla said, intercepting her. "I was just on my way—"

Sam set the utensils on the table, unsure what to say.

"Oh, here's my granddaughter." Marla reached toward a girl of about twelve, circling her shoulders with a loving arm. "Jolie, this is Ms Sweet from the bakery, Sweet's Sweets. She made this beautiful cake for us."

At an age when a lot of girls began testing their boundaries, dressing goth or piercing their body parts, Jolie seemed like a grandmother's dream. She wore a perky little dress of something blue-swirled and silky that kept her slim, budding body childlike. Her long, dark hair was drawn back at the crown with a little cluster of silk flowers. She smiled shyly at Sam, her teeth white and straight in her caramel complexion.

"Hi, Jolie, nice to meet you."

"You made this?" the girl said, looking at the cake.

"Yeah. Maybe you'd like to learn how sometime?"

Jolie sent another of her hesitant smiles toward Sam, then she spotted two other girls across the room.

"Go ahead," Marla said. "You can take Jenny and Sarah to your room."

"She seems like a good kid," Sam said.

"She is. I've been really lucky." Marla's eyes misted over and she blinked to clear them. "Her dad went missing when she was only two. Then her mom died when she was five. They lived in Albuquerque, and I hadn't gotten much time with Jolie until then. Suddenly, she had no one else, so I brought her here." She cleared her throat. "She's such a sweet girl."

Sam thought of the conversation in the kitchen but it didn't seem like her place to ask.

"You can stay awhile, can't you?" Marla asked. "Father Joe already gave us a private blessing. Now we're ready to start serving the food. I'd love to introduce you to everyone, along with the cake."

Intruding on someone's family time didn't feel right, but Marla seemed to sincerely want her there. Her hostess took hold of Sam's arm and pulled her into the living room where she proceeded with a flurry of names. Sam would do well to remember half of them, but she tried. The couple who had helped bring the cake inside were Joy and Bill; neighbors from the houses on either side were the two women she'd overheard talking in the kitchen, Diane and Deborah; another couple introduced themselves as Jorge and Camille. The priest, Father Joe, gave her a warm handshake. Someone offered her a glass of wine and then Marla's voice rose above the conversation for a moment to announce that the meal was ready. Jolie and her friends had come back, eager to be first in line for the food.

Platters and bowls crowded the table, except for the end where the cake sat, filled with homemade dishes—tacos, posole, enchiladas plus beans and salads and more. Sam stood aside, feeling like an extra, letting the others fill their plates first.

"Go, Sam, eat," Marla urged.

"After you." She touched Marla's elbow and edged her toward the serving line. She noticed that the other woman took only tiny spoonfuls of the salads and a scant dipperful of the beans.

"Saving room for the cake," she said when she caught Sam noticing her small portions.

Sam scooped enchiladas onto her own plate, wondering again about the conversation in the kitchen.

Someone else pulled Marla aside at that moment. She gave the newcomer a bright smile and went along. Sam found a spot to sit at one edge of the living room. She watched Marla interact with her guests and decided she'd probably misinterpreted the earlier conversation.

"Sad, isn't it?" The voice beside her was Camille, if Sam recalled correctly. "The way Marla keeps hoping Tito will come home."

"She told me she believes he's alive and well somewhere," Sam said, remembering Marla's comments yesterday in the bakery. "Can't she find out where he is and contact him?"

Camille shrugged. "She tried. She reported him missing.

I don't think the police treated it very seriously. And then she hired some investigator. But that didn't work out either."

Sam stared at a spot on the carpet. Maybe Beau would know something about the case.

"It was really hard when Tricia died. Tito's wife," Camille said. "Gosh, she was so young. It just didn't seem right. That little girl, all alone. She seemed so lost."

"Marla really loves her, doesn't she?"

"Jolie is all the world to her now."

Someone tapped on a glass and Marla's voice again rose to get everyone's attention. "We have a lovely memorial cake for Tito," she said. "And I want to introduce you to the talented baker who made it."

Sam blushed as all eyes turned to her.

"Samantha, would you do the honor and cut the cake?"

She nodded and made her way to the table. Within minutes she'd handed out dessert plates to nearly everyone. Jolie and her friends held back.

"I want one of the big roses," Jolie said.

At choruses of "Me too!" Sam worked out ways to make cuts that gave each girl a slice of the cake with a whole rose on her plate. They wiggled with delight and headed back to Jolie's bedroom with their treasures.

The other guests began to surround Sam when she went back to the living room with a small slice of the red velvet cake, and she found herself explaining what kind of shop Sweet's Sweets was and giving directions to the place. Several of Marla's friends promised to come by and others talked about upcoming birthday orders. By the time she caught sight of Marla again, Sam realized the crowd had thinned.

"I think I've overstayed a bit," she said when Marla walked up to her.

"Oh, nonsense, Sam. Everyone was delighted to meet you."

Sam looked at the ruins of the meal. Most of the serving bowls were gone, taken away by whoever brought them, but there were the remains of the cake alongside splotches of spilled food on the tablecloth.

"Let me stay and help you clean up," she offered.

Marla started to defer but Sam could see that she was tired. Through the doorway to the kitchen she could see the two neighbors scraping plates and loading them into the dishwasher.

"With several of us working on it," Sam said, "it'll only take a few minutes." She headed toward the table and began carrying the remaining dishes to the kitchen. A platter from a cupboard provided a good place for the leftover cake, and Sam expertly cut it into pieces, arranged them on the platter, and set the messy cake board aside to be taken away.

Diane finished wiping the counter tops and Deborah had put detergent into the dishwasher and started the machine. Sam lost track of them for a few minutes and when she looked again, they were saying goodbye to Marla who had stretched out on a couch in the living room, looking worn out.

"Is there anything else I can do for you, Marla?" Sam asked, as the two neighbors walked out the front door.

"Not really," Marla said with a weak wave of her hand. "Unless you'd like to sit and have a cup of tea."

Sam truly felt more like going home and putting her feet up, but something about Marla's demeanor made her pause.

"Tea would be nice." Sam remembered seeing a kettle somewhere in the kitchen, and she went back to fill and heat it.

"I'm sorry to be so lazy, making you do everything," Marla said. "I just don't seem to have a bit of energy right now."

"It's been a big day," Sam said. She glanced toward the short hall that led to the bedrooms. "Does Jolie need anything?"

"She went home with Sarah to spend the night. That's Diane's daughter. Even though it's a school night I don't mind. They'll walk to the bus together in the morning."

Marla pulled a crocheted afghan over her legs and picked at the edge of it.

"Sam? Could I ask you something?"

The kettle sent out a long, screeching whistle. "In a second, you sure can." Sam hustled to the kitchen and spent a minute organizing two cups of tea.

"Here we go. This will relax you." She set the delicate china cups on the coffee table and pulled an armchair in close for herself.

"Sam, you know the sheriff pretty well, don't you? I mean, I've heard that you—"

Sam smiled. "We're getting married, actually."

Marla brightened. "That's nice. I'm happy for you."

"But I have a feeling that isn't the real question you wanted to ask me, is it?"

Marla sipped from her cup, buying time. "No, it isn't. I need to find Tito, and I need to do it now."

"Ah. Someone at the party said that you'd filed a missing persons report when he first disappeared."

"I did. And nothing came of it. I called the sheriff's

department here in Taos, but since Tito and Tricia lived in Albuquerque at the time, I think they pushed the case off to the Albuquerque police. But he was here in Taos when it happened, and I thought they should have done more."

"And this happened ten years ago?"

"Yes. Late August. Tito, Tricia and Jolie were here for a family weekend. Tito went to the store for some beer and he never came back."

"What did the sheriff's people say?"

"It got ugly. They said he probably went off with some woman from his work. Tricia was devastated. She couldn't believe it and neither could I. I still don't. Tito wasn't like that. He served in the Navy, became an electrician, he had a good job and provided a good life for his family. He loved the outdoors, hiking, fishing—things like that. He wasn't a cheat. And he would have never left little Jolie. He loves that baby."

"What do you think happened?"

"I have no idea, Sam. If he'd gone hiking he would have told us. He always said where he was going and what time he would be home. We would have known where to look. But this—this is too weird."

"You said you don't believe he's dead, though."

"Jolie and Tricia always get birthday cards. They're never signed and they come postmarked from all kinds of places. But I know he sends them. He sent them for awhile even after Tricia died."

"Do you get mail from him too?"

"Sometimes. I got some cards too. Once there was a package with a beautiful scarf, my favorite color. But nothing signed. Nothing in writing at all."

Sam set her empty teacup down. "You said you need to

find Tito now. What has changed?"

Marla stared at the leaves in the bottom of her cup for a full minute. When she looked back at Sam her eyes were filled with pain.

"I'm dying, Sam. It's cancer and the doctors don't have any hope for me." She answered Sam's unasked question. "Yes, I've done the whole, horrible round of chemo—two years ago when I was diagnosed. It didn't work and the cancer is too widespread now. I won't do it again. What I need now is for Tito to come home and get Jolie. Once I'm gone, she'll have no one at all."

Chapter 5

Sam walked out into the gathering darkness, her heart heavy with the news from Marla. She thought of the twelve-year-old Jolie, having lost both father and mother, now about to lose the last of her family.

Her van sat alone at the side of the road, about twenty yards from Marla's driveway, barely visible out here away from street lights. The houses sat on five to ten acre plots, fairly well separated from each other, although Sam could make out lights in distant windows of the homes on either side of Marla's. It was sad to think of Jolie leaving her friends and the only neighborhood she probably remembered.

Sam turned her vehicle around, heading back toward Taos, noticing that a winter fog was moving into the low-lying areas. She dimmed her lights and visibility of the road improved a little. But before she'd driven three miles, the fog became a thick shroud, encasing her in cottony white. She slowed to a crawl, peering ahead and behind in hopes that no other vehicles were nearby.

Trees loomed at the sides of the narrow road, their dark shapes hovering, ghost-like, above. An occasional structure stood dark and silent, more of them as she came to the center of the tiny settlement of Arroyo Seco. She knew the small crossroads to be composed of about a dozen adobe buildings, but in the eerie darkness they seemed to move with the air, closer to the road, then farther away. Not a light shone from any window, not a person moved in the night. She had a brief bizarre vision that the entire earth had been abandoned and she was the only living being to remain.

With one hand firmly on the wheel, she reached for the electric door lock. It snapped with a satisfying click that told her she was securely locked in on all sides. The town's one restaurant, where Sam distinctly remembered there being four or five cars when she'd come out to Marla's, sat dark and deserted now. She glanced at her dashboard clock and saw that it was only seven o'clock. A profound sense of the creeps edged its way up her arms.

The van crawled along, despite Sam's urge to stomp the gas pedal to the floor. It would be crazy to speed through this winding stretch of road with her view so restricted.

She no sooner had that thought than a dark shape emerged from between two of the hunched adobe buildings on her left. Man-shaped, large, the figure stepped toward her van. He walked straight to her driver's side door, one arm waving, beckoning to her. She hit the brakes, praying that no other vehicle would come up behind and crash into her.

Sam peered through the mist, wondering what there was

about him that looked familiar to her. He reached up and pushed back the cloak that covered his head. The garment fell across his shoulders and Sam recognized the shape of a large brown coat that she knew well. She lowered her window two inches.

"Bobul?" she croaked.

"*Da*, Miss Samantha, is Bobul here. You are doing fine?"

"Bobul—what the hell?" She glanced in all her mirrors. "I have to get off the road. Someone's going to come along and hit me."

He took two large steps back and waved her forward. She steered to the left, to what she hoped was the parking lot of a small shop, although she could barely make out the shape of its windows.

Gustav Bobul, the chocolatier who had showed up at Sweet's Sweets on a snowy night in December, then vanished on Christmas Eve, walked over to her door.

"Miss Samantha need help with chocolates. Bobul know this."

She stared at him. Now just *how* had he heard her plea for help? Had he somehow been spying on her, watching her chocolate-making attempts that weren't going so well?

He seemed to be waiting for an answer but all she could do was nod like some stupid wobbly-headed doll.

"Bobul have answer." He unfastened three buttons of the huge brown coat that he'd always worn and reached inside, pulling forth a big canvas bag that hung by a wide strap across his chest, the one he'd brought every day to the bakery.

"Do you want to come back to work for me?" Sam asked, feeling a spark of hope.

"Cannot. Bobul have other plans." He pulled the bag away from his body and practically stuffed his head inside it. Both hands worked their way around in there. Finally, he came up with a small reddish cloth pouch, which he extended to her with one hand while he continued to stare into the bag. Another little drawstring pouch came out, then a third, muddied shades of blue and green, respectively.

"There. All fix now." He stepped back and tucked the messenger bag back under his coat, then redid the buttons.

"What? What's all fixed?"

"Miss Samantha chocolate problem, all fix."

She felt herself becoming impatient and remembered what it had been like, having him around all the time. "Bobul, explain. I don't know what you mean."

He pointed at the reddish pouch. "One pinch." Then, indicating the other two, "Two pinch."

"A pinch of this," she said, holding up the first bag he'd handed her, "and two pinches of these? And then what?"

"Put in chocolate, voilà—" His large shoulders rose. "Is perfect."

Huh? She wanted to get out and shake him. Or just drive away and ignore him. Or wake up from whatever weird-ass dream this was.

Bobul patted the side of the van. Then he turned and walked toward the building behind him. When Sam blinked, he was gone. She stared toward the empty shop but saw no sign of the chocolatier nor any clue as to where he'd gone.

She quickly raised her window and rechecked the door locks. *That was just way too strange.* She put the van in gear and slowly pulled away from the dirt parking lot.

At the next bend in the road, the fog evaporated and a black sky with a million pinprick stars surrounded her.

Okay, now I am *going nuts*, she thought as she sped up.

Her arms and legs suddenly felt jelly-like and she wanted more than anything to be off this road and out of the van. When she spotted the turnoff to Beau's place just ahead, she whipped the wheel to the left.

The lights in his log house glowed warmly in the dark night, and the trail of smoke from the chimney sent a reassuring trace skyward. The dogs, Ranger and Nellie, set the alarm and Beau stepped out to the porch as she parked in front.

"Hey, darlin', didn't know you were coming out tonight," he said, wrapping an arm around her shoulders and pulling her in close for a kiss. "Wow, you're toasty warm."

She raised a hand to her forehead. Maybe that was it—she had a fever and delirium.

"Come on in. I just poured myself a drink. What would you like?"

His normalcy felt so reassuring that Sam simply followed along, letting him take her jacket and hang it up. She trailed along into the kitchen and poured herself a glass of wine from the bottle she'd uncorked a couple of nights earlier when they'd eaten dinner here. She'd been gradually getting used to the idea that this would soon be her home too, trying to feel less like a guest.

"So, what's up? Busy day at the bakery?" Beau asked as they settled together on the sofa.

She took a deep breath. There was no point in revealing how close to freaked-out she'd been just a few minutes ago. Although Bobul had worked at the bakery for three weeks in December, and Beau had certainly seen him there, he'd not really gotten to know the quirky Romanian. In fact, there were a lot of things about Bobul that Sam had never told her fiancé, mainly the fact that the man was in the country illegally.

"I was just out this way, attending a sort of memorial for the son of a customer," she said. She took a long pull from her wine glass.

"Well, I'm glad you ended up here. I actually got home on time, for once. Made myself a burger. Did you eat yet? I could make you something."

She explained about the buffet dinner at Marla's, and the longer she talked the more she relaxed.

"Beau, do you remember a missing-person case from about ten years ago, a man named Tito Fresques? He's Marla's son and she says there is evidence that he's still alive but she felt that the authorities didn't do much to find him at the time, and then they dropped the case."

He set his drink on the end table. "Well, I wasn't yet with the department back then, so the name doesn't ring a bell. There's probably a cold case file on it somewhere. I suppose I could check on it."

"Why wouldn't they have investigated more thoroughly?"

"There could be a hundred reasons. Our department has been understaffed forever, and there's only so much we can do, maybe we just ran out of leads. And you mentioned that Fresques lived in Albuquerque. It could be that the case was handed over to APD. After that, it wouldn't have been our concern anymore."

"But—"

"Darlin', grown men go missing all the time, and it's usually because they want to. There's trouble in the marriage or frustration with the job and the desire to start over somewhere new. Unless there's evidence of foul play . . . sometimes there just isn't much we can do."

"I guess." She sipped from her wineglass. "But there's more. Marla has terminal cancer. There's no one to care for Tito's daughter once she's gone, so it's really important to her to find him."

"Sorry to hear that. Tomorrow I'll dig around and find the file. But I can't promise much. We're buried, and I don't see the workload letting up anytime soon. I don't know how I could assign anyone to it right now."

"Could I take a look?" Even as she uttered the words, she wondered when, exactly, she thought she would have time to do anything with the information.

Beside her, Beau yawned widely.

"I better get—"

"Just stay. There's no reason for you to drive all the way into town tonight." He pulled her closer and she welcomed the warmth from his chest. It had been an intense day, with the frantic pace at the bakery, the revelations from Marla, and then the strange encounter in the fog.

They climbed the stairs to the spacious master bedroom. Sam loved the golden lamp glow on the log walls. She turned down the bed. Standing side by side at the double sinks, brushing their teeth, she realized this was how it would be every night of their married life. The little things, like both reaching for the toothpaste at the same moment, brushing fallen hairs from the vanity into the waste basket, her robe hanging on the hook behind the door—it would all become part of the pattern of her life. From this day forward, as they said, a comfortable pattern.

Beau's eyes looked droopy as he reached to switch off the lamp on his side of the bed. He murmured as she turned off her lamp and then reached to drape his arm over her. In the dark, she let the muddled thoughts of the day drift out of her mind as she heard his breathing become deep and steady.

A dream—one of those you know is a dream, even as it unfolds—put Sam in a garden somewhere, wearing a long white gown. The dress didn't fit properly and the train snagged on something every time she took a step. She kept thinking, *this is not the wedding dress I bought, why am I wearing this fluffy monstrosity?* Chimes began to play and she tried to turn toward the spot where she knew Beau must be standing. Then the chimes became an alarm clock, and the tangled dress was the bed sheet wrapped around her legs.

Beau groaned and muttered something that included, "Already . . ." and some other choice words.

She really needed to bring her own clock. He could grab an extra hour's sleep if he didn't have to wake on her schedule.

"Roll back over," she whispered. "I'll leave quietly."

"No, no, it's all right." He rubbed his face and sat up. "I can use the time. Feed the animals early and get to the office in time to find that file you asked about."

Bless him, she thought as she stood under the hot shower. Making time for her inquiry about an old case was really beyond the call of duty.

From the bathroom window she could see him walking toward the barn in the dark, a strong flashlight beam marking the frosty path. The horses whickered softly, glad to see him, and she caught glimpses of the two dogs scampering near his legs. The barn door opened and a light came on.

Sam got dressed, found blusher and lipstick in the small cosmetic kit she'd left in Beau's bathroom, and was ready to head for the bakery by the time he came in through the kitchen door, stomping his boots on the deck outside.

"See you later?" she asked.

"If you can break away for lunch, I'll try to have that file by then. Maybe we can both take a look?"

"Perfect." She kissed him, loving the feel of his cold, scratchy whiskers against her face.

She unlocked her van and slid inside. On the passenger seat sat the three small cloth bags Bobul had given her. Damn. In the warmth of Beau's arms last night, with the reality of the world firmly within her grasp, she'd almost convinced herself that exhaustion and the drive from Marla's home had set her thoughts running wild and that she'd only imagined the fog and the encounter with the chocolatier. She lifted one of the pouches—it seemed nearly weightless. *What was this all about?*

She caught Beau watching her from the kitchen window, obviously wondering if she were having car trouble. She put the van in gear and rolled away, blowing him a kiss.

At Sweet's Sweets Sam was blessedly alone. She started the bake oven and brewed a pot of coffee. The employees could handle the routine baking as they arrived, she decided. She pulled a two-pound block of fine dark chocolate from her supply.

Much as she would have liked to do each step from scratch, she'd learned that the roasting, winnowing, grinding and conching were difficult steps that required lots of specialized equipment. Finding a supplier for chocolate that was ready for tempering was a huge time-saver. Even so, some things simply required time and concentration. She stood over the stove, watching the chocolate melt, checking the thermometer until it reached precisely 110 degrees. The steps of cooling, tempering, and blending while carefully watching the temperature were becoming second nature to her. When the mixture reached the ideal point for molding at 90 degrees, she pulled out the little pouches Bobul had given her.

Okay, what had he said? One pinch from the red bag and two pinches from each of the others. She sniffed at the first pouch as she opened it. Maybe a faint hint of cinnamon? But not really. It was something else and yet she couldn't name it. She stuck her fingers inside and took the requisite pinch of whatever the powdery substance was.

"Here goes nothing," she said, sprinkling the small amount of powder over the bowl of chocolate.

The contents of the other two pouches had no discernable scent at all and the powdered substance inside was almost colorless. Two pinches from each, scattered over the surface of the chocolate like fairy dust, then stirred gently until it vanished.

Sam stared at the glossy surface. "Man, I hope this doesn't kill somebody."

Chapter 6

Sam pulled the drawstring closures on the three little spice pouches, stuffed them into a metal canister and jammed them up into the corner of the overhead shelf. She pulled a teaspoon from the drawer and dipped it into the warm chocolate, then tasted. Tongue and taste buds reacted immediately. *Finally*, the result she'd wanted.

She carried the bowl to the work table where she'd laid out clean molds. She tempered it then watched the chocolate flow in a smooth ribbon into each small, heart-shaped cavity. Although she didn't see how the minute amounts of Bobul's powders could affect it, Sam swore that the consistency was silkier than anything she'd yet turned out.

The molds went into the fridge for a five-minute quick cool down, and Sam started another batch. Again, she tasted. Again, the flavor was exquisite and she felt no odd side effects. By the time Cathy, Sandy and Becky arrived to start making the daily muffins and breakfast pastries, there were sample chocolates for the tasting.

"Mmmm," Becky said. "I think you've got it."

"I still don't know how Bobul created his intricate designs, but at least the flavor is there."

"The molded hearts are perfect for Valentine's," Cathy said.

She was right, Sam decided. With six days to go, she couldn't hope to learn to sculpt the perfect little flowers and garlands Bobul had made at Christmas. But this was a good start. She rummaged through one of the storage shelves and found some gift boxes left from the holidays. Within an hour she'd filled several of them with the small heart-shaped chocolates and set them near the register for Jen to begin selling as soon as the doors opened.

"We could save some of those to put on the cakes, too," Becky suggested.

Good idea. Sam envisioned them on cupcakes as well, and maybe on the miniature tortes that she planned as her Valentine-dinner specials.

"Okay, I smell that special chocolate," Jen said, pushing her way through the curtain that separated the sales area. "Is Bobul back?"

Sam grinned. Jen, the great chocolate lover of the whole crew, would spot any inconsistency immediately. Sam handed her assistant one of the newly-made hearts and watched as Jen swirled her tongue and rolled her eyes.

"Oh, yeah. *Oh, yeah.*"

"Don't go all orgasmic on us here," Sam teased. "I just need to know if they're good enough to sell."

"At double the price. People will *love* these!"

"Just price the boxes the same as we did at Christmas." She let Jen take another heart from the sample plate. "I better get busy on some truffles now."

While Sandy and Cathy concentrated on the standard array of breakfast pastries and Becky began assembling and filling layers for the custom cake orders, Sam sneaked the canister of little pouches back into her own work area beside the stove. No one seemed to notice that she'd begun including extra ingredients.

"Okay, Mom, when were you going to let Riki and me in on the secret?" Kelly demanded, walking up to the worktable where Sam was dipping truffle centers into a bowl of the new chocolate.

"I just turned out the first batch this morning at six o'clock. Not my fault you didn't stop by earlier." She continued dipping.

"My first break of the morning. Can I take a couple back to Puppy Chic with me?"

Sam pointed toward the pile of rejects, those inevitable pieces that didn't unmold quite right or the dipped truffles that weren't perfectly symmetrical. Usually, she just melted them down or cut them into small bits for samples.

Kelly immediately popped one into her mouth, did the same eye-roll that Jen had earlier, and then grabbed up two more and wrapped them in a napkin.

"Thanks, Mom. Short break. Gotta go."

"No more soapy-dog emergencies today, I hope?"

Kelly laughed and headed out the back door.

Sam had just finished the last of the truffles when her cell phone rang down inside her pocket.

"Hey darlin'. Almost ready for some lunch?"

She glanced at the kitchen clock, startled to see that it

was after eleven-thirty. They made a plan to meet in ten minutes at the Taoseño, and she rushed to the sales room to be sure Jen had things under control there.

"Quit eating all the samples," Sam cautioned, chuckling at the guilty look that crossed Jen's face.

"I'm giving out plenty, too. Look, nearly all the boxes are sold already."

Uh-oh. Sam scratched a note to herself to order more boxes from her supplier. Clearly, the few remaining in the storage area weren't going to get them through the week.

She walked through the door of the popular local restaurant a few minutes late, but luckily Beau had snagged them a table. Her heart gave a little flip when she saw him. God, he looked good in his uniform. Maybe tonight . . .

He stood and pulled her chair out. "I ordered your favorite burrito. It's already getting crowded and the waitresses looked pretty busy."

"Thanks." She gave him a long look. "I don't know if I ever mentioned how absolutely wonderful you are. I mean, not only dashingly handsome but considerate as well."

He actually blushed, and Sam realized that it wouldn't hurt her to be a little more forthcoming with compliments. He really was a treasure.

He cleared his throat and looked up. Their orders had arrived.

"Oh, I got the Fresques file for you," he said after they'd taken a few greedy bites of their food. "Glanced through it."

"Is there any new information for Marla?"

"I doubt it. I got interrupted and really didn't have time to study it. The gist of it was that no one pursued the case very far because there was no evidence he didn't leave of his own accord. But feel free to take it home and read through it. Ask questions if you want. Maybe Mrs. Fresques has information that she didn't provide at the time."

"She told me that family members have received birthday cards but they are never signed. She's convinced that Tito sent them."

"Where were they mailed from?"

"She said a variety of places. That doesn't seem to make sense with the 'other woman' scenario, does it? I mean, wouldn't he have just filed for divorce so he could be with this woman? Why would he continue to send his wife birthday cards?"

He paused with his fork midway back to his plate. "Well, it's odd, that's for sure. I don't think there was a mention of these cards in the file. It would be nice if Sheriff Padilla had asked more questions at the time, rather than assuming so much."

Sam bit back a comment about the former sheriff. "I'll see if Marla can tell me more."

"Let me know if you come up with anything that would make it reasonable for us to reopen the case."

She nodded thoughtfully.

People were lining up at the door, waiting for tables, so Sam and Beau quickly finished their meal. In the crowded parking lot she hugged the case file to her chest as Beau walked her to her van. She climbed in and powered her window down.

"Touch base later?" he asked, leaning in for a quick kiss.

She stared at his back as he walked toward his cruiser. *Umm, nice view.*

She pulled out her phone and made a quick call to the

bakery. Sam heard laughter in the background although Jen assured her that everything was under control.

"I need to do an errand before I come back. Call me if you need to."

Jen giggled at something someone had said. "Sure, Sam. We're doing fine here."

As long as business isn't being ignored, Sam thought. A drive all the way out to Marla's place probably wasn't the best use of her time right now, but she needed to ask more questions and the week wasn't going to get any less busy. Plus, her wedding florist's shop was on that end of town and Sam needed to give him a check for the balance they'd agreed upon.

It took fifteen minutes to get past the midday traffic clog near the plaza, out to the small flower shop on the north side.

"I shall order your flowers on Friday," the diminutive owner said as he reached for her check. "They will arrive Monday, as fresh as can be, and your bouquets will be ready Tuesday morning."

"Thanks, Eben. My daughter will probably be the one to pick them up."

He handed her a single red rose, nestled beside a sprig of fern and wrapped with green tissue around the stems. "It's an extra. Enjoy."

She carried the flower out to her van, laid it gently on the seat beside her and picked up the file Beau had sent with her. As he'd said, there wasn't a whole lot to it.

A report, neatly filled out in someone's squarish printing, gave the basics. Tito Fresques was last seen by his family members when he left Marla's house to drive into town for beer. Although he hadn't stated as much, both

Marla and his wife, Tricia, assumed that he would go to the supermarket where the family normally shopped. It should have been a round trip of less than an hour. When Tito didn't show up after more than two hours, the women became concerned. He'd left his cell phone in the bedroom, his former childhood room, so Tricia decided to take Marla's car and drive the route, concerned that he'd had car trouble somewhere. There'd been no sign of him or his vehicle along the way or at the grocery store. She'd driven to the other large supermarket in town, with no sign of him there either, then she'd cruised slowly past the few liquor stores. No car. No Tito. At one point she'd called back to Marla's house to be sure he hadn't arrived in her absence.

Feeling a little panicky, Tricia had then driven to the sheriff's department and informed them of the situation.

A shadow crossed the page. Eben, the florist appeared at Sam's window and she rolled it down. "Everything okay, Sam?"

"Oh, yeah, I just had something to read over. I hope I'm not taking up a valuable parking spot?" It was nice of him to worry about her.

He assured her that he didn't mind, then pulled his sweater more tightly across his chest and hurried back inside.

Two other pages in the file contained notes about phone calls the deputies had made to the hospital and the morgue. Among Tito's friends who'd been contacted no one said they'd heard from him. Someone had made a note in the file that the sheriff's department had simply recommended that Tricia Fresques go back to Albuquerque and wait there for her husband to come home.

Sam closed the folder and tapped it against her steering wheel, pondering. Pulling out her cell phone she made a quick call to Marla, who didn't mind at all that Sam wanted to drop by.

Sam glanced at the time. She could afford another hour away from the bakery. She pulled out of Eben's parking lot and headed north toward open country. There'd been no new snow since mid-January and the bright February sun now shone on tan fields of stubble. Horses stood in the sunshine, their fuzzy winter coats soaking up its warmth. Flocks of small black birds suddenly abandoned perches in a spiky cottonwood tree, flowing like a dark stream low across a field on her right, landing to pick at fallen seeds on the ground.

The trip to Marla's home seemed to go more quickly this time, the miles streaming by pleasantly. Sam slowed the van nearly to a crawl as she passed through Arroyo Seco, watching both sides of the road for any sign of Gustav Bobul. She couldn't imagine him living so near and not coming to her shop, at least to say hello. But then he was a strange one. Nearly anything was possible.

Only the one sedan sat in Marla's driveway today. Sam pulled in behind it and Marla stepped out onto the shady front porch to greet her.

"Come in, Sam. I've made some coffee."

Sam handed her the red rose Eben had given her and gave her new friend a hug, noticing for the first time that Marla's shoulders were so thin that she could feel the bones through her quilted cardigan. Marla led Sam, a little unsteadily, toward the kitchen where she placed her rose into a bud vase then poured two mugs of coffee from a carafe. Her hands were a bit shaky, and she covered by pushing the sugar and creamer containers toward Sam rather than attempting to spoon the contents herself. Sam pretended to ignore Marla's increasing weakness, turning to remove her coat and hanging it over one of the kitchen chairs. She held up the folder.

"Sheriff Cardwell gave me this. His department ran out of leads a long time ago, but he said it was okay if I did some asking around."

"Thank you." Marla's voice came out tight and high. "It means so much to me."

Sam bit her lip. "I really can't promise anything. But I'll try."

Marla nodded, blinking her moist dark eyes twice. "I know." She sat in one of the chairs at the table, her body sagging as if she'd used every scrap of energy to answer the door and pour the coffee.

"May I take a look at the file?" She reached toward Sam with her thin fingers.

"I guess it would be all right." Sam handed over the folder, giving a short verbal recap of what she'd just read.

"The list of friends," Marla said. "We called most of them ourselves. The police wouldn't even take a report for more than two days. So Tricia and I started calling everyone we knew, hoping he had run into a buddy and got sidetracked." She shook her head. "No one had seen him."

Sam sipped from her mug. The coffee was really good. "Did the Albuquerque police ever investigate?"

Marla shook her head. "Not really. They said that he'd disappeared in Taos. I think they told Tricia that she could file a separate report . . . I really don't remember."

"I assume she also called friends there? People he worked with, maybe?"

"Oh, yes. He worked at Bellworth, you know. Very good company, a very good job."

Sam recognized the name. Bellworth was one of those huge corporations that did a lot of government contract work, often with agencies at Sandia Lab or Los Alamos. As she understood it, the contracts usually lasted a few years, but then were often renewed, so employment was steady and pay was good.

"Tito's training in the Navy was as an electrician. He was well qualified for the work he did at Bellworth and had worked his way to one of the higher pay grades." Pride in her son was very evident in Marla's expression. "He and Tricia bought a house in a nice neighborhood. Jolie was still a baby, but they chose the area because of the good schools. They were planning to have more children."

She closed the folder and toyed with the coffee mug in front of her. "Sam, Tito didn't run away. That sheriff, Orlando Padilla, he hinted that Tito had another woman and that he'd run off with her. But that wasn't true. He would never do that."

An excellent character reference, or a mother's blind love? Sam didn't know. She did know, however, that Padilla had been lax as a lawman, a product more of New Mexico's infamous nepotism in government than any outstanding accomplishments on the job.

"When Tricia died and I brought Jolie here, I sold their house in Albuquerque. Her death . . . losing the house . . . it would have hurt Tito so bad." She swallowed hard. "But I didn't see any other way. I used the money to hire a private investigator. I couldn't keep him very long. There wasn't much equity in the house, so the money ran out pretty fast. With a baby to raise, I couldn't go into debt."

"What did the investigator say?"

Marla leaned forward and gripped the edge of the table to stand. "I have his reports. I'll get them."

Sam kept her seat at the table, feeling an ache in her heart for this poor woman.

Five full minutes must have passed before Marla came back. She had a manila envelope in one hand and a stack of smaller ones—pink, lavender, yellow—in the other.

"These are the cards my Tito sent me." She set them on the table in front of her mug, just out of Sam's reach. She extended the large envelope to Sam. "His name was Bram Fenton, the investigator."

Sam knew the name. The man had died this past summer. She took the envelope and bent the metal brads upward. Inside was a small sheaf of paper, maybe ten pages at most.

"May I take these? I can make copies and get the originals back to you right away."

"It's all right. There's nothing I can do with them now. Keep it as long as you need to."

Marla had taken her seat again and her left hand rested on the stack of personal envelopes. "These, I will keep but you may look."

She picked up the topmost envelope, raised the flap and pulled out a birthday card. For Mother, pink with scalloped edges and a small bow formed of ribbon, stuck to a design of pink roses. The printed greeting inside was a heartfelt message of love, but there was no signature.

"They are all like this," Marla said.

She set the card down and handed Sam the envelope. It was hand addressed in neat block letters, no return address.

"It's postmarked from Chicago," Sam said.

"Yes. They came from many places." Marla spread the others like playing cards in a deck. "California, New York, Washington, St. Louis. Here's one postmarked Santa Fe. That's the closest he ever got to home." A tear rolled from the corner of her eye.

Sam studied the envelope and card intently, giving Marla a moment.

Marla raised her head. "I know they are from Tito," she insisted.

"I'm sure you are right. Maybe, with this proof, I can get the sheriff's department to reopen the case."

Even as she said it, Sam realized how unlikely that was. But it might be worth a shot. Anything she could do to provide this poor, dying woman with a little hope would be welcomed.

"Yes, that's a good idea," Marla said, visibly brightening. She flipped through the cards and chose one. "Take one with you. Show them."

Sam could tell that Marla was tiring. She carried their mugs to the sink, switched off the coffee maker and helped the other woman to the sofa in the living room, where Marla lay back against the cushions and pulled an afghan over herself.

"I'll be all right after a nap," she insisted when Sam offered to call someone. She closed her eyes.

Sam gathered the file and envelopes, shrugged back into her jacket and locked the front door behind her.

Chapter 7

Back at Sweet's Sweets the sales room was full of customers and Becky was inside the walk-in fridge searching for someone's order. Sandy hit Sam with about a hundred questions the second she walked in the door, and there went all hope of leaving early and spending the afternoon at home going through Tito's case file.

She helped Becky find the pastry she was after, a set of miniature tiered brownies decorated like tiny wedding cakes for a bridal shower, then she realized that the situation with the gift boxes for chocolates was getting desperate. She sat at her computer and placed an order, springing for the cost of overnight delivery and kicking herself that she hadn't done it sooner.

Once that was done and she set Sandy to work happily cutting out heart-shaped cookies, Sam went back to the stove and began work on another batch of chocolate. She remembered Bobul doing something with luster powder in the molds, making the finished pieces glow with a special sheen, so she prepped the molds with dustings of red, gold and silver, then began melting chocolate in the double boiler.

"We can use more of those out front, the minute you have them done," Jen said on a quick pass through the kitchen. "I'm down to no cookies, no brownies, and only two boxes of chocolates."

Sam sent a harried nod her way and continued filling the molds. While those set up, she unmolded some plain milk- and dark-chocolates she'd started this morning and quickly filled her last few gift boxes with them. Sticking a smile on her face she headed for the front, where she could hear a customer chatting with Jen.

"Here you go," Sam said, stacking the seven new boxes as Jen finalized the woman's order and sent her on her way.

"Whew—what an afternoon! I guess word is out about the chocolates." Jen wiped her forehead with a tissue and looked in the mirrored wall behind the counter, straightening the one errant hair that had come out of her neat chignon. "Oh dear, here's another," she mumbled, with a glance at the door.

Sam had turned to check the beverage bar—they were running low on their signature blend coffee—and to pluck a stray sugar packet off one of the bistro tables. The woman who'd opened the door was a stranger. Tall, super-slim in a tiger-print dress, black coat and heels, with chin length red hair which had that purposely bedroom-tousled look, she wasn't the sort of woman you didn't notice.

"Oh what a sweet little shop," she gushed, laughing at

her own play on words. "Perfect name."

"Hi," Sam said. "I'm Samantha Sweet, the owner. It's your first time here, I guess?"

"In this shop. I actually once lived here in Taos. *Ages* ago." She turned toward the display cases. "What do we have here?" she said, flicking a long, brilliant orange nail across her lower lip.

Sam caught Jen's eye and bit back a grin.

Jen, with previous experience at dealing with the rich and snobby, put on her best customer-service manners and began showing the woman some of their more popular treats.

"The amaretto cheesecake is our own exclusive recipe. And the scones are especially nice with afternoon tea. Of course all our ingredients are a hundred percent natural and everything is made from scratch."

The woman's glance barely grazed the selection. "Actually, I was only looking for coffee. Black. To go."

Jen nodded and Sam lifted a cup from the stack and proceeded to fill it. She affixed the plastic cap and carried it to the register where Jen was ringing up the dinky sale.

Tiger lady reached for one of the sample chocolates from the plate near the register and popped it into her mouth.

"*Mmm . . .*" Her voice went into a little lilt at the end. "Those *are* good." She spotted the boxes nearby. "Add one of those to my order."

She paid with a gold card, gathered the box and cup, then flounced out the door.

"Well, at least she ended up spending a few bucks," Jen said as they watched the colorful swirl of orange and black get into a Lexus at the curb.

"Taos has all kinds," Sam muttered, heading back to the kitchen.

The three employees who'd spent their day near the ovens were looking pretty wilted.

"Once those cookies and brownies are done, why don't you all head home?" Sam suggested. "I can finish up."

Cathy, the older woman who seemed to have a series of perpetual aches and pains, gave her a grateful look and headed for the coat rack. Becky's kids were due home from school any minute and that was always her cue to exit. Sandy stood at the sink, washing up the last of the cake pans from the morning's output, and her efforts put her back on Sam's gold-star list for the day.

Sam turned her own attention to getting a quick smear of frosting on the heart-shaped cookies and sending them out to the display cases. She set the brownies to cool and unmolded her most recent set of chocolates. From the sales room came the high voices of school kids, in for their daily cookie fix, and shoppers who tended toward the coffee, tea and heavier desserts. Jen's voice sounded calm and in control, so Sam lost herself in the zone of decorating two more proposal cakes.

By five-thirty it seemed that all was clear. With the other employees gone, Sam had used the last hour to clean up and organize. She took a deep breath and looked around. As much effort as the shop required, this had been her dream for such a long time. Once in awhile she needed to simply stare around her and appreciate that.

She appreciated it right up to the moment when she stepped into a near-invisible dab of butter and her foot went out from under her.

"What happened?" Jen said, rushing into the kitchen. "I heard a crash."

"Cookie sheets. I guess I grabbed for the table—" Her breath caught as a pain jolted through her hip.

Jen dashed toward her. "Let me help—"

Sam laughed. "Don't even try to pick me up. You'd break your back." She rolled to her left hip and got her hands and knees under her. "I'll be fine."

Jen backed away, keeping a hand outstretched, just in case.

"Are you sure you're okay?" she asked once Sam had pulled herself to her feet.

"Yeah. I think I hurt my pride more than anything else." She took a few steps, just to prove it. "See? All better." Her right side felt like knives were piercing every joint, but she wasn't about to admit it.

Jen eyed her boss's cautious movements. "Maybe I better call Beau to give you a ride home."

"Nonsense. I'll take something for it. We were about to close up anyway. Let's just do it now."

"If you're sure . . ."

"Jennifer, cut it out. I'm not a fragile little glass ornament." She hobbled to her desk and shut down the computer, then glanced around to be sure the oven was off, the refrigerator securely closed.

"Okay, I'll get the front. You take care and rest up tonight," Jen said.

Once her assistant's back was turned, Sam headed for the sink where she drew a glass of water and swallowed four ibuprofen. The leg ached like crazy as she turned out the lights and crept down the two steps to the alley and climbed into her van. By the time she got home she was seriously wondering whether she ought to have an x-ray taken. She gritted her teeth and limped into the house where she shed her coat and backpack. This really could not have happened at a worse time.

An ice pack would help the soreness, but she couldn't quite work up the energy to fill one. She made it as far as her bedroom, where the temptation was to simply fall into bed, let the painkillers take effect and sleep for the whole night. And she was about to do exactly that when she caught sight of her oddly lumpy, carved jewelry box.

From the day it had come into her possession, months ago, the box seemed to give Sam some extraordinary abilities. One of those abilities had been a healing touch; on several occasions after handling the box, Sam was able to make someone else's aches and pains go away. And at this moment in time, the person who most needed help in that department was herself.

She picked up the box and sat gingerly on the edge of her bed. As her hands rubbed the curves of the box's quilted design, the wood began to warm. She placed it on her lap, letting the heat seep through her slacks and into her legs. Within minutes her arms began to tingle, then her legs, a feeling familiar yet vaguely scary.

She lifted the box and set it on the bed. Small cabochon stones of red, green and blue were mounted in the wood, at each little X where the quilted grooves intersected. In its quiet periods, the box was a dull, sour yellowish color, the stones dim and almost colorless. But now, after her touch, the wood glowed golden and the stones winked with brilliant color. She stroked the bright stones then placed the box on the night stand.

"I better rest," she mumbled. She rolled over to her side, away from the box.

The room was completely dark when Sam woke and it took her a minute to realize that the buzzing cell phone in the pocket of her slacks had awakened her.

"Hey, darlin', I was wondering if you were coming out here for dinner tonight?"

"What time is it?" She groaned as she rolled over.

"Six-thirty," he said. The numerals on her clock confirmed it. "Did I wake you up? You sound kinda groggy."

"Yeah, I guess I was pretty tired." She scrubbed at her face, left-handed.

"Well, then you should just tuck in and stay there. It's getting cold out and there's no point in catching a chill by driving out here." Some metal implement made a noise in the background and she pictured him in the kitchen. "Although I sure was thinking about having you here in my arms for the night."

She relaxed into her pillow. That did sound nice.

". . . and catch you tomorrow," he was saying. "Go back to sleep."

The phone went dead in her hand and she was tempted to roll over again but realized that she really needed to go to the bathroom. She sat up and switched on her bedside lamp, noticing for the first time that the rest of the house was dark, too. Kelly must have gone directly from her job at Puppy Chic out to the nursing home. Sam swung her legs over the side of the bed and tested to see how her hip was going to feel with her weight on it.

Surprisingly, there was only a little pain, like a toothache that had subsided to a small throb. She stood, paused, then felt confident enough to walk. In the bathroom she pulled her slacks down and looked at the hip in the mirror. No sign of a bruise, no swelling. Amazing.

She went back to the bedroom to get out of her work clothes. In her soft robe and warm slippers she felt nearly human again, deciding she should eat a little something. The fridge revealed what she already knew; she hadn't cooked a real meal at home in days, so there wasn't much in the way of leftovers. She made a peanut butter sandwich and poured a glass of milk to go with it.

Her backpack lay on the kitchen table, reminding her that she'd intended to look through the investigator's file that Marla had given her. She took a big bite of the sandwich and dialed Beau's number. It rang several times before he picked up.

"Why didn't you tell me you were hurt?" he demanded. "I was just on the line with Jennifer. She called to say that I should go check on you. That you had a bad fall at the shop today."

Thanks, Jen. "Beau, I feel fine. Yes, I fell, and yes, it hurt like crazy right at that moment. But really, I had that little nap and I'm feeling almost a hundred percent."

"Are you sure? I mean, she really made it sound like you could hardly walk."

Okay, Sam, this is the perfect time to tell him about the box and its powers.

"Should I come over there?" he asked. "Is that why you called? You need some help?"

"No, actually, I was calling to discuss the Tito Fresques case." She went on to tell him about the visit to Marla and the folder of notes from the private investigator. "I haven't had time to read through his report yet, but I had an idea. About those greeting cards Marla believed Tito sent. They were mailed from several different cities. Maybe there's a way to check on that. Or maybe fingerprints? Would that be possible?"

Her voice must have sounded normal enough because Beau switched off the doting boyfriend voice and went into professional mode.

"Fingerprints on paper can be very well preserved," he said, "depending on whether the surface is shiny or rough, whether the paper was exposed to heat . . . that kind of thing."

"Maybe the case could be reopened with proof that he's been in contact with his family?"

"Darlin', can I ask what is the point of this? I mean, we know Tito Fresques is not in Taos, probably not in Albuquerque. It's likely that he really sent the cards. But knowing that doesn't disprove the original idea that he left his family voluntarily."

She thought about that for a minute. "I suppose you're right. I just wanted something concrete to tell Marla."

"She already believes Tito is alive and well somewhere, and thinking of his family. Nothing we do will change that."

Darn it, he made a lot of sense.

"I'll take another look and might be able to reopen the case, but don't expect any huge breakthrough because of it."

She sighed. "Okay." She almost hung up but something stopped her. "You know, something just crossed my mind . . . Assuming Tito were living a normal life somewhere, he can't be doing it under his real name. If he got a job using his own Social Security number the employer would have to be withholding child support and that money would be going to Marla and his daughter."

He thought about it for a few seconds. "Not unless the court ordered it. Court ordered child support is treated that way, but since he was never divorced or legally separated, I don't think . . . Well, I'm not sure. It might be an angle to pursue, but surely Marla would have mentioned to you if she'd tried to get money to support the child, wouldn't she?"

That was probably true, but the whole thing was a muddle. When Beau changed the subject she put the Tito situation out of her head.

The high protein dinner put Sam into drowsy mode and even though it was barely seven-thirty, she coasted through her bedtime routine and crawled between the covers. When her alarm went off she was still in the same position as when her head hit the pillow.

She rolled over and sat up, feeling a twinge from her injured hip. And although she'd promised herself to get away from using the wooden box's magic powers to accomplish her work, she knew there was no way she could be on her feet all day at the bakery without some help. She reached for the box.

Once the warm glow had permeated her limbs and sent its energy throughout her system, she rushed through a shower and grabbed her backpack. The hip felt absolutely fine—no pain whatsoever—and it only bothered her for a split-second that she'd used magic to accomplish the miraculous healing.

She arrived at the bakery, went through the normal routine to make things ready for the rest of the crew, then eagerly turned to the real task—making more of the special chocolates. By the time her three kitchen helpers arrived at six, she'd completed crèmes, truffles, nougats, and molded enough hearts in rich dark chocolate to fill at least a dozen of the new gift boxes which should arrive this morning.

"Wow, Sam, these are gorgeous!" Becky exclaimed. "I think you're doing them as well as Bobul ever did."

"Have a sample," Sam said to the three women. "I'm curious what you think about this new flavor I added, the caramel crunch."

Three pairs of eyes closed in ecstasy. No one thought to ask how she'd managed to make so much chocolate so early in the day.

Chapter 8

Jen reported for work at a quarter to seven and immediately marched into the kitchen with a stern look on her face.

"I told Beau to be sure you went for an x-ray and then stayed home in bed today," she said, facing Sam over the worktable.

Becky and the other ladies stopped to stare.

"She didn't tell you guys? She fell last night and really hurt her hip. She shouldn't be standing on her feet all day."

Sam looked around the room. "It wasn't all that bad. Surprised me when it happened, but no real damage. See? I'm fine." She stepped away from the table and walked across the room and back. "It really doesn't hurt."

The others turned back to their work, but Jen gave Sam a long hard stare. "If you say so," she finally said. "But if it starts bothering you at all . . . Sam would you just please take care of yourself."

Sam offered a hug. Jen had been her first employee and they had a special affinity. It was natural for her to worry the most, Sam decided.

"Here, have one of the new chocolates. The girls gave them a big thumbs-up."

She glanced toward the bake oven, where Sandy and Cathy were giggling over something. Becky was working at making risqué replicas of male body parts for a bachelorette party order, a drifty smile on her face as she handled the modeling chocolate—perhaps a little too enthusiastically.

"Becky! Come back to earth."

Becky dropped the piece she was working on. "Sorry, Sam. For some reason I was just—" She flushed crimson. "Oh, never mind."

Sam pulled out an order form for a child's birthday party and reminded Becky that she needed to finish that one before noon, diffusing her embarrassment.

Jen, meanwhile, had carried the boxed chocolates out front, along with a plate of sample pieces. Soon, Sam heard the jingle of the bells at the front door and knew the morning customers were beginning to arrive. She immersed herself in decorating two more of the proposal cakes, thinking all the while that she wished she'd had time to read through Marla's private investigator's notes last night.

When she finally got the chance to step out to the sales room to check on the display cases and coffee carafes, she realized that the sky had clouded up with that all-over white that meant snow.

"Winter's coming back," she said, half to herself and half to Jen and the man who stood at the counter.

A silly laugh erupted from behind her and she turned to see Jen flirting outrageously with the male customer. A bag of pastries sat near the register and he seemed to be in the process of choosing more. Obviously, the giggles and dimpled smile were helping Jen's sales technique. Sam smiled and checked to be sure they weren't running low on teabags.

The door jingled again as Sam finished wiping up the small blots of coffee and sprinkles of sugar that inevitably accumulated wherever people served themselves beverages.

"Cute, huh?" Jen said, staring at the retreating back of the man who'd just left.

"Looked like a good customer. Is he a regular?"

"No. It's the first time I've seen him here."

Sam grinned at her assistant. "He seemed pretty taken with you."

"Maybe so. He asked me out tonight."

"Really." Sam *so* wanted to caution Jen—all the usual 'be careful on a first date' stuff—but it really wasn't her place. "Well, have a good time."

She looked up to see Kelly's little convertible pull up to the curb next door at Puppy Chic. It lurched to a halt and out came Kelly, her curly brown hair looking a bit more frazzled than usual. Instead of going right into the grooming shop, Kelly headed toward the bakery.

"Ohmygod, Jen, you won't believe what I did last night," she said, her breath coming in white puffs on the cold air. She screeched to a halt when she spotted Sam.

"Oh?" Sam said. "No, you know what? Unless it was something illegal, it's none of my business." She sent a smile toward her daughter and walked into the kitchen.

I'll just pry it out of Jen later, she thought as she pulled a tub of cookie dough from the fridge.

Some harried whispers trickled through the curtain and

the shop bells chimed again a minute later.

They're both adults, both entitled to love lives. Sam's eyes scanned the kitchen, noting the perky smiles on the other three women, the faint sense of pheromones floating through the air. What on earth was going on here?

By five o'clock, all her kitchen staff were hinting that they needed to get home to their husbands—early dinner, favorite TV show, got to get the kids to bed early . . . and Sam knew something was up. Was it only because Valentine's Day was coming up—all the hearts-and-romance stuff at the shop?

She let them go early, still feeling pretty energetic herself and well into the final touches on one of the larger wedding cakes. She enjoyed the quiet for awhile, lost in the concentration required for old-fashioned piping work.

Jen walked into the kitchen, the first time all day she'd not dodged being alone with Sam.

"I know, need to get home to get ready for that exciting date?" Sam teased.

"Well, it would be nice. The shop has been pretty quiet for the last hour."

"So you and Kelly both have someone . . . interesting?"

"She'll tell you about it, Sam. I know she will. It's a guy she met at the nursing home last night."

"Oh god, don't tell me he's ancient."

Jen relaxed and laughed out loud. "He works there as an orderly. About our age, good looking." She put her hands up. "Okay, that's all I'm saying. Kel can tell you the rest."

"Ah, so there *is* more."

"Sam, don't make me—"

Sam aimed the pastry bag toward her, like she planned

to get off a good, gooey shot. "I won't. Thanks for telling me at least that much." She lowered the bag and turned back toward the cake. "And, yes, go on home. Turn out the front lights and lock the door, okay?"

Jen stepped over and gave her a light kiss on the cheek. "You're a great boss, and Kel's lucky to have you for a mom."

Sam watched her saunter back to the sales room with a jaunty little lift in her step. These girls. Pretty cute.

She finished the wedding cake and managed to slide it from the worktable to a rolling cart and get it to the fridge. The thing weighed over sixty pounds and she really should have insisted that at least one of her workers stay long enough to help with the task, but she managed to move it without a crash.

Her phone rang as she was closing down the shop, sticking the money and credit card receipts into a bag to take home.

"Hey darlin'. How's it going?"

"Pretty routine around here. How about your day?"

"Well, that's what I was calling about. I promised you dinner at home tonight but we've gotten a bunch of extra calls. I've got all the deputies out on traffic watch. Storm has moved in and the northern part of the county is getting socked. I hope you can get settled in before much longer."

She assured him that she would go straight home and stay there.

"My place or yours?" he asked.

A rush of lusty thoughts and pictures popped into her head and she almost blurted out that she wanted him—now.

He was talking on, though, about how it would be a late night and maybe she shouldn't chance the drive all the way out to his place. He would be busy. She ought to go on to her own house. Disappointment welled up as she said goodbye. *What's with that*, she thought as she stuffed the phone into her pocket. They'd never been clingy with each other. Fatigue? Hormones?

Now she *knew* something weird was going on.

Chapter 9

Outside, clouds still blanketed the town, heavy with the promise of snow, the air chill with undelivered moisture. However, as yet the actual storm had not reached her house.

The envelope with the private investigator's notes waited on Sam's kitchen table, but she gave herself time to take off her sugar-coated bakery clothes, have a quick shower, heat a frozen low-cal dinner and eat it before turning her attention to the stash of information.

The first two pages were evidently the investigator's worksheet, the information he'd taken from the family, and a copy of the same police report she'd seen in Beau's file. She set them aside.

From that point on, the pages contained dates, times and results of interviews, all in Bram Fenton's vaguely familiar neat printing. Sam had helped Beau with the investigation of the PI's death a few months ago. She pushed back the memory of those circumstances and read on.

Fenton had started with the same set of friends Sam knew about, the list of people Marla said she had spoken with. But the investigator dug a bit further, going to the supermarket employees, a man who regularly sat on the street corner by the store, and Tito's co-workers at Bellworth. Sam scanned the early pages; none of the market employees remembered seeing Tito that afternoon, and the man who regularly begged spare change from caring souls was one of those who lived in his own minute, foggy world. If you weren't pausing to drop some cash into the can he held out to you, you were not of interest to him. Fenton reported that he'd gone back a week after first questioning the man, to find that he no longer resided at that intersection.

She stared for a moment at the dark kitchen window. There would be no point in going back to the market now. Odds were that their employee turnover was tremendous and no one from ten years ago would still be around. Any who remained would almost certainly not remember one particular August afternoon. She laid those pages aside and got up to make herself a cup of cinnamon tea.

Settling into her favorite corner of the sofa, she set the tea cup on the end table and resumed with Fenton's reports. With the assumptions taken from the police report—the questions Marla and Tricia didn't want to ask—the PI had quizzed Tito's friends specifically about whether he'd had a woman on the side. Sam read the notes carefully, but it seemed that none of his local friends could or would verify that.

Beside two of the notations, Fenton had penned a small asterisk but there was no footnote corresponding to them. Sam could only guess that it was a bit of private code for himself, maybe to indicate that a particular interviewee had more to say, or perhaps he suspected those witnesses of fudging the truth a little. It might be worth following up.

The next page indicated that Fenton had traveled to Albuquerque and talked with Tito's supervisor at Bellworth, along with a few co-workers. It was a huge company, and Sam surmised that the investigator would only have taken the time to talk with those who worked personally alongside the missing man. She wished she had phone numbers for them. A few calls might ascertain whether those folks still worked for the company. She took a sip of her tea and pondered whether it would be worth her time to personally look them up. The idea of taking a day or more out of her crazy schedule to go there made her feel tired.

Then she thought of Marla and Jolie. The grandmother clearly wasn't holding up well. Having her son come back to reconnect with his daughter was vitally important to her, and it seemed that Sam's involvement in the case was the thread she was hanging onto.

Sam turned back to the pages, hoping for something firm, some clue that could quickly resolve this whole puzzle, but she didn't spot a thing.

A noise at the kitchen door caught her attention.

"Greetings, mama mia," came Kelly's voice.

Sam heard the door close a little too firmly and something thudded to the floor.

"Kel? You okay?"

"Oh yeah. Me doing wonderful."

Sam stretched to see around the corner into the kitchen. Her daughter was bent forward at the waist, picking up her huge hobo bag from the floor, obviously the cause of the crash. When Kelly raised up she tilted to the left; luckily the wall was right there.

"Had a few drinks after work?" Sam asked.

"Oh, Mom, we had the greatest time!" She came into the living room and flopped into an armchair. "Riki and I met up with Ryan and Tanner at this new little bistro. They make the *best* pasta with melted tomatoes."

Too many questions flew into Sam's head. Ryan? Tanner? Melted tomatoes?

"Ryan is just . . ." her voice drifted and her gaze floated toward the ceiling.

Sam noticed that Kelly's oversized T-top had slid off one shoulder.

"Ryan is the orderly from—"

"Yeah." The word stretched out into a long sigh.

"And Tanner? Riki's date?"

"More than a date," Kelly said, leaning forward with a confidential air. "Those two are *hot* together!"

She's thirty-four, Sam reminded herself. You can't preach. She smiled a little wanly.

"So anyway, we had this *fabulous* dinner, some wine . . . ended up at Ryan's for music and more wine . . ." She scratched at her scalp and her brown curls wiggled. "I guess maybe a little too much." Her vision seemed to focus a little more sharply. "Whatcha got there?"

Sam held up the pages from Fenton's report and gave Kelly the quick, uncomplicated version of the story.

"I was just thinking I might have time to call a couple of these Bellworth people tonight. Fenton didn't give phone numbers in this report, though, and I hate to go through directory assistance with no more than a name. They make it difficult."

"So, look 'em up online," Kelly said, rising a little unsteadily. A fuzzy smile crossed her face. "I think I'll take a shower."

Online. Why didn't Sam ever think of the obvious? She took the notes to her little desk in the corner and found a white pages service where she could browse the names. Within five minutes she had numbers for two of the people from Fenton's file.

"I'm following up on an investigation by Mr. Fenton, on behalf of a woman in Taos." A little devious, but it wasn't completely a lie. "There's an urgent family matter here and we really need to locate Tito Fresques as quickly as possible. I understand you worked with him at Bellworth a few years ago?"

The man at the other end of the line, Harry Cole, came back with about ten seconds of silence before he said, "Yeah?"

Sam went on to explain that Mr. Fenton talked to him right after Tito disappeared, and that she wondered if he might have thought of anything new about the case since then.

"Lady, that was ten years ago. I ain't given Tito another thought. He went off for a weekend and never came back. Didn't make my job no easier, I'll tell you. Had to do his work and mine until they got a replacement."

"Mr. Cole, do you remember if there was anyone at the company that Tito was especially close to? A buddy he hung around with after work or anything?"

Again, a long pause. She could almost imagine him

rubbing his chin while he pondered the question.

"Maybe a woman?" Sam asked.

"I'm tryin to remember. There was some from the department, went out for a beer on Friday nights sometimes. I never went along. Like the casinos better myself. There mighta been a woman or two in that bunch. Lisa Tombo was one, I think."

It didn't exactly sound like the makings of a hot, secret affair. She read off the names of Fenton's interviewees and Cole thought a couple of them were in the Friday night group. Sam thanked him, realizing she'd gotten about all she could from him.

The second call was more productive. Bill Champion instantly remembered Tito.

"Well, heck yeah. Tito and I worked side by side for five years. I just couldn't believe it when he never showed up for work that Monday morning. I mean, it seemed way out of character, him not quitting or anything, just not showing up. I talked to your investigator guy and he asked a bunch of questions, like did Tito have a girlfriend or something like that. Well, I told him I sure didn't think so. I mean, you work with a guy for a long time, they'll usually hint around, maybe ask you to cover for 'em now and then, make up a story. Tito never did anything like that."

"Harry Cole said that a woman named Lisa Tombo sometimes went along with the group, out for a beer. Do you know how I might get in touch with her?"

"Lisa. Yeah ... she and Tito ate lunch together a lot. Gosh, I haven't heard from her in quite awhile. I don't remember. She quit Bellworth and moved out of town, I think, shortly after Tito left. She might have got married. Now, Lisa, she was a looker. If Tito was going to fool around, she might be the one. Hell, I might have been interested there too, but she never gave me those kind of vibes, you know, where a woman kind of lets you know she might want to?"

"Mr. Champion, can you think of anyone else that Tito might have confided in? Someone he might have told if he were planning to leave?"

"Gosh, I sure can't," he said after a short pause. "But you know, the human resources person back then was a lady named Glenda Cooper. I heard that she left Bellworth to start her own company, some kind of internet thing that she runs from her home. She and Lisa were pretty tight, as I remember. She might be the person who could tell you where Lisa is now."

Since he seemed like the kind of guy who loved to share information, Sam asked if he knew how she could reach Glenda Cooper and he very cooperatively looked up her number and she jotted it down. She immediately dialed it as soon as she got Champion off the phone; the chatty guy didn't quite know when to quit. A busy signal buzzed in her ear. Hmm, who doesn't have voice mail anymore? The thought crossed her mind that Champion might have dialed Glenda Cooper himself, in order to be the bearer of the news, but a quick dial back to him and his phone rang. She hung up before he could answer. Cooper's line immediately went to an answering device on the second try but Sam didn't leave a message. She realized she was tired.

Sam yawned and gathered Fenton's notes into a stack. Okay, so she would try Glenda Cooper again in the morning and see if she could track down Lisa Tombo. At least she felt like she was doing something to help Marla.

She poured the unfinished half cup of tea down the drain, noticing for the first time that a few snowflakes drifted past the window. She switched off the light and stared out into the darkness. A scant half-inch of the white stuff coated the landscape and her vehicles, nothing near the amount of doom-and-gloom called for by the weather forecasters.

She peeked into Kelly's room on her way to the bathroom and found her daughter sprawled on top of the covers. *You'll be freezing by morning*, she thought as she tugged the spread out from under her snoring body and draped it over the top. Some things never changed. She would always be a mom, she supposed.

Don't get hurt with this new romance, little one.

Chapter 10

It was mid-morning before Sam remembered to try calling Glenda Cooper again, not exactly optimal timing. She tried to tune out the bakery noises all around her as she sat at her desk, but it was impossible. Finally, taking her cell phone and bundling into her heaviest coat against the blustery air outside, she stepped out to the alley.

The overnight snowfall had only amounted to an inch or so, but the temperatures had dropped dramatically and she'd opted to drive her pickup truck in case there was more weather and she might need the four wheel drive. She shivered and leaned against the big vehicle, hoping to draw a little warmth from it.

Glenda answered on the second ring with, "Website Answers. How may I help you?"

Sam had already decided that an HR person wasn't likely

to fork over information on a former employee, especially if the inquiry sounded official, so she'd cooked up a story about being a friend of a friend, someone Lisa would know. She needed to know how to get in touch with Lisa now, and really hoped Glenda could help her.

Other phones were ringing in the background and Glenda stopped twice to put people on hold before Sam even got her cover story out.

"I'm sorry," she said when she came back on the line the second time. "Now, what was it you needed?"

"I can see that you're really busy. Lisa Tombo—I just need to quickly get in touch with her."

"Lisa Tombo?" The wheels turned for another couple of seconds. "Oh, Lisa from Bellworth?"

"Yes, thank you," Sam said. "I guess the address I have for her is old since my Christmas card came back. Do you happen to have a current address or phone number for her?"

Another phone rang. "She's back in Albuquerque but we've kind of lost touch," Glenda said. "Can I put you on hold again?"

"I'll just let you go. Thanks so much." Sam clicked off and jammed the phone and her frozen hand into her pocket.

She stepped gingerly through the thin layer of snow and up the steps to the bakery's back door. The heat from the oven felt so good that she stood still for a moment, soaking it up.

"Sam, Jen was just looking for you," Becky said. "Something about a birthday cake order."

Sam shed her jacket and headed toward the fridge. "I think I know which one it is. Lemon cake, white fondant,

'Happy Birthday Betty'. I finished it early this morning because the customer said he would be in around ten."

She retrieved the cake, carried it out to the gray-haired man who gave a noncommittal nod and fished a twenty out of his pocket. Women were so much more complimentary, probably because a lot of them had attempted to decorate a cake and knew that it wasn't just a simple task. She gave the guy a smile and went back to the kitchen.

It was time to buckle down to the daily production of chocolates. Although she'd re-created the flavor and a little of the pizzazz of Bobul's chocolate techniques, she was nowhere close to the speed of his production. Even when she'd relied on the wooden box for a boost in energy, she still felt like she was moving in molasses-time compared to the way the chocolatier had turned out hundreds of pieces a day. And now the supply out front was nearly gone.

She pulled out the new heart-shaped gift boxes and experimented with placement of the variously shaped pieces, fitting a pound of candy into each box. Once she'd come up with a pleasing arrangement, she used one box as an example and told Sandy to fill the others in exactly the same manner.

While Sam stirred dark chocolate at the stove and added Bobul's prescribed pinches of this and that, she monitored the progress around her. Becky was stacking and filling layer cakes and quarter-sheets, smoothing buttercream icing on some, merely dirty-icing the ones that would require fondant. Sam considered that it might be a good idea to teach Becky how to roll and apply the sugar-dough coating. It would free up more of her own time.

But, for now, chocolates were the pressing matter. She watched the candy thermometer for the precise moment to pull the double-boiler off the stovetop.

"Clear me a spot," she said to Sandy, preparing to pour and temper the chocolate.

She'd just finished dipping caramels and fruit crèmes when her phone rang.

"Hey, darlin'. How's your day?"

"A little crazy, but crazy is the new normal, isn't it?"

He laughed. "Any chance of you taking a break for lunch? My treat."

She looked at the stack of order sheets and the cakes Becky had iced, now awaiting her expert touch with the pastry bag.

"Oh, Beau, I don't see how. I'm really up to my eyeballs today."

"Okay." He sounded disappointed.

"Tonight? Maybe I can make dinner at home. I do have a little new information on the Tito Fresques situation."

He gave the verbal equivalent of a shrug and she felt badly when he hung up. Here they were, getting married in four more days. He must already be feeling like she was taking him for granted.

"Sam?" Sandy waved a hand toward the chocolate on the table, which was setting up far too quickly.

"Oh no." Sam reached with the spatula to begin spreading it and Beau's concerns got shoved aside again.

Someone brought a pizza into the kitchen at some point and Sam thought she remembered taking a few bites from a slice. She didn't actually remember finishing it but when she looked around the room no trace remained.

Jen bustled back and picked up the boxed chocolates that Sandy had organized, and Sam remembered glancing at the clock and saw that it was already after three. Becky had left at some point. She'd saved the tempered chocolate, poured the molds and then had moved on to decorating cakes. Dozens of little fondant hearts lay scattered on the table.

The phone rang and she became busy taking an order.

"Sam? Jen just buzzed—something about a consultation or something?" Sandy almost wrung her hands whenever she had to deliver news.

"Thanks, I'll be right there," Sam said, heading for the front, order pad in hand. But the customer had gone.

"It was Ivan," Jen said. "Reminding you that tonight is Chocoholics Unanimous."

"Oh no." Sam closed her eyes and thought hard. "Okay, I can do this."

There was a chocolate Kahlua cake already baked. She couldn't remember whether she'd planned for it to go into the display case or if somehow in the muddle of her mind she'd automatically known that the bookstore's weekly meeting of chocolate fanatics was coming up. She dashed to the back and found her mother's recipe for Texas Chocolate Frosting. She'd never used this one for the book club, so they would find it new and different. Plus, it was easy.

While the butter and powdered sugar blended in the mixer bowl, Sam chopped pecans and filled the layers with her special chocolate-crunch filling. The nutty, chocolate frosting flowed over the top and down the sides of the cake, leaving little freeform spaces. It wasn't the most elegant in looks, but it would definitely be one of the better tasting cakes she'd ever made for them.

She stuck it into the fridge while she finished placing the fondant hearts and adding little frosting touches to the four generic Valentine cakes that waited on the table. By the time she carried the Kahlua cake next door to Ivan's shop, the frigid outside air felt fantastic on her damp forehead.

"Ah, Samantha, is being a wonderful cake for our mystery group," Ivan raved. "Can you be coming tonight?"

"I haven't had a chance to read the book," she admitted. When was the last time she'd had the chance to read *any* book? She wiped a wrist across her forehead, sending her bangs straight upward. "Things will settle down soon. No more sweet shop holidays for awhile, and then after the wedding . . ."

"Is a busy time. Ivan know this. You come when you can." He patted her shoulder and she just wanted to collapse into one of his big wingback chairs and pretend that her phone was broken and her shop didn't exist.

But that wouldn't do. She thanked him and stuck his check into her pocket, eyeing the table full of bargain books as she walked toward the door.

Back inside Sweet's Sweets, Sam noticed that Jen had two customers mulling over the displays; everything seemed under control there. The beverage bar was another matter. The coffee carafes were nearly empty, tea selection needed to be replenished and a scattering of stir sticks and spilled sugar certainly must be cleaned up before the afternoon dessert crowd came. She scooped the small items into the trash and reached under the counter for a pack of her special coffee.

Almost on auto-pilot she filled the filter basket and water reservoir and started a fresh pot brewing. She was stooped in front of the storage cabinet, rummaging for the boxes of tea bags when she heard the front door jingle again.

"Oh, lovely! I'm so happy to see that you've made more

of the chocolates," the customer exclaimed. "And heart-shaped boxes—perfect!"

Jen finished ringing up a sale to the older lady who had been there first, then greeted the newcomer. "How are you? Two days in a row. It's good to have you back."

Sam turned to see who it was. The woman who'd worn the tiger-print dress and bright orange nails. Today she had fuchsia nails, and a hot-pink dress that came halfway up her slender thighs, under a silver fox coat that flowed around her like Superwoman's cape. The tousled red hair, amazingly, didn't clash but seemed to set off the dazzling outfit. Sam felt every grain of the sugar that encrusted her own hair and the flour that inevitably clung to her black slacks by this time of day. She tried to melt into the wall next to the beverage bar but it didn't work very well.

"Felicia Black," the woman was saying to Jen, extending her hand. "Now that I'm back in town I can't seem to stay away from here, can I?"

She picked up one of the heart-shaped boxes of chocolates and hugged it to her way-too-visible chest while she studied the contents of the display case.

Jen glanced toward Sam, who was trying hard for a shred of dignity, to look more owner-like than servant-like. But the minute she picked up the box of sugar packets, intending to pull out a few and place them in the little glass holders on the tables, something slipped. The box practically leapt out of her hands, came open, and sent the little white packets flying.

"Oh, my, how unfortunate," Felicia Black said. Somehow, she was even taller and thinner than yesterday.

Sam murmured an apology and began grabbing up the

loose packets. This was ridiculous! She wasn't about to let a snooty customer make her feel inferior. She shoved the fallen packets toward the baseboard, set the box on the counter and calmly walked toward the kitchen for a broom. *I will not lower myself to sweeping the floor in her presence,* she thought. *It can wait a minute or two.*

But Ms. Black seemed intent on taking forever. She asked a dozen questions about the various pastries, which Jen answered with utmost courtesy. Sam peered around the edge of the curtain. Finally, the customer set the heart box on the counter and reached toward the microscopic purse that hung by a skinny strap over her shoulder.

"I've got someone special in mind for these chocolates," Felicia said. "Have you tasted them?"

Jen nodded and punched some keys on the register. "They're really good, aren't they?"

"Better than good." Felicia lowered her voice. "I think they can make a person fall in love."

Sam almost pulled the curtain down. Was that what was going on with Kelly and Riki last night? With her married employees who couldn't wait to get home to their husbands after work?

Jen started to open her mouth, then closed it. She'd noticed the same thing—Sam would bet on it.

"So anyway . . . there's a special man here in Taos. We dated a few years ago. I thought it might go somewhere . . . permanent . . . but it didn't. Maybe we were simply too young at the time. Now, however . . ." A grin spread over her perfect features and she raised an auburn eyebrow at Jen. "Now, I think I know how to get him back."

Jen passed the gold card through the machine and waited for it to process. "Oh? He still lives here, then?"

Felicia sighed. "Yes. He stayed when I left. I couldn't seem to convince him to try life in the big city." She signed the slip Jen had set on the counter. "But this time he'll come. I will just bet he's not found anyone to compare with me, here in Taos."

Jen managed to suppress the expression that would have said, that's a pretty safe bet.

"You might even know him," Felicia said. "His name is Beau Cardwell."

Chapter 11

Sam nearly fell through the split in the curtain. Jen was staring at the back of Felicia Black, her mouth hanging open, as the woman flung the door open and swooped out toward her Lexus.

"What nerve! I'll—" Sam marched toward the door, intent on grabbing the witch in the silver fur and yanking her off her feet.

"Sam." Jen said it so quietly that Sam stopped in her tracks. "You've got a little—" She brushed her finger across her cheek.

Sam reached up to her own face, wiped at it and came away with a smear of chocolate. How long had that been there? She slumped and turned away from the windows.

"I . . . surely she can't . . ."

"She can't be for real," Jen said. "And she darn sure

won't get Beau. He's in love with you."

Sam straightened her shoulders.

An SUV pulled up to the curb as Felicia's silver Lexus drove away. Sam quickly scooped up the rest of the spilled sugar packets and ducked though the curtain as another customer opened the door. In the small restroom at the back, she took a hard look in the mirror. A faint trace of the chocolate smear remained, and the short layers of her hair stuck out at odd angles. She didn't remember running her fingers through her hair earlier but she must have, while her head was all sweaty. A blob of red frosting had landed on the white baker's jacket, smack on her right boob, in addition to the normal-enough smudges that she half expected to always be there.

"I'm such a disaster," she wailed at herself in the glass. Her eyes began to well up. *I have to draw the line at this,* she thought. *I cannot walk back out there and let my crew see me with red eyes.* She grabbed a paper towel and wet it, ridding herself of the smears and sugar granules. The jacket would have to go into the wash, but luckily she'd brought a spare one for precisely this reason. She reached into the medicine cabinet and found her hairbrush, worked with the graying layers until she didn't look quite so ridiculous. She stood up straight, raised her chin, and walked out to the kitchen to change her jacket.

The writing on the order sheets dimmed in front of her eyes and the normal bustle of the kitchen went unnoticed. *Should I warn Beau about Felicia Black? Tell him she's back and looking for him?* She set the pages back on the desk. When they'd started dating they used to sit under the stars, talking about their lives, getting to know each other. Beau had already told Sam that he'd dated beautiful women, that he'd in fact been married to a former model for a few years. When she'd compared herself to them, Beau assured her that the glamour life and the beautiful, self absorbed women were of no interest to him.

His simple roots on a ranch and the fact that he'd settled into basically that same life in his adult years reassured her that despite the fact that glamorous women tended to latch onto him, he genuinely did not want their lifestyle. Felicia Black had, no doubt, chosen Beau because they would look so good together, but did she really know him? Would she ever be content to wake up day after day in his log house and help him feed the horses on frosty mornings? Sam formed a picture of the redhead in her high heels and fur coat trudging through spring mud and scooping up oats for a horse. The image was so comical that she caught herself chuckling.

Beau loved *her*. He was the one who wanted to get married without a long engagement. He'd never done anything to make Sam believe otherwise.

So there, Felicia Black. You won't get him.

Sam dimly became aware that someone was speaking to her.

". . . closing up now?" It was Jen. Sandy and Cathy had apparently already said goodbye, although Sam barely remembered their leaving.

"Sure. Can you make sure the tables and beverage bar are ready for the morning?" Sam said.

"I did. Everything's in good shape." Jen pulled the sleeves of her wool coat over her arms. "Sam? About earlier?"

Sam looked up.

"I would have done the same. If somebody like that threatened to get my man. I know, Michael and I are still really new together . . ."

Less than a week, if Sam recalled.

"But I'd still claw her eyes out."

Sam couldn't help it—laughter welled up at the image of the polite and diminutive Jennifer clawing anyone's eyes out. The mood was contagious and Jen gave in to giggles, herself.

"I know, crazy huh?" She finally said, wiping her coat sleeve across her eyes. "I'm much more likely to be a sneaky poisoner." She straightened her shoulders and buttoned her coat. "Okay, reality check. You know I'm kidding about all of this, right?"

They both laughed and Jen headed for the door.

With the bakery quiet at last, Sam concentrated on re-checking the status of the upcoming orders. Including her own wedding cake. She stared at the sketches for a few minutes. As much as she and Beau wanted to share their lives together, the real test was all the ceremonial hoopla which, no matter how simple you wanted it to be, invariably became complex. Cake, dress, flowers and invitations had taken over most of the last month. The crush of new business had kept her sidetracked all week. When had she lost the focus that she simply wanted to be Beau's wife?

She set the cake sketches aside and went online to place her supply order. That accomplished, she shut down the computer and pushed her chair up to the desk. A quick survey of the sales area showed everything neatly organized, the night lighting casting a warm glow on the front window displays. A Bakery of Magical Delights, said the slogan on the door. She smiled and sighed.

Despite her aching muscles and the months of work it had taken to get the pastry shop up and running, Sam knew she wouldn't change a thing. She still loved creating beautiful things to brighten people's lives. Even with its frustrations, she felt so happy that she'd begun to master the techniques of making her fabulous chocolates. And once things quieted down this spring she intended to work on new designs, some signature chocolate pieces that she might be able to sell online as well as here in the shop.

Now all she had to do was stop by the supermarket and grab a few items for dinner. She'd decided to make one of Beau's favorite pasta dishes, something she'd invented by accident a few weeks ago, with chicken and vegetables in a creamy sauce. Picking up the fresh veggies was her final errand. But her phone rang just as she was starting the truck.

"Darlin', I'm sorry I have to take a rain check on dinner tonight." His voice sounded a little edgy.

"Oh—what's up?"

"Just work stuff. But I can't break away anytime soon."

A surge of disappointment.

"Sam? I love you." This time his voice definitely had a strained quality. But when she started to reply, he'd already hung up.

Damn. The nice dinner would have been her perfect opportunity to warn him that Felicia Black was back in town. She'd envisioned Beau across the dinner table, the pasta dish, a nice wine, having a few laughs over the silliness of this piece of fluff thinking she would just move right in and win him back. She drummed her fingers on the steering wheel then put the truck in gear. Not much she could do about it now.

Traffic around the plaza was sparse and Sam waited at the light.

What if Beau already knew Felicia was in town? What if she'd found him and . . . No. The idea that he'd canceled their dinner because of his ex-girlfriend . . .

She caught herself thinking about swinging around the corner to be sure his cruiser was at the office. When the light changed she turned left.

Sam . . . what are you doing? *This is so high school. You love the man. You trust him completely. He has never lied about anything—the guy is the epitome of honesty and integrity.*

She turned in at the first alley and used it to circle the block and head for home. Even though she knew she could trust Beau, she was absolutely certain that she could *not* trust Felicia.

Chapter 12

Thoughts raced in turmoil as Sam drove home and walked into the dark house. Kelly was either reading stories at the nursing home or was out with Ryan again. Remembering the romantic effects of those chocolates wasn't helping Sam's peace of mind any. Felicia had bought the largest heart-shaped box in the store today and plainly stated her intentions to get Beau back. If he ate them, the tiger-lady's plan just might work.

Tossing her backpack on the table and hanging up her coat, Sam debated. Taking any action at all would make Beau think she didn't trust him. But not taking action could be disastrous. She felt as if a low voltage current was racing through her veins as she changed out of her work clothes. The wooden box stared at her from the dresser top, but this was one time when Sam couldn't think of a single way in which the box could help her.

She stared around her bedroom, at the unfilled packing cartons and at the closet where she'd begun going through her clothes and getting rid of things she no longer needed, donating them to the thrift shop and generally clearing the clutter of the old life in order to start the new. They'd planned on spending the weekend moving her things to his house. Not everything, as Sam would leave the furniture and a lot of the kitchen gear for Kelly. Beau had said nothing of changing that plan, and Sam would not let negatives sneak into her thinking. She gave the carved jewelry box a stroke for luck and turned toward the kitchen.

Her cell phone lay on the table, in the little pile of things she'd pulled from her pockets. She picked it up and composed a text message before she could talk herself out of it: **Don't eat any chocolate. Will explain later**. She hit the Send button and dropped the phone to the table. For better or worse, she'd interfered with fate.

* * *

A rough night caused by man-worries had not happened in Sam's life in many years and she wanted to refuse to believe that was the reason she woke approximately every hour on the hour and why, now at three-thirty, she felt resigned to being awake.

Moving day. She should be sleeping at Beau's tonight and every night till death did them part, but she knew she needed to be absolutely sure of what would happen with Felicia before she could do it. She sighed and rolled up on one elbow. There was no way to get the answer to that question at this ungodly hour and decided she could make better use of the time than continuing to twist the bedcovers in knots.

Her father had always quoted some old saying about idle hands and as Sam tiptoed through the quiet house she decided that huddling in the corner of the couch with endless cups of tea was not the answer. Even though Jen had promised to open the shop and the other ladies would get the breakfast pastries underway, Sam knew she would be more content to be working than sitting around.

Like some kind of secret Christmas elf, she entered the shop stealthily and got out her decorating tools. Two hours passed as she pulled sheetcakes and layers from the freezer. Filling, frosting, decorating . . . she found her zone. She'd already left the shop well set with stock cakes for the Saturday sales needs. Now she finalized a wedding cake and the last of the proposal cakes. They all went to the fridge, ready for the customers to pick them up in the coming two days.

At six-fifteen she put away the pastry bags and wiped down the worktable. When the girls arrived at six-thirty, no one need know she'd been there. She locked up and started her truck, heading back home toward coffee, packing cartons and an important conversation with Beau.

With a steaming mug in hand as fortification, she dialed his home number. No answer. He might be outside with the animals. But his cell went to voicemail as well. He'd taken the day off work to help with the move, but maybe last night's emergency had spilled over into the morning hours. She'd almost convinced herself to call the department when her phone rang in her hand.

"Samantha, it's Marla Fresques."

Her friend's voice sounded small and tired, like she could barely get the words out.

"Marla, is everything okay?"

"Not really, Sam. I'm not doing so good. My doctor wants me to be in the hospital."

Oh, no. Don't say this is the end.

"I wondered . . . did your sheriff friend find Tito yet?"

Poor thing. Sam realized that Marla had no idea it wasn't that simple.

"I'm afraid not, Marla. We're working on it. I've got some names of his old co-workers in Albuquerque."

"Can you go there, Sam? Find my Tito and bring him back. I need this. Jolie needs him, very soon."

Sam set her mug down. The last thing she needed was to blow this whole day by driving to Albuquerque. She paced as the silence on the line grew longer.

"I'll go, Marla." *What am I saying?* "You just rest. Do what your doctor says."

"Thank you, Sam." The words came out in a breathless rush.

She quickly dialed Beau's cell again, this time leaving the message that she needed to go to Albuquerque on an emergency and would have to delay the packing and moving until tomorrow. She knew she had to act while momentum was on her side.

Surely she wouldn't simply go there and come back with Tito Fresques in the truck with her, but she certainly wasn't having much luck by phoning his friends here in Taos. She found Lisa Tombo's address and phone number online. If she showed up at the door then maybe a personal plea would bring the information to get him back home to his mother and his daughter. That was her line of thinking, anyhow, as she grabbed a granola bar and an apple for breakfast and tossed her heavy coat, Fenton's file and her backpack into the truck.

Two hours later, approaching the outskirts of the sprawling city she fished one-handed into her pack for the address. The street name wasn't familiar to her, not surprisingly, since she knew so little about the layout of this city. She spotted a McDonald's ahead at an exit so she whipped off the freeway and headed that direction.

A strong cup of coffee and a table where she could study the map from her glove compartment, and she eventually figured out where the house was, in the northeast quadrant of town. She jotted a series of notes about which turns to take—this would have been so much easier from home, with the computer—and she was back on the road a few minutes later.

It felt strange to find herself in a neighborhood of tract homes with squared-off block walls separating them. So different from Taos. But she made the turns and found herself in front of a flat-roofed house stuccoed white with a few bits of bright green wood trim. Freeform brick borders separated the winter-brown lawn from sections of colored rock and some evergreen shrubs. A fairly new blue Pontiac sat on the concrete driveway, taking up both sides of the double garage door in front of it.

She got out of the truck and followed a precise strip of sidewalk to a flat front porch.

Lisa Tombo came to the door wearing a turquoise track suit, with a ball cap over her brown hair and earbuds dangling from their cords over her shoulders, like she'd just come in from running. She held the door to a narrow wedge, to keep the heat in and her visitor out.

Lisa seemed puzzled when Sam said she was trying to locate Tito Fresques, her brown eyebrows drawing together in the middle. After a minute, she invited Sam inside where they settled on a pair of armchairs that looked they were never used.

"Well, yeah, I worked with him," Lisa said when Sam mentioned having talked to some people from Bellworth. "We were pretty close, you know. He'd talk about his wife and baby all the time. We ate lunch in the company cafeteria quite a bit. Even though we worked in the same department, he was in the electronics lab most of the day and I had a desk job. Assistant to the department manager. So we met up in the cafeteria and swapped stories for a half hour or so. Sometimes a few of us would go out for a beer on Friday nights after work. But Tito never stayed late. One beer, he'd go."

"Some people said there were rumors about an affair."

"Yeah, an investigator brought that up right after he left. But me and Tito? Hunh-uh. He was a hundred percent in love with his wife."

The way she said it made Sam think that Lisa would have been perfectly willing had Tito made a move.

"And you haven't heard from him since? Not even a card or letter?"

She noticed no signs of deception when Lisa Tombo said no. "He disappeared from my life at the same moment he disappeared from work. And I moved on shortly after that, myself. I'd already gotten a job in Denver and given my notice at Bellworth a couple weeks before Tito left."

Sam tried to think what else Beau might have asked, but couldn't come up with anything other than whether Lisa knew anyone else Tito had been close to, someone he might have confided in.

"What about Harry Cole or Bill Champion?" Sam asked. "They worked with him."

Lisa shrugged. "Different section from mine. I knew the names but wasn't really close to either of them."

Lisa got up to walk Sam to the door. "You know, there was something unusual that last day he was there. I didn't remember it when that investigator questioned me. That day, I met up with Tito for lunch like usual. Well, he came in all flushed and nervous. I joked around, asked if he'd gotten a jolt from a wire or something. He laughed it off, but now that I think about it, he kept looking around the room. Like maybe somebody was going to come in and chew him out. I just figured he'd broken something in the lab and was hoping not to catch hell for it."

Sam opened the door and felt the chilly breeze rush into the house. She pushed it closed again when Lisa spoke.

"Actually, later that afternoon, somebody did come around looking for Tito." Her brows did that wrinkly thing again as she worked at remembering. "Dark suit, white shirt, tie. I'm thinking blond hair, maybe? He popped up at my desk and I told him which way to go down the hall to the lab. He had all the right clearances and an ID card on his lanyard, like everyone else who worked there. I guess I never gave it a second thought."

"That was on a Friday?"

"That's right. I remember Tito skipped going out for beers that night because he and the family were driving somewhere to go visit his mother or somebody like that."

Sam nodded and thanked Lisa Tombo for the information. Back in her truck, she wondered what, exactly, she had learned. Tito was nervous on his last day of work and later some guy in a dark suit had come looking for him. That could be explained in so many ways, including the way Lisa viewed it—Tito had broken something in the lab and someone from management wanted to speak to him about it.

But then, what had happened over the weekend? Sam couldn't help but believe Tito's disappearance was tied to his job at Bellworth. If he'd simply been grabbed off the streets in Taos and robbed, he would have turned up—dead or alive—shortly afterward.

She opened Fenton's file and found the notes from her phone calls the previous night. It took a few minutes with the city map but she located streets and jotted directions before pulling away from the curb, mulling over all the information as she left Lisa's little tract neighborhood.

Harry Cole's home was the closer, so she followed Montgomery Boulevard east until she reached his area. Another tract home, another winter-dry yard, this one not as neatly kept as Lisa's. No answer at the door.

Sam caught a neighbor openly watching her, eyeing her red pickup truck suspiciously. She crossed the space between the two yards and walked toward the woman who quickly began coiling up a stiff length of green garden hose.

"They ain't home," came the brusque greeting. "Prob'ly down to Isleta."

Sam remembered Cole's comment about liking the casinos and guessed that the Isleta Pueblo had a good one. She thanked the neighbor, deciding against leaving a message. The nosy woman didn't need to know any of what was going on in Taos. Cole hadn't been especially helpful on the phone anyway. She drove away, noticing that the neighbor stared at her until she rounded the corner.

Her only other contact, Bill Champion, met her at the door of his fairly new, upscale home and ushered her into a world of hardwood floors, pale beige furniture, and minimalist décor. Seeing no wifely touches, Sam decided he had hired an expensive decorator.

"Yeah, I sure do remember your call," he said, offering her a beer while he muted the volume on the football game on a huge flat-screen TV. "You found out anything about Tito Fresques yet?"

He ushered her toward a leather couch, while he resumed his spot on a recliner beside an end table full of snack food packages and beer bottles.

"Not a lot. Glenda Cooper seems to be in the computer business now and Lisa Tombo lived away from Albuquerque long enough that she's lost touch with everyone."

"Yep, yep. Not surprised." His eyes darted toward the silent TV screen about every fifteen seconds.

"Lisa did mention someone who was looking for Tito the last day he was at work at Bellworth. She thought he had blond hair, wore a suit and tie." Even as she said it, Sam realized what pitifully little information that was.

Champion actually turned his attention toward her, chewing at the inside of his cheek as he thought about it. Slowly, his head began to nod.

"Could have been Rick Wells. He still comes around once in a great while. Inspector, auditor maybe?" He stopped, as if that explained everything.

"He still works for Bellworth?"

"Oh, no. Outside guy. Used to come in a few days at a time, keep everyone jumping, finding reports and all. Well, I guess he did. Wasn't part of my job description."

"But he audited Tito's work? Or Tito reported to him?" Sam's experience with auditors was nil, although she'd once had to send copies of her bank statements to someone at the IRS, years ago.

"No idea. I suppose so. I would see Wells show up, Tito would talk to him awhile. That's about all I remember."

His eyes were back on the game, his face lighting up at whatever was going on there, and Sam knew she wouldn't be getting much more from Bill Champion. She stood, which distracted him from the TV long enough to listen to her request for Rick Wells's address, hand her the telephone directory then see her to the door.

Back at the truck she pulled out her map again and repeated a tedious perusal of the city map. Forty-five minutes later she'd made her way across the river to the suburb of Rio Rancho, missed two crucial turns in the horrendous traffic on Coors Road, and finally pulled onto the street she'd identified as Wells's. His home was a cookie-cutter bachelor condo, the kind of place a guy buys after a divorce has forced him to split twenty years of accumulation with the ex who's finally had it with his non-stop—fill in the blank—work hours/womanizing/drinking or general slobbery.

When Wells came to the door, Sam put her money on womanizing. The guy was good-looking and knew it, probably always on the prowl. He wore his blond hair short and business-like, and his casual warm-up suit looked as if it had been custom made for him.

She briefly explained her mission, asking if he remembered Tito Fresques and if he knew anything that might help the authorities to locate the missing man.

"Absolutely, I remember Tito. He was in electrical engineering at Bellworth, one of the companies I routinely audit. Personable guy, very forthcoming." His smile brightened in a way that reminded Sam of those infomercial hosts who sell ice cube makers to Eskimos.

"Were you at Bellworth the last Friday of August, ten years ago? Or maybe the following Monday? Tito disappeared sometime that weekend."

"Really? I'm so sorry to hear that. He was a nice guy."

She asked a couple more questions and got the same type of answers. Sam watched his face as he talked. He seemed genuine enough but was he actually giving her any information? Maybe that's how auditors were—trained to get more information than they gave.

After ten minutes of conversation she began to feel that they were going in circles. She couldn't think of anything more to ask, and the sun had definitely given up trying to warm the day. She shivered her way back to the truck.

She made a couple of quick stops; there were always things available in the city that couldn't be easily obtained in Taos, and after grabbing a quick burger for lunch she was northbound again on I-25.

The weekend traffic on the interstate roared past her. *Sheesh,* she thought as a big black Suburban with opaque windows nearly took off her rear fender, *am I that much of a country rube? I'm not going that slowly.*

She watched as the vehicle crossed three lanes and disappeared at the next exit. She left the northern boundaries of the city putting the close encounter behind her and beginning to relax.

With no companions in the truck, she found herself again thinking about Tito, his last day at work, his drive to Taos and his final day with his family. What would possess a man to abandon everything and go underground? When she phrased it that way, she wondered if perhaps the guy had led some kind of secret life. Bellworth got a lot of government contracts. Much of the work in Albuquerque and Los Alamos, particularly, was classified. Maybe he'd seen or heard something on that Friday at work that he wasn't supposed to know about.

Chapter 13

The Rio Grande rushed counter to Sam's northbound heading as she neared Taos, and the final climb to the high desert revealed the crooked slash of the gorge with the town and mountains sharp in the distance. The magnificent scene soothed the city stress out of her. *A person can just never get tired of this,* she thought.

Her speedy trip to Albuquerque had netted information; she just wasn't sure what to do with it yet. She should check on Marla, find out whether she'd been taken to the hospital. But Sam felt that she should report her findings to Beau first. She pulled out her cell phone and speed dialed his. He sounded a little distracted but told her to stop by his office. Apparently his plans for a day off had changed too.

With any luck he would either reopen the investigation or press hard with the Albuquerque police to do so. She slowed as the road narrowed into the outpost of Ranchos de Taos, past the old church famously depicted by Georgia O'Keefe. It soon widened again within the town limits where curbs and sidewalks were a recent addition.

The sun had dropped low over the western volcanoes, making her crank up the heater setting one more notch. The turnoff to her street beckoned but she ignored it and headed toward Beau's office. Whether he was interested in opening Tito's case or not, Sam needed to see him.

Not many people had business with the sheriff's office at dusk on a Saturday, it seemed, and she easily found a parking spot. The desk officer greeted her with a smile, glancing at her watch to see if her shift might be nearly over. Apparently not.

"I think he's in his office," she told Sam. "Go on back." She sighed and went back to some papers.

Since Beau had taken over the job of sheriff, after the previous man was run out of town in disgrace, he'd inherited an actual office rather than one of the desks in the open-space squad room. She walked up to the open door, prepared to tap, but he wasn't there. She glanced around and a flash of red caught her attention.

She felt the breath go out of her. A heart-shaped box of her special chocolates sat on the corner of the desk, open. Felicia Black had been here.

Sam stared around the squad room and into the empty interrogation room. Called out to him. Beau was nowhere to be seen. The lid on the chocolates was propped partway open. Two pieces were missing. Her heart sank.

She slowly replaced the lid. He'd eaten some of the candy and she would bet money that Felicia had stood there and watched him do it. Then she'd probably worked her bright smile and flirtatious ways on him. Sam felt her temper rise.

That tramp! Beau surely told her he was engaged and yet she still came on to him. Sam picked up the chocolates and tucked the box under her arm. Her self confidence began to wane. She walked out, past the front desk, down the sidewalk to her truck, each step an effort. The combination of the special ingredients for the chocolates and her handling of the magical wooden box must have created an extra-strong batch.

Her joy at seeing how much her customers appreciated them—how could it all have backfired on her so drastically?

She started her truck and pulled away from the curb. A half block away she spotted that distinctive silver Lexus. Felicia was still here in the neighborhood. Perhaps even inside the small inn at the end of the block. Sam felt a momentary urge to ram the car and then sprint along the row of buildings, to find Felicia and slap her way-too-pretty face. The image made her feel a little better but that sort of confrontation wasn't her style.

She waited at the corner for a break in the traffic, realizing that it had been a long day and she was exhausted. The drive to Albuquerque, the knowledge that a rival was after Beau—Sam decided to go home and lock her fragile emotions away for the night. In the morning, in a better state of mind, she would have to decide how to address this with Beau.

Down inside her pocket her phone buzzed but she ignored it.

Kelly's red car sat in the driveway at the house and lights glowed from the kitchen and living room windows, a welcoming sight. But the peace was short lived.

"Mom, what is going on between you and Beau?" Kelly demanded before Sam had even taken off her coat. Her daughter stood at the refrigerator, browsing the food choices. "He just called here, sounding kind of shaken up. He wants you to call him."

Sam hung up her coat, taking her time about it, then reached into her pocket for her phone. Sure enough, the missed call came from Beau's number.

Kelly stared at her.

"Either choose something or close the door," Sam said, nodding toward the fridge.

Kelly closed it and watched her mother cross the room. "You okay?"

Sam took a deep breath. "Probably."

"You obviously need a minute. I'll be in my room."

Sam filled the kettle with water and looked for a packet of her favorite raspberry spiced tea. The good part about a call from Beau was that he probably wasn't locked away in a hotel room with Felicia. She held that thought while she dialed him.

"Hey, where were you? Ortiz said you stopped by." His tone was a little hesitant.

"Where were *you*? She said you were in your office but I didn't find you anywhere." She took a deep breath. "Sorry. I didn't mean to be—"

"I, uh, just had to step out for a minute. Why didn't you wait?"

The kettle whistled and Sam turned off the burner.

"Darlin', really. I wasn't avoiding you."

"I found the chocolates on your desk. I brought them home with me, in case you were wondering."

"Oh, that."

"She was there, wasn't she?"

"Sam, I think we need to have this conversation in person. Can I come by?"

This could degenerate into a fight at this point or she could cool it down. "I'm tired, Beau. It's been a long day."

"Sam, nothing happened. I promise you."

She stared at the dark kitchen window. The wall phone rang. "I better get that," she said. "I'll talk to you in the morning."

What now? She clicked off Beau's call and reached for the other phone.

"Ms Sweet? This is Diane Milton. Marla Fresques wanted me to call you."

"Oh, dear, is she okay?" Sam's mental gears switched from her own problems to the much more serious ones Marla faced.

"She's in the hospital. I wanted to let you know that Jolie is staying with us. She knows that her grandmother is sick but Marla has been really obstinate about any of us letting the girl know how bad it is."

That's not good, Sam thought.

"She's pinning a lot of hope on your getting her son to come home. I guess she thinks that if Jolie has the positive news that her dad is back it'll make losing her grandmother easier to handle."

"What does the doctor say, about how long . . .?"

"They don't tell us much, mainly because I'm not related. But I get the feeling we might be down to a matter of days or weeks. They've recommended hospice care."

Sam stared at the teabag in her cup, where the water had become darker than coffee.

"Diane, I have to be frank with you. I've made almost no progress toward finding Tito, and the authorities aren't pursuing the case at all."

"I was afraid of that."

"I don't want to put it quite that bluntly to Marla," Sam said, "but I can't really give her any false hope, either."

"I know. Just do what you can." Diane hung up after giving her Marla's room number at the hospital.

Sam carried her tea to the table and dropped into one of the chairs. Marla dying, Felicia coming after Beau, the crazy schedule at her shop. And she was supposed to be moving to Beau's house today and getting married two days after that. Something had to give.

She picked up her cell phone and speed-dialed.

"Beau, you're right, we better talk tonight." As she clicked off she choked back a sob.

Chapter 14

Three minutes later, flashing red and blue lights bounced through her kitchen window. Well, one benefit of dating a law enforcement man was that when you said now, he came *now*. Sam bit back the smile that tickled at her mouth, dumping the scrap of ironic humor into the muddle of her other emotions.

Heavy steps hit the service porch and a second later he was in the kitchen. When he spotted her at the table he crossed the room in three strides.

"Darlin', what's—"

She stood up and let him pull her to his chest. The outdoor chill on his coat felt good against her hot skin. Somewhere behind her she heard Kelly's bedroom door open, a little exclamation, then the door closed again. Sam allowed herself to cave, sobbing until she became aware of

Beau's hands making wide circles on her back, his breathing steady in her ear.

"Shall we sit down?" he finally asked.

Her head shook against his chest. "I can't move."

He took her shoulders and stepped back, trying to make her meet his gaze.

"Have you eaten anything all day?" he asked. "You look plain tuckered out."

She sighed. "I can't remember. I think I had something in Albuquerque."

"Well, that was too many hours and too many miles ago. Let me find you something." He steered her back to her chair and pressed her into it.

He sat patiently while she worked on a bowl of vegetable soup. When she'd finished, he cleared the dishes and sat facing her.

"Better?"

She nodded.

"Okay, now that you can be a little bit coherent again, you want to tell me what this is all about?"

She took a deep breath. Where to start? "Several things, I guess. I just learned that Marla Fresques is dying, probably soon. I feel so obligated to follow up to find her son. She begged me, Beau. She may only have a few days."

He nodded slowly. "I'll do what I can to help. Somehow, I'll make time for it."

"I'm also getting a little freaked about moving and the wedding. It's coming up so fast."

He stared at her intently. "Are you changing your mind?" His voice came out barely above a whisper.

"I don't think so. But I need to know if you are." Her blood felt as if it were racing through her veins. "Felicia

Black. I need to know."

His gaze slid to the box of chocolates sitting across the table. Sam lifted the lid, revealing that two pieces were missing.

"She gave you those, right?" Sam asked.

"Darlin', don't worry. I got your message. I didn't eat any." He reached out to run his fingers down her arm. "I don't understand why, but I didn't touch 'em."

Sam flipped the lid back onto the box. As if the mere sight or smell of the candy might bewitch him.

"There's just something about this particular batch . . ." She wasn't quite sure how to explain it. Was the love-inducing power specific to the giver and receiver of the gift? Or did it simply work on anyone who got in its way?

"Were you there when she brought them?" she asked, hating the whine of jealousy that crept into her voice.

"I was."

"Did she . . ." Damn, it was hard to phrase the questions without sounding like a shrew.

"Sam, she did come on to me." He paused a fraction of a second too long. Realized it. "She kissed me. I stepped away, walked to the back door of the squad room and showed her out. Last I saw of her she was throwing me the finger along with a few choice words."

Sam found herself smiling at that image.

"So? Are these things tainted or something? Why didn't you want me to eat them? You would never let bad food out of your shop."

"No, they're not tainted." She chewed at her lip. "I don't really know how to explain it. Everyone who eats them seems to become very attracted to someone . . . And, well, I knew Felicia was coming after you."

She told him about the remarks she'd overheard Felicia make to Jen at the shop.

"So that's it." She shrugged. "I have to admit that I was afraid she might really win you back and with these things— You might actually fall for it."

He lifted the lid and peeked cautiously at the chocolates.

Sam said. "Who took the two pieces?"

Beau thought for a minute. "My bet would be on Rico. I'd said something about how you didn't want me eating any chocolate and he asked if I didn't want them anymore. I didn't say anything, but I'll bet he came back and took a couple." His mouth twitched. "In fact, an hour or so after the box arrived I caught him in one of the back rooms, kind of off to himself, talking on the phone in a very suggestive voice. He like to have jumped a mile when I spoke to him. He blushed and covered the phone."

"You think—"

"I think he was having phone sex. He's got this cute little girlfriend. Maybe they—"

"Oh my." Her eyes went wide.

"He came in a few minutes later, kind of jittery, said he had a bad headache coming on, wanted to go home for prescription medication." He rolled his eyes. "I had to let him go."

Sam pictured the deputy dashing home for a quickie and they both erupted in laughter at the same moment.

At least Rico's antics proved that the chocolates worked on anyone who ate them, not specifically the person who received them as a gift. And she hoped Rico's lust was solely directed at his girlfriend and not just any woman who crossed his path.

"Unless you want your whole department going on some kind of love-binge, I think you need to keep this candy away from the office."

"This stuff, it's just for you and me." He closed the box. "So. Felicia problem solved. Marla's problem, we will work on." He stared at the center of the table. "Wedding. What do you want to do?"

"I want to marry you." She waited until he met her gaze and then she repeated it. "But I can't cope with the push to do it in two days' time. There's too much going on right now. I feel like I was crazy to buy into the whole idea that it would be so romantic to do it on Valentine's Day."

"Fine with me." He reached out and took her hands. "Darlin', I want our life together to be happy. The marriage can't be a source of stress for us."

"Thank you." She sent him a little smile. "You're sure?"

He nodded.

"Kelly's probably starving by now. I kind of banished her to her room, I'm not sure how long ago."

"We'll fix it." He walked to the closed bedroom door and tapped. "Safe to come out now."

Kelly emerged cautiously. "You guys okay? I was getting a little worried in there."

At Sam's inquiry about dinner, Kelly admitted that she'd broken into her stash of late-night snack food, filling up on peanut butter crackers and trail mix.

"We've decided to put the wedding off for a few days," Sam said. "I'm sorry. I know you pictured how beautiful it would be at Valentine's Day but I just can't handle the bakery business and my own wedding at the same time."

She purposely didn't mention Felicia, although there

was no doubt Kelly had overheard a few juicy tidbits on the subject.

"So, I could help out by calling the guests," Kelly offered. "Gramma and Grampa will be kind of upset."

"Oh, why? They're used to me by now aren't they?" Sam half-joked. From the day she'd skipped out of west Texas at the age of eighteen she'd had the feeling her parents disapproved of most of her lifestyle choices. This could just be another checkmark on her mother's I-told-you-so list.

"Who else do I need to add to the call list?" Kelly was asking. "Florist? Judge?"

"At least the baker got the word in time. I won't have a cancellation charge there," Sam said, feeling her old sense of humor returning. "If you'll contact the others, I'll call Zoë. She better hear this from me or she'll freak."

Kelly headed toward the computer desk in the living room, the portable phone in her hand. For most of the guests an email would suffice. But the grandparents better get the word by phone. They were supposed to be in the car heading to New Mexico first thing in the morning.

Zoë took the news well, Sam thought, considering that she'd probably rearranged her living room, stocked a bunch of extra food, and turned down bookings at the B&B to dedicate her home to Sam's wedding.

"Samantha, are you *sure* you're all right?" she kept asking. "Never mind about the extra food. Most of it can go into the freezer. And if you don't reschedule the wedding and use it soon—well, our skiers will just get some exotic breakfasts for the next few weeks."

Beau stayed with Sam at the table, holding her hand, until she decided she'd been a baby about it long enough.

"Really, hon, I feel fine. Just giving myself a few extra

breathing days makes my whole outlook a lot less strained. How about some dessert?" She started to head toward the cupboards but noticed that he was eyeing the box of chocolates.

He wiggled his eyebrows. She craned her neck to be sure Kelly was tied up on the phone.

"You staying over?" she whispered.

At his nod, they both reached for the box at the same time. Four truffles later, they were ready to jump each other. Then Kelly showed up in the doorway.

"I reached Grampa. You'll have to call him tomorrow, Mom. He was a little freaked. Left messages for the florist and judge. They won't get them until Monday morning, I'm sure, but at least it's a little bit of notice. Friends are all notified. I'd recommend you don't answer the phone tonight or you won't ever get to bed."

She stopped, mouth open, ready to say something else, but she'd caught the electricity in the air. "Okay, I'm sensing that's not going to be a problem and I'm leaving you two alone right this minute."

She backed out of the doorway, holding her hands over her ears, la-la-la-ing all the way to her own room. A minute later they could hear booming rock music from behind her door.

"Oh god, now that's just too embarrassing," Sam said.

"We'll get over it," he whispered in her ear, switching out the kitchen light.

Chapter 15

Kelly was gone when Sam and Beau emerged from the bedroom Sunday morning. A note on the kitchen table: *I got into your candy last night. Sorry. Will be at Ryan's until further notice.* She'd signed it with a smiley face.

"Oh, man, I'm learning too much here," Sam said, picking up the note by a corner and dropping it into the trash. "Is it really a good idea for mothers and daughters to know details of each others' sex lives?"

Beau walked up behind her and snaked an arm around her waist. "You're both adults. Plus, you aren't exactly sharing details—yet."

"Yikes, Beau. It's almost the same. She saw us fawning all over each other last night and now I know she's gone off to do the same. And I haven't even met this Ryan yet."

He peeked into the candy box. "Looks like a third of it

is gone. She may not be home for a week."

Sam covered her eyes. "I don't want to see this or hear about it."

"Then we'll just set this out of harm's way." He set the lid in place and tucked the box into a lower cupboard, far toward the back. "You know, just because we're putting off the wedding doesn't mean you can't go ahead and move out to my place. You and Kelly wouldn't be quite so knowing of each other's movements that way."

"You're right," Sam told him, "but I've barely started packing all those boxes in the bedroom."

"In that case, how about a breakfast burrito out somewhere?"

Sunday mornings at their favorite little Mexican place were usually crazy and today was no exception. They got a table after about a fifteen minute wait, and with a cup of good, strong coffee Sam's mind was beginning to focus on things other than Beau's physique.

"Help me think through this situation with Tito Fresques," Sam said while they waited for their order. She filled him in on her interviews with Lisa Tombo and the co-workers.

"Well, Lisa's comment to you about his being nervous his final day at work might be the best clue we have," Beau said, glancing around the room in hopes of getting a coffee refill. "But she didn't know what it was that set him on edge?"

"She says she didn't."

"And she didn't recognize the man who came looking for him later?"

"Lisa didn't but I think it was probably the auditor that

Bill Champion told me about."

"An auditor's presence could easily account for Tito's nerves. I can make a few calls, maybe get hold of his security file. Everyone who works at a place like Bellworth, from the scientists to the typists gets a very thorough clearance investigation. Now that he's been gone ten years, maybe even a small town sheriff like myself can find out what was in it, and that might lead us somewhere."

"Thanks, hon. It would really help me out. I feel obligated to Marla now. She's so scared that she'll die and there won't be anyone to raise Jolie. It's a sad situation." Sam reached across the table and took his hand. "I have your case file in the truck."

She walked outside to get it while Beau flagged down the waitress for more coffee.

"Maybe there's something in here, something you'll see on a second reading?" she said, laying the file on the table beside him.

"I'm off duty today, so I guess it's as good a time as any. Cold cases generally have to be worked on personal time. Let me try calling in a favor with somebody in Albuquerque." He pulled his phone from a pocket and dialed.

While he was speaking quietly, their waitress showed up with the two steaming plates—eggs, bacon, hash browns and cheese, wrapped in a flour tortilla and smothered in green chile sauce. Sam tried to wait politely but the scent was about to make her drool.

"I should get a report later this afternoon," Beau said, picking up his fork. "Jonathan is a buddy I met at the law enforcement academy. He changed career paths and went to Quantico and ended up in the Albuquerque FBI office.

He can usually get his hands on background and security information. I've used him as a resource a couple times."

Sam dug into her meal. "I'd be interested to know if the report has any explanation as to how Tito might have sent cards to his family after he vanished," she said when she took time for a breath. "Had I mentioned that part of it to you?"

Beau shook his head and stared at her. "No. And there's nothing in our file about it. Why wouldn't Mrs. Fresques have reported that she was hearing from him?"

"Maybe she did. My guess is that if she said anything to Orlando Padilla about it, he told her that her son just had a guilty conscience after running off with that 'other woman.' Sent a card now and then so they wouldn't hate him." She pushed her empty plate aside and held her coffee mug with both hands. "But that makes no sense. Aside from the fact that Lisa Tombo told me there was no affair between them, a guy who is close enough to his mother to send cards would take the approach of eventually introducing her to this lover and trying to get mom to accept her. Don't you think so?"

He nodded. "Makes sense to me."

"Most of us would work harder at getting the family to accept a stranger than we would at hiding out for years just to be with this person. It's just the way we work, typically."

"And does that statement have anything to do with us? With my meeting your folks?" His lopsided smile became even more crooked as he held back a grin.

"Okay, maybe I'm the exception to the rule. I left home as a teenager, with no expectations, certainly no desire to ever return to my parents' way of life. They could accept it or they could just lump it. Besides, you have met them and I thought it went really well."

"Because your dad is a strictly law-and-order type."

"And because Mother is a pushover for a handsome man with a Southern accent."

"Just wait until they *really* get to know me." He wiggled his eyebrows.

Their waitress pushed the check onto the table without asking whether they wanted anything more, and Sam noticed that people were lined up at the door.

"We better give up our seats," she suggested. "I need to get home and keep packing."

Beau's phone rang before they'd reached their vehicles. His side of the conversation consisted of a lot of *uh-huh* and *really*, punctuated at the end by a *no kidding!* and "give me ten minutes." He rattled off a phone number.

"I need to go to my office," he said, as he clicked off.

"Emergency?"

"That was Jonathan."

"Quick response."

"Yeah, and the information is surprising. He's faxing a report and it's got to go directly into my hands. He says it includes confidential information and to expect gaps in the data. But basically Tito Fresques's job at Bellworth was a cover for something entirely different."

"Like what?"

"He didn't say. I expect we're about to learn whatever they're willing to tell us. Follow me over there?"

It took Sam two seconds to decide she'd rather know what was in the report than to go home and pack boxes.

Sundays around the plaza were always congested, although the chill weather was keeping a lot of folks from strolling around. Beau opted for the back streets and she followed, which took her past the little strip of shops where Sweet's Sweets sat quietly closed. Past the half-empty municipal parking lot they made the turn and found spots in the lot behind Civic Plaza.

He pulled out his key to the back door and they entered through the squad room where one deputy, a new man, was speaking on the phone, something about a guy they were holding at the county facility for an overnight disturbance. The fax machine at the far side of the room was sitting quietly. Beau's cell rang again, he gave a quick affirmative, and the machine started to whir. Four sheets of paper edged their way out and Beau picked up each one as it slid into the tray.

Beau nodded toward his office. He unlocked the door, ushered Sam inside and closed it again. He sat at the desk and she stood behind, looking over his shoulder. The pages seemed to be more of a typed report than actual employment forms or government documents. Jonathan Ernhart had taken a risk, transferring this information to a report and sending it.

"Drug enforcement?" Sam said. "Am I reading that right?"

Beau was running his finger down the lines as he read, not skimming ahead as she'd done. Tito Fresques worked for the DEA, performing certain undercover duties that frequently took him to Mexico, occasionally to Washington. His fluency in Spanish and ability to blend had gotten him the job. The Bellworth job as an electrician was purely a cover.

"His family never questioned this, an electrician being sent to Washington?" she mused.

"Doubtful that they ever knew where he went. Bellworth is a big enough entity that they might send guys out on jobs around the state. Tito could use that as a reason to be gone a day or two."

The second half of the report gave dates and places.

"Look, in mid-August he went into Mexico twice, once through Tijuana and again later to Juarez. That Juarez trip was just three days before he came to Taos and disappeared." Sam pointed to the line.

Beau nodded. Flipping to the previous sheet, he said, "He'd made both of those runs before. Four times to each place during June and July of that year."

"So he was familiar with the territory, met the same people each time?"

"Looks like it. They're only using code names. Tito was Panther. See here? He met with an Oso Negro twice and a Diablo Rojo several times."

"Were those guys, the Black Bear and the Red Devil, were they good guys or bad?" Sam wondered.

"Informants, I would guess. The real criminals would have probably been named. These codes are to protect the identities of the men DEA had to work with."

Sam thought about all this, questions flying at her. "And his family knew nothing of this?"

"Too dangerous. For them. A wife casually tells a friend that her husband is away on a trip, a wrong word here or there, and a guy is toast."

"Tito may have become toast anyway. Someone may have followed him to Taos that weekend."

"I think his body would have been found. These drug deals go bad, they don't usually take the time to transport a body very far, or to give it a decent burial." Beau set the pages down. "But it's a big state. Lots of room to lose things."

"Plus," Sam reminded him, "who sent the cards to his wife and child and his mother? Somebody who wanted him to disappear isn't going to keep up that pretense."

"Right. It's a lot more likely that Tito went into hiding. Saw something he shouldn't, could name the wrong person . . . I don't know. To stay hidden this long, I'd bet that he was feeling that there was no one he could trust. Maybe he stills feels that way. It would have to be someone pretty high up."

"Don't agencies have a protocol for that sort of thing, some kind of witness protection program for agents? Somebody they absolutely know they can trust, the person they can call when everything falls apart?"

He shrugged. "I would think so. I need to ask Jonathan some more questions."

Chapter 16

While Beau picked up his personal phone Sam excused herself to go to the restroom. She came out to find the deputy who'd earlier been in the squad room standing near Beau's closed door.

"Excuse me?" she said. She recognized him as the newest recruit, Denny Waters, a guy Beau had hired after Padilla left.

He started and spun around. "Oh, hi Sam. I just needed to ask the sheriff a question but it sounds like he's on the phone."

"He should be out in a few minutes," she said, standing her ground.

She watched him head down the hallway toward the break room and vending machines.

Come on, Beau, she thought. *I've got packing to do, a zillion other things* . . . She didn't want to leave without saying goodbye. She paced. She'd programmed Diane Milton's phone number into her cell, and decided to see if the neighbor had any news about Marla's condition. But when she dialed it, there was no answer, not even a machine. They'd probably gone to church. The young deputy returned to the squad room, a mug of coffee in hand.

His lurking at Beau's door earlier was probably nothing, Sam thought, trying to shake off the jumpy feeling. Chalking it up to general impatience, she resolved to calm down so she asked the deputy if he thought the weather was going to get warmer again. Luckily, Beau came out of his office before they'd completely worn out that topic.

"Waters, don't you have patrol this morning?"

The deputy stammered something about just finishing up a report. He tamped some papers together and abandoned his coffee in favor of putting on his jacket and walking out the back door.

"Not a great self-starter, that kid," Beau grumbled. He glanced around to be sure they were alone. "Jonathan says he'll do some more checking on Tito's status. Says there was absolutely nothing in the file to indicate that Fresques had gone missing. So, if that's the case, I asked why no one raised the alarm when he quit reporting in. Jonathan suggested that he could have begun reporting to someone else, been shifted to a new division or something and the info in his file was allowed to go stagnant."

"That just doesn't seem possible," Sam said. "A guy working undercover, wouldn't they expect updates? Surely someone at Bellworth would have questioned. If they didn't hear from him for a long time, wouldn't someone go looking?"

He gave her a firm look. "You honestly think every department of government knows what the others are doing? The left hand . . . the right hand . . . one federal office versus another . . ."

She got the picture. And speaking of reporting to a federal officer, Sam remembered that she'd promised Delbert Crow that she would send an update on the two properties under her care. He was one guy who didn't care about her business or her personal life. First thing Monday morning she would be hearing from him.

"I better go," she said. "It's my one day off from the bakery and I'm not accomplishing much."

He pulled her close, a reminder that the day hadn't started off badly at all. After a lingering kiss she broke away reluctantly.

"You're right," he said. "It's my day off too." His eyes grew wistful. "Sure was hoping we would be moving your stuff to my house today."

"Let me get past this holiday on Tuesday. Things will settle down a lot after that." She gave him another quick kiss and headed out.

Would life really settle down anytime soon? The wind tunneled down the street as she rushed to her truck. Slamming the door to block the chilly air, she sat in the sun-warmed cab for a moment before turning the key. She wanted to get to the hospital to see Marla, needed to handle her caretaker duties on the two properties and report to Delbert Crow, plus she really should get serious about packing her things. Even though they'd postponed the ceremony, she didn't want Beau to think she was backing out.

I'm not backing out. I'm just waiting for a day, one whole day, in which I don't have four thousand other things to do.

And you're stalling about revealing your little secret, Sam, a little voice said. *You know you are.*

She rested her forehead against the steering wheel and tried to suppress the thought but it wouldn't go away. Until she could be completely open and honest with Beau about the powers of the wooden box, she couldn't make vows to him. She swallowed the lump that came into her throat.

That damn box had been thrust into her hands, had come into her life, completely against her will. She'd tried more than once to get rid of it. Gustav Bobul, the chocolatier, had hinted that the object had an evil history, while Bertha Martinez, the woman who'd given it to her spoke of the many good things she could accomplish with it. So far, her actual experiences had been for the positive. She would have to stress that part of it if she told Beau.

When she told Beau.

The top of the steering wheel felt hot against her forehead. She raised her head, wondering how long she'd been sitting there.

She cranked the ignition and pulled away from the curb. Traffic was light and she drove with purpose toward the hospital. Visits to sick and dying people were always difficult for her and Sam knew that she could very well find excuses to stay away. But she also owed Marla a report.

How much would she actually reveal, Sam wondered as she got closer to her destination. Should she tell the mother that her son's good job with Bellworth was a façade? That he was working undercover, probably consorting with drug dealers and traffickers in Mexico? The knowledge certainly wouldn't help a mother. Then again, maybe Marla had already figured out some of it. She pulled into the visitor's parking lot, still debating.

The decision was made for her when Sam walked into Marla's room. Two of the neighbors she'd met at the memorial were there, sitting by the bed, talking in low tones. Marla seemed smaller and thinner than ever, shockingly pale, her color almost blending with the hospital sheets. Her hair had gone completely white, and her eyes were large chocolate orbs surrounded by slack muddied skin.

The other two women greeted Sam quietly and used her arrival as a reason to leave.

"Samantha, I'm so happy to see you." Marla's smile stretched her dry lips to the point that they looked painful, but the happiness never reached her eyes.

"I'm sorry I didn't get here sooner," Sam said, taking a hand that felt like bones inside a gauze bag.

"Is there news about Tito? Is he coming?"

Sam's throat clenched at the desperation in her friend's frail voice.

"Not yet," she said. "We're still looking. I've got the sheriff's office involved now, and there is even an investigator in Albuquerque working on it."

That scrap of news seemed to give her a boost. Marla let go of Sam's hand and used both arms to push herself a little higher in the bed.

"I need something from the house, Sam. I meant to ask Camille." She glanced around. "I guess they are gone already."

Her hands fussed with the edge of the sheet for a minute. "Could I ask you to get it for me?" Marla finally asked.

"Certainly. Whatever I can do."

"My purse is in this—" She waved one hand toward the bedside stand. "I can't reach it."

"Don't try," Sam said, walking around to the far side

of the bed. She pulled open a drawer but it contained only small items like a mini box of tissues and a paperback book. The larger compartment below held a black leather purse and she pulled it out.

It took Marla almost a minute to grasp the zipper pull and to work it along until the purse opened. Sam nearly bit her nails at the delay, but finally out came a key ring with three keys on it.

"This one works the front door." Marla said, selecting a silver-toned one. One of the others obviously belonged to the car and the third one probably didn't matter for Sam's purposes today.

"I left my cards in the bedroom," Marla said. "The ones from Tito. I would like to look at them again, for awhile."

"Sure. I'll go get them and bring them back for you."

"And Sam? When I'm gone would you see that Jolie gets them? Don't let the hospital people throw them out."

"Oh, Marla, of course."

She wanted to come up with something encouraging, try to tell Marla that she would soon be going home and that her granddaughter would be there with her. But the lie would be cruel. Marla wouldn't believe her anyway. Sam could see that in her eyes.

"Go now, dear. I'm a little sleepy." Marla's hands let go of the purse and Sam placed it back in the nightstand.

When she turned to say that she would be back this afternoon, Sam saw that Marla had already fallen asleep, her head lolling to one side. Gently, she straightened the pillow and tucked the blanket higher around the thin shoulders. So sad.

The new errand gave Sam a reason and a method for organizing the rest of her day. One of the properties under her care was located at this end of town, no more than five minutes from the hospital. She backed out of her parking slot and steered that direction. The other place was on the north side of town, and in the interest of killing two birds and all that, she could run by there on her way to Marla's.

Her duties as a property caretaker under her USDA contract were straightforward: Get into the place and see that it was cleaned and maintained in reasonable condition for sale. Normally, the homes were abandoned by owners who couldn't keep up with their mortgage payments. If the government had guaranteed the loan, the department had to eventually take possession and see that the property was auctioned off or sold through a Realtor. Sam was usually the first person to appear after the abandonment, and she'd found places in every sort of condition. A couple months ago, she'd walked into an upscale home that looked as if the owner had walked away in the middle of breakfast. Most often, she didn't get that lucky. Some places were hoarder's nests, others had refrigerators full of rotten food. And then there was the one where a body had been buried in the backyard, the day she'd met Beau.

It took no more than fifteen minutes at her first assignment to take the key from the lockbox, walk through the house, check all doors and windows, and do a perimeter check outside as well. All secure.

An hour later she'd completed the same routine at the second place and was on the road toward Marla's home. Again, as she passed through the wide-spot called Arroyo Seco she caught herself scanning the few buildings for a sign of Bobul the chocolatier, but of course he wasn't there.

Marla's property already had an air of desolation about it, that untended feeling that Sam always noticed first when she took on a new caretaking job. She wondered about Marla's financial state, whether she'd written a will, how Jolie would be cared for, who would get the house. She hoped that Marla had structured her legal documents on her granddaughter's behalf, not basing them on the belief that Tito would come walking back into the picture anytime soon.

Sam pulled into the driveway and squared her shoulders as she got out of the truck. She couldn't take on everyone else's legal and financial matters. Whatever Marla had done, it was her choice.

The key worked in the lock with the familiarity of a mechanism that had operated thousands of times. Sam stepped inside, noticing for the first time the faint air of sickness. Poor Marla, trying to brave it alone in her home, hoping to recover or at least to hang in there long enough for her son and granddaughter to put their little family back together.

Sam stood in the dim living room, eyes closed against the sadness, finally remembering her mission. She knew the kitchen and dining areas of the house; now she walked toward the arched opening that led to a short hallway. Three bedrooms opened onto the hall. Out of habit, she peeked into each quickly to get the layout in her mind.

The back bedroom felt decidedly masculine, had probably been Tito's as a child, although now it contained a double bed and the minimal furnishings of a guest room. Sam pulled open drawers, glanced through the closet, in hopes of finding any little clue the grown man might have left behind. Nothing. It appeared that when Tito left the parental home he did it for real.

A bathroom linked this room to the middle bedroom.

The bath and second bedroom were very girly, with Jolie's hair ribbons and ponytail holders strewn about. Along the edge of the tub, eight bottles of shampoos, conditioners and body washes jammed the small space, testament to a girl with the luxury of often changing her mind about her favorite fragrances. Her seven years of life at grandma's looked to be very comfortable indeed.

Sam exited Jolie's bedroom into the hall, making her way forward to the room obviously occupied by Marla. Even as she'd probably waited for a neighbor to drive her to the hospital, she'd attempted to make her bed. The spread lay in wrinkles, pulled up to cover the pillows. A couple of empty pill bottles sat on a nightstand; most likely the full ones had been gathered up and taken with her.

Across the room, a wide dresser with a mirror above it held a dusty silk flower arrangement and a small jewelry box with a crewel-work top. A cardigan sweater spilled over the edge, perhaps something Marla removed as she dressed for the trip to the hospital. Standing upright between the jewelry box and the mirror were the stack of envelopes Marla had previously showed Sam, the cards from her son.

She picked them up.

Flipping through the stack, she again noticed the neat hand-printed addresses, the postmarks from so many different places without return addresses. She pulled out one of the untraceable cards. It was hard to imagine such a need for secrecy that he hadn't even signed them.

Sam pictured him, stealthily approaching a mailbox, dropping an envelope inside, looking over his shoulder in case someone should see him. Perhaps even dreading that he would be grabbed off the street, the attacker snatching the card and opening it, knowing where to find the family.

A man would live in fear of such a thing.

She ran a finger over the stamps. Without really thinking, she began to sort them in order by postmark date, seeing the postage denominations climb by a couple of pennies every two or three envelopes. When they all sat in a neat stack by date, she stared at the one on top.

Sam flipped back through them, glanced at the dresser to be sure she hadn't somehow missed others. The last card Tito Fresques mailed came more than two years ago.

Chapter 17

Sam sensed the blood pounding in her temples as she thought back over the conversations with Marla. The definite impression was that the family continued to receive these cards all along. Sam felt sure Marla had said so, but she couldn't remember for sure.

She pulled a scrap of paper from her pack and jotted down the cities and dates of the postmarks. Maybe she and Beau could put together a trail of Tito's movements for the FBI man to follow. The only problem was that the trail would end abruptly twenty-seven months ago in Denver.

What could this mean? How on earth would they come up with a man who clearly wanted to stay hidden?

Unless it wasn't Tito himself who wanted to hide. Perhaps someone else wanted to be sure he stayed away. Maybe permanently.

She slowly folded the slip of paper and stuck it back in her pack. How could she locate evidence that would help Beau and his contact in Albuquerque find Tito? She glanced into Marla's closet but it felt too invasive to start going through her things. Wandering back to Jolie's room she noticed that the closet door stood open.

Well, I don't have any problem looking through a kid's stuff, she decided. *I'm a mom. I've done this.*

The girl was no more or less messy than any pre-teen, Sam decided as she surveyed the clutter. Blouses hung one-shouldered, barely clinging to their hangers. Jeans sat in lumps on the floor. And a tangle of belts seemed permanently snaked around the strap of a purse. On the shelf above, the grandmother's hand was a little more evident. Clear plastic bins held art supplies and photographs. In the far corner was a cardboard box, labeled in kid writing, "Mommy and Daddy's Things."

Sam felt her throat tighten. How hard it must have been for this little one. Her daddy gone since before she could remember and her mother dying when she was in kindergarten. Their memories condensed into a twelve-inch cube of a box. She debated whether to touch it, but the thought that Tito might have left something with his daughter, something even his mother didn't know about, won out.

Pulling the carton from the shelf, Sam carried it to Jolie's bed and set it down.

A sheet of pink tissue paper with Happy Birthday printed in bright purple covered the contents. Beneath it, the kinds of memorabilia that a kid would choose: a box of Emeraude bath powder with an elegant screen-printed design, two lipstick tubes as reminders of her mother's face and her scent. A preschooler's gift project, Jolie's small handprint inked onto a sheet of paper with a verse neatly written by the teacher, the whole thing rolled like a scroll and tied with red ribbon.

Sam set each object carefully on the coverlet with the idea that she would replace them exactly in the order she'd found them. It wasn't until near the bottom of the box that she came across anything masculine: an old sports sock, dirty and wadded, and a comb. The cheap black plastic kind that men often tucked into a pocket. It didn't seem likely that the old objects would comfort Marla now.

She diligently replaced everything into the carton and set it on the shelf in the exact spot where she'd found it. Back in Marla's bedroom Sam gathered the envelopes. Locking the front door again, she headed toward town.

It was well after noon when she arrived at the hospital. A nurse was in the room with Marla, trying to coax her to take a bit of soup for lunch. The patient leaning against the steep angle of her bed, propped with pillows, clearly had little taste for the food. She brightened when she saw Sam in the doorway.

"Would you like to give this a try?" the nurse asked, holding up the soup spoon.

"Sure." Sam glanced at Marla. "I'm sure we can manage something."

Once the lady in blue-flowered scrubs bustled out, Marla smiled. "I'm so glad you came back, Sam." Her voice seemed a little stronger now.

Sam laid the envelopes on the nightstand. "Are you sure you don't want some soup? Or maybe the crackers?"

"Stuff tastes like water. I don't know how they expect a sick person to find this appetizing when it's so bland even a two-year-old wouldn't want it."

Sam nodded sympathetically. No doubt the nurse had already tried all the arguments about how Marla needed nutrition, ought to build her strength.

"Maybe I should smuggle in some enchiladas." She gave a conspiratorial wink.

Marla smiled for the first time. "I would love that. But I don't think they'd stay down. I can't eat the things I used to." Her gaze went somewhere to the middle of the room.

"Maybe if you ate the soup first? Get your stomach used to food again?" *Come on, Sam. You're not dealing with a toddler. Let the woman do what she wants.*

After a minute Marla shook her head. "I think I'd rather just look at my cards."

Sam pushed the meal table aside and placed the envelopes by Marla's side.

"I'll go then. You enjoy your cards."

"Is there any word about Tito yet?" The wistful look on her face nearly broke Sam's heart.

"Not yet. We're still looking."

She leaned over and gave Marla a hug then left the hospital, wondering whether her friend would ever get to go home again.

* * *

In her own bedroom, Sam stared at the cardboard boxes she'd left lying around, half packed. Earlier she'd wondered what was holding her back from finishing the job and simply hauling everything to Beau's house. Now, for some reason, her own concerns didn't seem nearly as important, not in comparison with the Fresques family's misfortunes.

She thought of Jolie, that twelve-year-old who'd already suffered too much loss. For the third time in her life, she would soon lose the person most important to her. She was too young to be going through this.

Sam realized that she'd not yet had the proper conversation with Marla. Instead of buying into the idea that Tito would come back and raise a daughter on his own, maybe Sam needed to find out if Marla had any alternate plan at all. When the day came, with the father gone, who would actually take the girl in? It was sad to think of her becoming a ward of the state and being shipped off to a foster home somewhere.

She picked up the phone and dialed Diane Milton. This time there was an answer.

"Diane, can you talk for a minute? I mean, without the girls around?" she asked after re-introducing herself.

"Sure, Sam. My husband took them into town for a movie. I was sitting here with my feet up, enjoying a cup of tea."

"Do you know if Marla has a will? What provisions she's made for Jolie?"

There was a space in which Diane must have taken a sip of tea. "I don't know. She's a little bit old-school that way, a little superstitious about bringing on bad luck by planning for it."

Sam itched to tell the neighbor what serious consequences that could have but Diane seemed aware of it.

"I'll talk to Marla more seriously about it when I go see her tomorrow. We're got a good attorney. Maybe I'll see if he can go along with me."

Sam thanked her and said she would let Diane get back to her relaxing afternoon. With that burden temporarily transferred to someone else, Sam remembered that she owed Delbert Crow a weekly report on the two properties she'd checked earlier in the day. She switched on the computer and began typing. By four o'clock when Sam hit the Send button on the email she felt ready for a respite herself.

She'd no sooner brewed her own cup of tea and headed toward her favorite corner of the sofa than the phone rang.

"Samantha Jane, what's this about canceling your wedding?"

Sam sighed. Her mood sank about five notches.

"Didn't Kelly explain it to you last night, Mother?"

"Well, she called and talked to your daddy, and all I got out of it was that you and Beau aren't getting married."

"We will, Mother. It's just that this particular week has gotten to be a bit too much for me."

"Sugar, every bride feels that way. I tell you, I've seen it a hundred times. But there are just certain plans that can't be undone once they're set in motion. Aren't you concerned about having to cancel your caterer, your photographer? What about the limo, or, I don't know, out there you probably have a horse and carriage."

Sam pressed deeper into the sofa and rolled her eyes heavenward. *Lord save me from her preconceived ideas of what a wedding should be.*

"You might not be able to get the top people back once you've cancelled them, Samantha. Your pastor might not ever speak to you."

She could picture her mother, dithering. She would have the phone propped between her ear and shoulder, pacing the kitchen floor, literally wringing her hands.

"Mother, there are no 'top people' involved. Beau and

I planned a very simple ceremony with a judge and a few friends at a local bed and breakfast—"

"Oh my, that sounds plain. No rehearsal dinner, no orchestra, no wedding dance?"

"No, Mother. We aren't into all that stuff."

"I'm putting your daddy on the line." Sam heard an uncharacteristically shrill "Howard!" in the background, followed by some fumbling of the phone.

"Okay, Samantha, you tell your father what all you just told me."

"Hi, Daddy. How's everything there?" Sam could hear the resignation in her own voice.

"Just fine, honey. The car's unpacked and we spent the day—"

"Howard! That's not what I meant. I want her to tell you— Oh, I don't know. I'm just so very upset about this." There was a click on the line.

"I'm still here, Sammy. Don't you fret. It's just that she bought a new outfit. Got some pointy-toe shoes to go with the dress and all, had her nails done with that awful plastic-like stuff. Painted 'em purple to go with the dress. She'll get over it."

Nina Rae would not get over it, Sam knew, and she was likely to be hearing about this for years.

"Daddy, just try to convince her that I don't need a big fancy wedding to make me happy. Beau and I will reschedule. I was silly to ever think I could pull this off on Valentine's Day. My business is just too crazy right now."

"I know, honey, I know. And whatever you decide to do is fine with us." He lowered his voice. "Well, it's fine with me. And I'll work on your mother."

"Thanks, Daddy."

She hung up, wondering how on earth this always happened. Her mother had a way of erasing fifty years of Sam's life, sending her right back to childhood. Could the woman not trust that Sam might just have some inkling about managing her own affairs?

Her tea had gone cold by the time she set the phone receiver down and she didn't have the energy to walk as far as the kitchen to reheat it. She closed her eyes, but the jumble of thoughts about her family, Marla's situation, finding the missing Tito, and the mountain of work at the bakery all formed an unsettling mishmash of a dream.

Chapter 18

The room was growing dark when Sam stirred, feeling guilty that she had napped away a couple of hours that could have been used more productively. She stretched, her limbs feeling heavy and useless.

The back door clicked shut.

"Kel?"

"Hey, Mom. I'm home." Her voice had a dreamy quality.

Sam knew she better get rid of the rest of those chocolates before her daughter turned into a full-fledged nymphomaniac.

"Whatcha up to?" Kelly asked, drifting into the living room and finding Sam sprawled on the sofa.

"I guess my mind shut down after the call from your grandmother."

"Oh god, I bet that was fun."

"The usual, how could I do this to her?"

"Mom, haven't you already figured this out? It's always about her."

"I know. And that's fine. She went to a lot of trouble to get ready for the wedding and I didn't give her much notice."

"Yeah, but did she once ask how you're doing, how you feel about canceling the plans?" Kelly plopped onto the armchair across from Sam. "No, I can bet that she didn't."

"It's just her way. Heaven knows, I should be used to it by now."

"How was Grampa? Did you talk to him?"

"He said she got her acrylic nails painted purple." She caught the snicker from Kelly and they both burst out laughing.

"Gramma and those silly nails," Kelly gasped. "I swear she does not see herself—"

"Okay, now, be nice." But Sam couldn't keep a straight face. She pictured her very proper mother decked out in something that had required a trip to Neiman Marcus, the shoes that would match perfectly, the large precise hairstyle, and those nails which were really done mainly as a backdrop for the big jewelry that Nina Rae managed to get for every birthday. Each time Sam looked toward Kelly they started laughing again, until Sam rolled off the sofa and landed on her hands and knees on the floor.

Kelly keeled back in the armchair, her amusement completely out of control now. As Sam used the coffee table to hoist herself off the floor, her daughter managed a straight face.

"I'm starving," Kelly said. "Have you eaten yet?"

Sam remembered something about a bowl of soup, but recalled that was Marla's soup, at the hospital, hours ago.

"Pizza. That's what I'm craving. I'll call." Kelly got out of the chair and headed toward the kitchen phone.

"Everything," Sam called out. "Get the works."

While Kelly left to pick up the pizza, Sam washed her face and ran her fingers through her hair. No wonder her mother felt so superior; she'd raised a daughter who frankly didn't give a whit about being stylish. Her mouth relaxed into her usual smile. But then a picture of Felicia Black, with her fur coat and designer accessories, flashed into Sam's head. She tossed the washcloth into the sink and went to the kitchen where she poured two glasses of wine.

An hour later, the wine bottle was empty and the pizza was gone.

"I think I needed that," Sam said.

She and Kelly had carried their food to the living room where they sat on the floor by the coffee table, leaning their backs against the sofa.

"What you need is to put other people's attitudes out of your head. Just do what *you* want to do. You and Beau are great together, and it doesn't matter if anyone else has an opinion on what you should do."

"How'd you get to be so smart?" Sam asked.

Kelly shrugged. "Had a mom who let me learn things the hard way, by doing it wrong and then figuring out how to get it right."

"Seriously?"

"Well, moving to California for a few years didn't hurt. You didn't get the chance to watch me make all those mistakes."

Sam reached an arm around Kelly's shoulders and pulled

her close. When she let go she said, "Do you suppose that all this wisdom comes from the fact that we've finished a whole bottle of wine?"

They broke into giggles again.

* * *

Sam felt slow as a slug when she woke up for her early morning start at the bakery. This would be one of their biggest days of the year, the day before Valentine's; she needed to get a strong start, and the pizza dinner still sat like a rock in her stomach.

The bakery felt chilly, as it always did on Monday mornings when the ovens had not been fired up for two days. She reset the thermostat in the sales room, brewed a pot of coffee and started her routine. Muffins, scones and crumb cakes went into the oven quickly. She raided the big walk-in fridge, pulling out enough heart-shaped cakes and Valentine themed cupcakes to fill the glass display cases.

Cathy had made a double batch of sugar cookie dough on Saturday, leaving it wrapped in plastic to chill. Sam pulled it out now and began rolling and cutting out hearts. Four dozen muffins came out of the oven and she checked the scones that were cooling on one of the racks. She loaded a huge tray with the warm pastries and balanced it on her shoulder as she pushed through the curtain to the sales room.

Three cars sat outside, lights off, engines idling, women sitting in them. Two other customers waited at the door, holding their coats tightly closed against the chilly dawn. Sam set her tray down on the back counter and rushed to unlock the front door.

"We aren't really open yet but come on in. We can't have you freezing out here."

"Do you have those chocolates you were selling last week?" one of the ladies asked.

Sam glanced at the three boxes near the register and realized she might have a rebellion on her hands if that's what all these customers had come for.

"Help yourselves to some coffee, and I'll have more goodies out very soon," she said.

She quickly filled the sales displays with breakfast pastries and fancy cupcakes. While the customers browsed, she dashed to the back for a couple of the decorated cakes, speed dialing Jen's home number on her cell phone as she walked.

"Help! Is there any way you can get here now?" Sam looked at the wall clock and saw that it was still an hour before their regular opening. "I've got five customers out front already."

"On my way." Bless her for not questioning or whining. Sam made a mental note to be generous with some bonuses this week.

During the fifteen minutes it took for Jen to arrive, Sam sold two boxes of chocolates, a Valentine cake, and nearly three dozen muffins and scones. The town's sweet tooth seemed insatiable this morning.

"Wow," said Jen, peeling off her coat as she walked through the door.

"Yeah. I've got more cakes in the kitchen but haven't had a half second to go get them. And I need to be putting cookies in the oven."

"Go. I can handle this."

"When that final box of candy goes, tell anyone else

that we'll have more by three o'clock this afternoon."

At least the rest of the crew should be arriving any minute, Sam thought. She carried two more holiday cakes out to the display cases while making up a task list in her head. Becky and Sandy could bake and decorate dozens of cookies. Cathy could keep the supply of breakfast pastries going and, hopefully, would also be able to wash utensils quickly enough that the bakers wouldn't get hung up for lack of a spatula or cookie sheet. Sam's own time best be spent on the chocolates.

She quickly reviewed the day's special orders, making sure they'd not missed something. Five proposal cakes were to be picked up Tuesday morning and Sam located them all, finished and ready, in the fridge. She had two wedding cakes to deliver today and two more tomorrow; Becky would fill and ice the latter two and Sam would decorate them in the morning. She closed the door to the walk-in and headed back to the stove.

Dark chocolate became smooth as silk in the double boiler pan, under her touch. As she started to add the pinches of Bobul's special spices, she took slightly smaller portions. Maybe she'd been a little too generous with them on Friday, that crazy day filled with romantic overload.

"How's this?" Becky asked, pulling Sam's attention toward the worktable where she had stacked the six tiers of their largest wedding cake.

It was a tricky one, requiring different shaped layers in odd combinations. A half-inch off center and they risked the whole thing becoming unbalanced and toppling. Sam set the pan of chocolate aside while she double-checked Becky's measurements and gave the cake a little jiggle to be sure it would hold.

"Perfect. Dirty ice it and make sure at least three of us are helping before you try to move it to the fridge."

"Absolutely. I'll bet this thing weighs seventy-five pounds."

At the other end of the table, Sam set out her molds and began carefully pouring dark chocolate from the hot pan. While the candy cooled, she enlisted Cathy's help in carrying one of the other wedding cakes from the fridge. It was smooth-iced in ivory buttercream and a box beside it held the array of lavender, deep purple and blue flowers that the bride had ordered. Sam took a deep breath and got to work with her pastry bag, piping the borders and trim, then placing flowers and adding tiny touches of dots and leaves.

"One down, one to go," she said.

Out in the alley she opened the back of her van and her assistants helped to place the three-tiered confection inside. Sam locked the van with a sigh.

Today's second delivery went to a couple who'd designed their cake together. A big chocolate tier at the bottom, with middle and top layers of vanilla and lemon poppyseed respectively. Becky had already covered the tiers with fondant and Sam hoped she'd followed the instructions.

The pale green fondant made an easy background for molded Victorian filigree, basketwork, and bundles of lilies, daffodils and strawflowers. By the time Sam had finished creating the cascades of foliage, the piece looked like a gigantic basket of spring flowers. She stepped back to check her work.

"It's marvelous, Sam. I'll take a copy of it for my own." Riki Davis-Jones, the dog groomer, had come up behind her without Sam ever noticing.

"Thanks." Sam studied her petite neighbor for a minute. "Is this new guy already getting that serious?"

Riki's laughter tinkled like small silver bells. "He might be, but I'm not. Not yet anyhow." She held up a small wrapped package. "I just stopped by to bring you something."

"What's this?" Sam turned the burgundy-wrapped box around.

"Just to say thanks for helping out the other day. With the wet-dog melee."

"Oh, gosh, that was nothing. Had to keep my kid from getting into a bind."

"Well, it was nice of you. And this is nothing much."

Sam wiped her hands on her apron and ripped the paper off. The box contained a packet of English tea, the real stuff, which Riki often brought back from trips to visit her parents in Manchester.

"I love this," Sam said. "In fact, I think I will love some of it right now." She glanced at the clock. She could spare fifteen minutes before setting out to do her cake deliveries. "Join me?"

"Can't. Kelly has been bathing the mutts all morning, now I've got the clipping." Riki nodded toward the packet. "Enjoy!"

Before Sam had spooned the loose leaves into a tea ball, her cell phone rang.

"Hey, darlin', how about lunch?" Beau sounded cheerful, which probably meant that his new deputy was actually doing whatever Beau had assigned him today.

She told him about the two cake deliveries. "If I could get them to the customers soon, that would be a big load off my mind. Maybe lunch after that?"

He named a place and she worked out the route in her

head so she could get there before he'd starved to death. She abandoned the idea of a relaxing cup of tea.

"Give me a hand with this?" Becky asked as Sam put the phone away.

The multi-tiered cake was ready for refrigeration. They commandeered both Sandy and Cathy and the four of them carefully maneuvered it across the room and safely onto a shelf, then they turned their attention to the Victorian flower basket and transported it to the van for delivery. Sam looked at the orders for the two cakes in the cargo section. Both were going to hotels for their respective wedding receptions. She could get help from the kitchen staff so she sent her own workers back to their duties here.

Leaving Sandy with instructions for unmolding and boxing the chocolates, she grabbed up her jacket and backpack. In the van, she let it idle for a couple minutes while she leaned into the seat cushion and let herself unwind. She'd been on the go for nearly eight hours already.

Both deliveries were north of the shop, so she rolled to the end of the alley, ready to turn left. The nose of the van had barely cleared the edge of the curb when a low-slung car roared out of the side street. Sam hit the brakes hard. An impression of a shaved head with tattoos running down the guy's neck, and the whir of red low-rider screamed out of sight around a curve two blocks farther down.

"Watch out, you jerk!" she shouted at the flash of taillights.

But her more important concern was behind her. Something had made a sickening sliding noise back there. Sam turned, expecting to find the worst—a pile of cake and frosting.

Chapter 19

Sweat broke out on her forehead as she peered behind her seat. A ruined cake at this point would be a calamity from which it would take the rest of the day to recover, by the time they baked, iced and redecorated. Two broken cakes would mean working late into the night and possibly being late for one or both deadlines. And forget any other plans for the day.

The ivory-and-purple themed one looked all right. She'd wedged it with blocks and its position seemed stable. The Victorian green had slid, coming up against the blocks around the other cake, and something didn't look right. Sam slowly backed up the alley toward her shop, stopped carefully and got out.

Opening the van's back door she surveyed the damage. One section of the cake had brushed against the shelving on the side of the cargo compartment. She gave it a careful turn and checked. Several of the sugar-paste flowers were crushed.

Dashing back inside she called out, "Becky!" probably louder than necessary.

Her assistant started, squirting red piping gel across two heart-shaped cookies.

"Do we have any spare flowers from that Victorian order? I need two stargazer lilies and about three daffodils."

"Oh my god, what happened?" Sandy's tone got everyone worried and within a minute they'd crowded around the back of the van. Becky rounded up enough extra flowers and Sam brought out a pastry bag of icing she could use as glue to secure the replacements. She worked quickly, ignoring the fact that it was freezing outdoors and her hands wanted to shake while she removed the damaged bits and carefully arranged the new ones.

"That was a lot easier than it could have been," she said with a sigh as she handed over the discards and closed the van door.

She wanted to track down the punk in the red car and give him a lesson in safe driving, but there was no time for that. Practically holding her breath she negotiated the back streets to each of the delivery sites. It wasn't until both cakes were safely in the hands of someone else that she let herself relax.

By the time Beau arrived at the tiny restaurant near his office, Sam had mentally rehashed the close call enough times that she was ready to drop it.

He greeted her with a kiss to her temple and picked up his menu before his rear had hardly hit the seat.

"Crazy today," he muttered, looking over the selections.

"Is there some weird phase of the moon happening or something? There have been more traffic violations than I can shake a stick at. My officers can barely keep up with them."

Sam opened her mouth, then closed it again. No point in telling him about the one that didn't quite happen. They ordered green chile stew from a genderless server who had shaggy burgundy hair, a silver ring through the lip and wore all black.

"I went to visit Marla Fresques yesterday and she had me bring those cards she's been receiving from Tito."

Beau gave her a long look. "She *thinks* they're from her son."

"We would know for sure if we had fingerprints from them . . ."

"Sam, I haven't had a spare—" His voice sounded so tired.

She counted to three. "That wasn't the point I started to make anyhow. What I wanted to say was that I actually paid attention this time to where and when the cards were mailed. I made a list." She pulled it from her pack. "And, although Marla gave me the impression that she's been receiving these cards all along, the postmarks stopped two years ago. If Tito went into hiding ten years ago, he *really* went deep underground more recently."

Beau looked politely at the list, but she could tell he wasn't going to do anything about it. Strictly speaking, from a law enforcement point of view, she couldn't fault him. The case was old, the evidence flimsy. No one even knew if there'd really been a crime committed or if it had happened in his jurisdiction. But the fact that the sheriff couldn't pursue this didn't make it any easier on Marla Fresques. And poor little Jolie would soon find herself in a foster home unless her father could be found.

"Could I ask you to do something?" she said. "When you hear from your FBI friend Jonathan again, could you ask if it would be all right for him to speak directly to me? I could ask my questions, maybe learn something helpful, and I wouldn't have to involve you every step of the way."

Their bowls of stew arrived and they ate silently, like an old couple who've run out of things to say to each other. *We can't start being like this already,* Sam thought. When Beau set his spoon down she reached for his hand.

"It'll get better," she said. "Maybe it *is* just some odd moon phase."

He let his shoulders relax. "Sorry. I didn't mean to snap. And, yes, I'd be happy to let you and Jonathan work out this Fresques thing on your own."

He jotted down an Albuquerque phone number and she stuck it into her pack.

"I wish I had some of my special chocolates for you," she said with a flirtatious lilt. "That might be the way to get your mind off the workday."

His lopsided grin reassured her. "Only problem with that is that you would also have to take your mind off work for a day, and I plainly don't see that happening."

She tilted her head in acknowledgement. He was right about that. If she could have skipped work this week, they would be getting married tomorrow.

"We need some time to work out—" Her voice trailed away as she caught sight of a whirl of bright purple at the front of the restaurant.

Felicia Black stood at the open door, a gust of frigid

wind swirling the fabric of her long coat. Several patrons looked up, annoyed by the chill but fascinated by the creature causing it. Felicia stepped inside, letting the door coast slowly shut.

"Samantha, I was *so* hoping to find you here," she said, never taking her eyes off Beau.

"Really." Sam toyed with the idea of flicking the plastic bottle of honey off the table. She was pretty sure she could aim it toward Felicia's thigh-high suede boots.

"Yes." Felicia's gaze turned to Sam about a nano-second before she could implement the honey move.

She pulled her hand back.

"You ladies excuse me a second?" Beau stood and headed toward the men's room.

Felicia's eyes followed his moves before she noticed that Sam's hand was getting close to the honey bottle. She picked it up and set it on the far side of the table, then sat in the chair Beau had vacated.

"Sam, I'd like us to be friends. There's no reason for you to feel animosity toward me."

Oh yeah? Other than flatly stating that you're back in town to get Beau, then sending him candy that you knew to be an aphrodisiac, then showing up during our lunch. Pardon my suspicions, Sam thought.

"Now that I'm back in Taos, I'm going to start entertaining again. I'd like to invite you and Beau to a little party at my place. Tomorrow night. Six or so for cocktails, a little buffet dinner. Dancing to a DJ until whenever."

Sam stared at the redhead levelly. "Felicia, things are really busy for both of us right now."

Beau walked up to the table just then and Felicia jumped up.

"All right, you two. I must go." She touched both index

fingers to her lips, kissed them, and then leaned forward to place one finger on Beau's cheek then one on Sam's. "Ciao!"

Pretentious little vixen. Sam noticed that Beau's eyes were wide with surprise.

"What did she want?" he asked.

"She invited us to a party at her place."

"What did you tell her?"

"That we were both pretty busy right now."

"I'm afraid my answer would have been less diplomatic."

Leaving cash on the table, he took Sam's elbow as they made their way outside. Down the block where she'd parked her van he opened her door and closed it securely after her. She lowered the window and he leaned in.

"I love you, darlin'." The half-wink and special smile warmed her.

"Love you too. And I'd rather spend Valentine's Day alone with you." He patted the side of her van and walked toward his vehicle.

His cruiser pulled away from the curb before she remembered that what she'd started to say was that they should plan some time to talk about rescheduling their wedding. And she knew that talk would need to include her telling him about the powers of the magic box.

Chapter 20

Sam ran through her mental checklist of duties for the day. The shop was in pretty good shape, with the girls keeping up the cookie and cupcake supply. Before closing time she would have them pre-make more cookie dough and bake additional layer cakes for the last minute shoppers. Women would do their buying today; tomorrow it would be the men.

With her own wedding on hold, the hours she might have spent having her hair done, putting together her accessories, or making last minute phone calls were suddenly free. Almost on its own, the van made a left turn at Kit Carson Road and headed toward Zoë's house.

Lights glowed from two windows at the adobe B&B but the visitor parking area out front was empty. Zoë and Darryl's winter guests were normally skiers who slept there but vacated during the day, spending their hours on the slopes nearly twenty miles away at Taos Ski Valley. Sam pulled around back and parked beside Zoë's Subaru near the kitchen door.

"Hey, what's up?" Zoë said, looking up from a ball of bread dough that she was kneading into submission.

Sam dropped her jacket over the back of one of the tall chairs at the breakfast bar.

"You okay?" Zoë paused and gave her friend a firm look. "With the wedding cancellation and all that?"

"I'm fine. A lot more relaxed, actually. I just feel bad that we gave you such short notice. Had you already made a lot of preparations?"

Zoë plopped the ball of dough into a bowl and covered it with a white cloth. Wiping her hands on a towel, she smiled. "Nothing that won't keep for another day."

Sam drew little circles on the shiny tile with her fingertip. "Beau and I need to figure things out."

"Problems between the two of you?"

"Oh, not at all. It's scheduling. We're both absolutely swamped right now. My shop will slow down after tomorrow, but then I've taken on this other thing."

Zoë sent her a puzzled glance as she turned on a burner under the tea kettle.

"A lady who ordered a cake . . . we've become friends, and I learned that she's very sick. And of course there's a mystery to be solved. Her son disappeared a few years ago and she'd like for him to come back before she . . ."

Zoë made sympathetic murmurs as she pulled tea cups from the cupboard. "Too bad you couldn't send this lady a big dose of that healing energy you used on me that time."

Sam nodded. "Yeah. But Marla's case is a lot more

serious than a pulled muscle. I wish I could . . ."

"Earl Grey or Chamomile?" Zoë asked, holding up the boxes.

Sam pointed at the Earl Grey automatically, her mind zipping off on the tangent that her friend had just suggested. What if she *could* send some kind of healing power toward Marla Fresques? Bertha Martinez, the old *curandera* who'd given Sam the wooden box, said that its powers were many, that it could be used for good purposes.

". . . with just a few days' notice." Zoë's words came to Sam and she realized she'd missed something.

"The wedding?" Zoë said. "Just give us a heads-up and we can have everything all set up for you."

Sam realized her tea was gone, and when Zoë got up to check on her bread Sam shrugged into her jacket.

"Thanks. I appreciate the understanding."

"You do seem a little distracted right now. Better to wait until you can give Beau your full attention. I'd guess that's what he would prefer anyway." Zoë laughed and gave her friend a hug.

Sam found her mind zipping forward as she started her van and turned toward the street. It might work. She got to the end of Zoë's lane and looked both directions. She really should turn right and get back to the bakery. But a little stop by home first . . . A quick visit . . .

It wouldn't take very long.

She turned left, made the jog over to Elmwood, and was in her own driveway within minutes. In her bedroom, the wooden box sat in its usual spot on her dresser, the finish dull and lusterless in the dim room. Sam slipped her jacket off and picked up the box.

Rarely had she ever specifically called upon its powers; far more often she just happened to touch it and then was amazed at the results. Amazed, or frightened. Sometimes this little object's powers could get pretty spooky. She sat cross-legged on her bed and held the box in her lap, placing both hands over its top.

She closed her eyes and fixed a picture of Marla Fresques in her mind, visualizing her friend well and energetic. She saw Marla in her home, bustling about the kitchen preparing a big meal. And at the table she saw a man—Tito. He sat across from Jolie, and the young girl had such love in her eyes. Marla brought food, first some freshly baked warm rolls with butter, then she pulled a ham from the oven and began slicing the succulent meat and handing slices of it to her family.

All at once the box became fiery hot. Sam's hands shot back, her palms burning. She stared at the object. The wood glowed with an intensity she'd never seen, its normally dull brown surface changing from golden brown to orange to yellow-white. The small inset stones shot blazes of light, like gems under an intense lamp. Her hands burned and she blew on the reddened palms.

They cooled almost immediately, and when she pressed them to her cheeks there was only a pleasant warmth. She rose from the bed and placed the glowing box back on the dresser. The wood and stones immediately began to settle down, losing their burning intensity in minutes.

"Okay," Sam said to the box. "I have a purpose. I'd better get busy."

During the drive to the hospital she refused to analyze what she was about to do. Doubts tried to work their way into her head—Would this do any good? Could she possibly harm Marla with this power?—but she refused to let them take hold. And when she walked into her friend's room and saw her lying semi-conscious on the bed, Sam didn't think twice. She rushed to Marla's side and picked up the cold, still hand that lay on top of the blanket.

Marla moaned, half asleep.

"It's okay. It's me—Sam." She ran her fingers up the arm that felt thin as a skeleton's.

"I want you to get well, Marla," she murmured. "I want to give you the power to feel better."

Three times she coaxed warmth into the right arm and shoulder, then she circled the bed and did the same thing with the left side. She placed her warm hands on either side of Marla's emaciated face and held her skull firmly and gently, willing the energy to enter Marla's entire system.

The dark eyes opened and Marla stared at her. "Sam? Why are you here?"

"Shush now, just relax. Just let your body heal itself."

Marla's thin eyelids drooped halfway closed. "That feels good, Sam. Thank you."

Sam stared at her own hands. They still felt tingly; the palms remained abnormally pink. What more could she do? She pushed the bedcovers aside and took Marla's chilly left foot between her hands, performing the same strokes up to the knee and back. Same for the other side. When she finished, her hands had cooled down.

She tucked the sheet and blanket snugly around her friend and sat in the chair beside the bed.

Marla's breathing was steady, and stronger. Sam watched her. It seemed that much of the wan, gray hue had left her face.

"I feel like I could sleep now," Marla said in a low voice. "Without pain."

Sam glanced at the monitors near the head of the bed. One machine whirred to a stop, but the patient's breathing became even more tranquil and stable. She reached out and laid her hands once more on Marla's shoulders.

"I'll leave you to your rest. Be well."

She stepped out of the hospital room and took a deep breath. What was done was done now. She could only hope for the best. The hum that had reverberated through her for the past hour had completely dissipated and she walked calmly out of the hospital.

Chapter 21

S am was about halfway back to Sweet's Sweets when her cell phone rang.

"Samantha Sweet?" She didn't know the male voice.

"My name is Jonathan Ernhart. Beau Cardwell said I should speak with you regarding information about Tito Fresques."

"Yes, Jonathan, he told me about you." Sam steered to the right and pulled into the parking lot of a small Chinese restaurant. "Is there new information about Tito?"

"Not much. But Beau said you had a list of places he'd been, where he'd sent mail to his family?"

She pulled the page from her pack and read off the locations and dates from the postmarks.

"Do you have these greeting cards in your possession?"

"No, I don't. His mother is gravely ill and it seemed important to her that she be able to see them. I took them to her in the hospital."

There was a short pause on the line. "That's okay. I'll work with this data. I'm having a hard time getting the DEA to cooperate with us. They may have hidden him in a sort of witness protection system or sent him on assignment to another part of the country, so deep under cover that he's not even allowed to contact his family. I don't know."

Sam chafed, thinking that it should be easy for two federal agencies to agree to share information but apparently that wasn't the way it worked.

"The man I'm talking to at DEA is Clyde Jonah. He's in the New Mexico division. You may hear from him, or you may hear from his supervisor, a man named Wells." He cleared his throat. "Neither of them is going to share much with you, understand, but I'm asking them to let you know if there is any way to get in touch with Tito Fresques. I've told them there's a family emergency behind the request."

"Thanks, Jonathan. I appreciate anything you can do."

The agent clicked off the call before she could quite formulate the question that nagged at the back of her mind. She folded her phone shut and it rang again immediately; Kelly, wanting to let her know that she'd be out again this evening. She'd no sooner ended that call than Jen called from the bakery.

"I'm on my way," Sam said. "Five minutes."

The 'emergency' would have been laughable if the young woman hadn't looked so absolutely stricken.

"A wedding cake on two hours notice—I don't think we can do that," Jen was saying when Sam walked in.

"But Jorge and me, we're going to the judge at five

o'clock. And then to my sister's for the reception."

The desperate bride probably wasn't more than seventeen. Sam got the feeling it was sort of a last-minute wedding. "I make it a policy never to tell a customer no, but this will be a stretch." She took the girl's elbow and led her to one of the bistro tables. "Let me see what we can do."

She left the customer with a cup of tea and went to check the refrigerator. A quarter-sheet and one small six-inch round were the only cakes that were already frosted.

"Are these committed to anyone?" Sam asked.

Becky shook her head. "They were going toward tomorrow's stock."

"Bake a couple extras for the displays. I'm taking these." Sam picked up her sketch pad and headed for the front.

Sitting at the table with her young customer, she quickly sketched an idea for using the small sheet cake as a base and stacking the little round tier on top.

"I'll put roses around, like this. What color would you like for them?"

"Pink. And can you write 'Congratulations Jorge and Christine' on it? And maybe put a little bride and groom on the top?"

Sam remembered a little plastic topper left over from the days when they were more popular. "I've got you covered. Give me thirty minutes."

Jen's eyes widened as the girl stood up, but Sam ignored her and squelched the knowledge that she would normally spend twice that time on the simplest of wedding cakes.

The girl pulled out a wad of bills and began counting ones and fives.

"Five dollars," Sam said. "That's the price."

Now Jen's eyebrows went straight to her hairline, but

Sam placed an arm around her young client's shoulders. "We'll make you a beautiful cake."

"That was nice of you," Jen said, once the girl headed toward the bookstore.

Sam shrugged. "Those kids need some kind of a break. Might as well give it to them now."

She dashed to the kitchen and began stacking layers. Luckily, with the Valentine's Day hubbub, she had plenty of shades of pink buttercream already made up. The roses flowed from the tip of her pastry bag, and it took no time at all to pipe borders and add little embellishments to personalize the cake to the young bride's content.

"Twenty-eight minutes," she said, raising the pastry bag in a sign of triumph.

When three pair of eyes stared at her, she realized she'd just revealed one of the magic box's effects.

"Well, it was probably actually longer than that," she backtracked. "You know how time flies when I get wrapped up in something."

When she heard the chime on the door, she boxed the cake and took it out front.

"That was close," Sam told Jen as they watched the happy bride carry away her prize. Jen smiled at her.

"Okay, back to the real world." Sam handed out assignments for the rest of the day: bake layers and heart cakes in chocolate, vanilla and red velvet. Blend up a triple batch of dough for cut-out cookies and get it into the fridge. Make sure there was plenty of tinted fondant and buttercream for the two wedding cakes that would be delivered tomorrow afternoon. Her three kitchen staffers set to work, and when the last two left at six o'clock, Sam surveyed the suitably stocked shelves.

As Jen handed Sam the bank bag with the day's receipts, the phone rang.

"Thanks, Jen. Don't worry about that—I'll get it if you'll lock up the front." She turned to sit at her desk. "Sweet's Sweets, how may I help you?"

"Sam, hi, it's Marla." Her voice was strong and cheerful.

"My gosh, Marla, you sound so much better."

"I am better, Sam. I don't know how, but I feel wonderful."

Wonderful, as in, slightly better than dying?

"My doctors can't explain it, but they sent me home."

"*What?* You're at home?"

Whatever Sam thought she might have gotten from the wooden box, this was way beyond. Way beyond anything.

"Isn't it amazing? They came into my room this afternoon and I was sitting up in bed. After that little nap, when you were there? Well, I felt pretty chipper and I was just about to try taking a walk down the hall. The nurse was supposed to draw some blood, I guess, and when she saw me sitting up she called Doctor Caulder in. He tested the blood and came back after an hour or so. He said my white count was so much better, he couldn't believe it." Sam heard something metallic in the background. "I told him I wanted to come home, that I wasn't sick enough to be in that bed. He thought I should stay a few more days and have some more tests. But I didn't want any of that. I called Diane. She and Jolie came and picked me up. We're at my house now, making dinner."

Making dinner. Sam remembered her vision of Marla cooking for Tito and Jolie. She felt her mouth flap open but words wouldn't form.

"So, I just thought I'd let you know, in case you went by the hospital and didn't find me in that room."

"Well, you sound . . . you sound amazingly good."

"I am good. I'm great, in fact." She let out a little giggle before she said goodbye.

Ohmygod, what have I done? Sam leaned back in her chair and stared at the screen saver on her computer. Was there any way that her touch had brought such a change in her friend's condition? She pictured the nearly skeletal woman in the bed shortly after noon today. Was there any way that her touch had *not* brought this change? What she would give right now to have a chat with Marla's doctor.

She pulled out the phone directory and looked up the number for the hospital. There was always a chance he might still be on duty. It took a few transfers, a little explanation and some outright lies but Doctor Caulder finally believed that he was talking to Marla's niece from Colorado.

"I recommended against her release," he started out, covering his liability right from the start. "The turn-around in her condition was so absolutely sudden that I can't rule out a quick and equal relapse."

"So, the cancer isn't gone?" Sam asked.

He rattled off some numbers that Sam didn't begin to understand but the gist of it was that Marla's cancer was still there, although the tests showed huge improvement. "I'm recommending another round of chemotherapy," he said. "Even though she is resistant to the idea, it's my opinion that it would prolong her life."

When baffled by good news, stick with standard medical procedure. Sam wanted to snap back at the man but held her tongue.

"It would be a good idea for the family to keep a close watch," he cautioned. "If you notice any signs of fatigue, loss of appetite, a downturn—I want you to call me. It will be very important to get her right back here."

Sam thanked him and set the phone down. The cancer wasn't completely gone, true, but the change in Marla was startling. Despite the doctor's pessimistic attitude about the temporary nature of the upturn, as long as Marla felt well enough to be at home there was hope. One thing about it—this development bought Sam more time to work on finding Tito.

Something Jonathan Ernhart had said earlier on the phone continued to nag at the back of her mind but she couldn't pinpoint it. Glancing up from her desk reminded Sam that she was facing one of the busiest days of the year tomorrow. She checked her supplies and reassured herself that they had plenty of everything. Her earlier burst of energy as a result of handling the wooden box seemed to have evaporated and she remembered the phenomena from other times. When she transferred vitality to someone else, it was as if she'd used it up and left none for herself. Which was fine—if she could make Marla well, it was worth it. She should go home and get a good night's rest to be ready for the full day tomorrow.

Locking up and driving home she pondered this newest development. If she were to handle the box often—say, every day for a week—and transfer the energy to Marla, would it be possible to completely cure her friend's cancer?

But how far would she take this newfound ability? She had a quick snapshot of herself sitting under some little canopy, extending her hands to the masses who would inevitably find out about her and bombard her with pleas for help. If she had the power, it would be the right thing to do.

Then, too, what would be the repercussions? There had to be side effects to channeling all this energy through her own body. Would she weaken herself irreparably? And how could she ever hope to cure everyone of every affliction—it was an impossible task. And what of her own life—would she willingly give up her business, her relationships, and all hope of privacy in the quest to help others? By the time she pulled into her driveway she felt weary from thinking about it.

She gazed disinterestedly into the refrigerator but nothing appealed to her. Instead, she shed her work clothes and took a long, hot shower and put on her cozy robe. The wooden box sat on her dresser and she placed her earrings inside.

Back in her kitchen, Sam dialed Beau's cell phone on the off chance that he might have been thinking of coming by for dinner. They hadn't touched base all afternoon and she couldn't remember what his plans had been for the evening. But it only rang once and went immediately to voice mail, which probably meant he was swamped at the office and had switched it off. She sighed and opened a can of soup, heated it and carried her bowl and some saltines to the living room.

A ringing phone brought her out of a doze. She stared, a little disoriented, at the empty soup bowl on the coffee table before she realized the sound came from the kitchen table where she'd dropped her cell phone when she came home.

"Ms Sweet, this is Jonathan Ernhart again."

She squinted her eyes tightly shut, placing him. Beau's FBI contact.

"Yes, of course."

"I'm afraid I may have some bad news." He paused but she didn't fill the gap. "We've tentatively matched a John Doe in Washington DC with Tito Fresques."

Chapter 22

Sam felt as if an ice-blue fog enveloped her head. Her vision and hearing blurred for a few seconds. "A John Doe? He's dead?"

"Yes, ma'am, I'm afraid so. I mean, the John Doe is definitely deceased. We're not absolutely certain that it's Tito Fresques, not yet."

"I don't think I understand."

"The partly decomposed body was found in a park in a DC suburb about two years ago. DNA samples were taken, photographs, all the standard crime-scene work. He was not identified at the time and was eventually buried. When I used Bellworth's file prints of Tito Fresques to run a nationwide missing-persons search, an eighty-percent match came back with this unknown man's prints.

"These fingerprints alone aren't enough to positively say

that it's him. As I said, the body wasn't in great shape. To do an ID, I should try to get something with Fresques's DNA, and I'm wondering if his mother might contribute a sample for matching. I thought I would drive up in the morning and visit her, but you said she's in the hospital?"

Sam could envision Marla's recovery taking a sudden and sharp downhill turn.

"I might be able to offer something better," she said, the idea popping into her head instantly. "I was at Mrs. Fresques's home a few days ago and found a couple of items that belonged to her son. They've been stored in a cardboard box for years." She described the sock and the comb. "Do you think they might still have anything useful on them?"

He hesitated. "I don't know."

"It's just that Mrs. Fresques's health is very precarious. If she felt that there was some hope for finding Tito alive . . ." Sam swallowed hard at the thought of telling Marla about this. "It would be best not to break this to her until you are absolutely certain."

"I understand." He seemed to be pondering.

"I could go out to her house, ask her for the items." She didn't want to say that she could be more tactful than a lawman could, but it was what she was thinking.

"I'd like to pick them up myself," he said, "rather than hoping the mail could get them here safely. Faster too."

Sam looked at the clock on her oven and saw that it was not quite eight o'clock.

"Let me talk to her first," she suggested. "Call me when you get to town tomorrow and I can fill you in on her state of mind."

Surprisingly, he agreed.

Before he had the chance to call back and talk her out of it, she dashed to her bedroom and slipped out of the robe, putting on warm sweats and a fleece top. The wooden box sat on her dresser; she picked it up and held it close.

"Come on," she pleaded. "I can use a second dose of strength right now. For Marla." She held on until the hot glow became almost too much, then set the box down.

While her truck warmed up she called Marla's house. Diane answered.

"She's a little tired right now," the neighbor said, "but I know she'd love to see you. I'm sure it would be fine, as long as you don't plan to stay too late."

Sam covered the distance in half her usual time, hoping she wouldn't have to explain her way out of a speeding ticket from one of Beau's deputies. Although she didn't need for Marla to be awake for what Sam had in mind, it would simplify things with the neighbor if it appeared to be just a simple visit.

Somewhere between her earlier self-talk about whether she wanted to devote herself to healing and Ernhart's call a resolve had formed. Sam knew that she had to at least try to help her friend—both in the search for her son and with her health problems.

She entered the Fresques home to find Marla walking out of the kitchen, drying her hands with a small towel.

"Hey, there," Sam said. "Well, I have to say I'm amazed. You look a thousand percent better than the last time I saw you."

Marla carried the towel into the kitchen. "I feel . . . I don't know how to explain it. At the hospital I suddenly got so much energy." She laughed out loud. "I really thought I could walk out into that hallway and dance."

Across the room, Diane sent Sam a fleeting, cautionary look.

"Well, don't overdo things, Marla. You need to take this slowly." She edged Marla toward a recliner in the living room. "Can I get you anything?"

Diane piped up. "I was just heating water for hot chocolate. Let me get some for all of us."

With the neighbor out of the room, Sam knelt beside Marla's chair. "I don't know if you remember my last visit to the hospital . . . you were pretty much out of it. But I held onto your hands and it seemed to help warm them. Would you mind if I tried that again?"

Marla lifted her hands and stared at them.

"Here. I'll do the left one first." Sam held the cool hand between her two palms and let the energy flow to her friend.

"It *does* get warmer. That's really nice."

Sam spent another minute in that position, then walked to the other side of the recliner and took Marla's right hand. Again, the warmth.

"The doctor didn't want me to leave the hospital, but I'm glad I came home. I feel so much better here."

"I know," Sam said. Her mouth opened, but she thought better of mentioning her conversation with Doctor Caulder. How could she dampen Marla's hope?

She took a breath. "Marla, there's something else. I'm working with some people, trying to find Tito."

Marla's face brightened. She looked ten years younger.

Sam held up her hand. "They haven't found him yet. I didn't mean to give you that impression. But there might be . . . something, a lead. I told this man I would try to find something that belonged to Tito, something personal."

This could get tricky.

"Did either you or Jolie keep any of his personal possessions?"

Marla's brows knitted.

"Look, don't stress over it. Is Jolie home? Could I ask her?"

"She's getting ready for bed." Marla waved toward the hall that led to the bedrooms.

"Here comes Diane with your hot chocolate. I'll be right back." Sam smiled at Diane and headed toward Jolie's bedroom. She knew what she wanted but it was a little awkward admitting that she'd already looked through the girl's closet.

Jolie sat on her bed, wearing a white flannel nightgown with tiny blue flowers on it.

"My grandma's not going to stay home for always, is she?" She gave Sam an intent stare.

"We don't know, honey. There's a lot we don't know about this kind of thing."

"I didn't really know my dad, only what Grandma's told me about him. My mom had brown hair, like mine, but I can't remember her voice or things we did together. I'm afraid I'll forget Grandma too."

"You're older now, sweetie. You won't forget her."

Jolie nodded. "I don't think so." She stared upward, blinking, toward her open closet door.

It didn't take Sam more than a few seconds to create a transition. She followed the girl's gaze. "What's that box? Things your mom and dad left for you?"

Jolie nodded. "Nothing really important. Just stuff."

"Can you show me? I'll get the box down for you." She

watched the girl's expression soften as she handled the items in the box. When she brought out Tito's sock, she glanced up at Sam.

"Jolie . . . I need to ask a big favor. There are some tests . . . In order to find your daddy, they might be able to get evidence from his things. Like this sock and the comb."

"You mean DNA. I watch TV a lot."

Sam smiled and nodded. Never underestimate a kid.

"If they want to get DNA evidence, it's because he's dead, isn't it?" Jolie's gaze was intent and steady. Sam wasn't getting off the hook with this.

"They don't know. But there is a possibility."

"Don't tell my grandma that, okay?" She slipped the sock and comb into a small paper sack and handed it to Sam.

Sam held it together long enough to bid Marla goodbye and walk out to her truck, but by the time she'd driven to the end of Marla's road she had to stop. Her eyes prickled and then the tears overflowed—for the brave little girl who knew her father was long gone, and for the grandmother who couldn't face the fact.

Chapter 23

Sleep came on hard. The minute Sam hit the mattress, fatigue from the intense day drained her of the energy to be restless. She woke up to her normal four-thirty alarm, lying in the exact position in which she fallen asleep. With a stretch that sent adrenaline to her toes, she sat up. It had become so routine to dress in her bakery work clothes and zombie her way through the morning routine that she left the house in record time.

Fortified with coffee and getting her assistants started with the day's regular tasks, Sam pulled out the baked layers and décor pieces for her own projects.

Top priority were the two wedding cakes, which she would need to deliver by mid-afternoon. The smaller one featured a homespun theme using fondant to create quilting, brocade and draped fabric effects on three simple tiers of yellow sponge cake. She began by coating them in white fondant, then making a peep-window effect on the middle one by draping fondant in swags around a red-quilted section that showcased miniature white roses. Simple, eye-catching, stunning with the contrast of colors. The large topper consisted of a red heart created of fondant with ruffled edges and sugar-coated smaller hearts on its surface. She set it aside to be added at the point of delivery, and admired her work. A couple hours to set up in the fridge and it would be ready to go.

"Is that your phone ringing?" Becky asked as Sam returned from the walk-in. She nodded her head toward the desk, where a low buzz throbbed against some order forms.

Sam grabbed it up.

"Ms Sweet? Jonathan Ernhart. I'm on the outskirts of Taos. You said to call?"

"Yes, Mr. Ernhart." Sam stepped out into the shady alley behind the shop. "I've got a couple of items for you if you want to come by my shop."

"What about Marla Fresques?"

"She's out of the hospital, probably only temporarily. She doesn't know you are trying to identify a body."

He started to say something but Sam cut in to give directions to the shop. He showed up fifteen minutes later and she met him in the sales room, the paper bag Jolie had given her in hand.

Ernhart looked like a suit-and-tie version of Beau—tall and slender, mid-forties—although he had quite a bit more gray in his short, razor cut hair. He shook her hand and gifted her with a businesslike smile when she handed him the small sack.

"I'll try to get a rush on this," he said as they walked together out to his government-issue sedan. "I'll call you or Beau when I know something."

"Thanks. I appreciate that. Marla's health is really precarious right now. I've avoided telling her this latest. If it's not Tito, I'd prefer that we didn't upset her for no reason."

His eyes told her that outcome wasn't very likely.

She watched him climb into the gray sedan and pull into traffic.

"Hey, Mom." Kelly held the end of a blue leash with a Schnauzer at the other end. He tugged her toward a dirt area at the end of the building and the shrubs other dogs had undoubtedly used a few hundred times.

Sam walked alongside.

"Happy Valentine's Day." Kelly stopped in mid-stride. "Sorry. I wasn't thinking. Maybe it's not."

"No, it's okay. I'm super busy. No chance for regrets at the moment." She picked at red fondant that had stuck along her cuticles. "Beau and I thought we'd do a quiet dinner together tonight. I'm actually relieved that we put off the wedding. What about you and Ryan? Plans?"

"We're double dating with Riki and Tanner, dinner at Casa Giuseppe. It seemed safer to make it a group thing— no chance anyone would get carried away with the romance of the moment and do anything dumb like propose." The Schnauzer tugged at the lead. "Sorry, that didn't really come out right either. Proposing isn't dumb."

"But it would be with someone you've known for two weeks."

"Oh yeah. Cannot *even* see that happening." Kelly's aquamarine eyes twinkled. "C'mon Snickle," she called to the dog. "Riki's working on his twin brother, Fritz, right now. Where *do* people get their pet names?"

Sam laughed along with her. "Well, don't work too hard."

When Kelly turned in at Puppy Chic, Sam walked back toward the bakery. The sun was out again and the warmth on her back felt good. Her sales room was filled with customers, so she stood near the wall that divided her place from the bookshop and dialed Marla's number.

"Sam! I'm so glad you called." At Sam's inquiry, Marla said she was feeling even better than yesterday. "Diane brought groceries and I'm making a big pot of my famous green chile stew. Would you like to come for dinner tonight?"

Sam explained about the plans with Beau, leaving out the part about how this would have been their wedding day. She ended the call without mentioning Jonathan Ernhart or the DNA tests. No point in ruining Marla's upbeat mood.

The second wedding cake order waited in the kitchen. Eight-, twelve- and sixteen-inch square tiers, separated by white Doric columns, the whole thing like a regal pyramid in royal purple and white scrollwork. Studying the sketches she'd shown to the client, she came across the ones for her own cake. Her mood took a dip, but there was no point in that. Their own joining in matrimony would come—just not today.

She bit at her upper lip and set to the task, rolling and fitting basic white fondant to the layers, stacking them, making sure the columns were strong and solid. Light purple bands trimmed the lower edges, with deep purple draping and medallions. When the crew suggested ordering sandwiches Sam was amazed to see that it was after one o'clock already.

"I better pass," she said. "Gotta work while this stuff is soft, and then plan my deliveries. Becky, I'll probably need you to go with me to handle this big one."

"No problemo. I got a neighbor to watch the kids after school. You sure you don't want a sandwich, for later?"

"Nah, I'll snack on something. Need to save space for dinner tonight."

Which reminded her that she hadn't talked with Beau all day. But she didn't have time to make a call now. She worked with the delicate pleats in the fondant drape, concentrating on one at a time. By the time the final medallion was in place, it was after three o'clock and Sam realized she was pushing the deadline for her deliveries.

She and Becky carried the two cakes out to the van and secured them. The first stop, for the large, columned cake was for two hundred guests at one of the more elegant hotels, down near the Rio Fernando. Sam had delivered a cake for a big political campaign there last fall so she knew the general layout of the place. With help from the kitchen staff, they set the cake on the elaborate dessert table in the midst of a room decorated entirely in purple and white.

"Wow," Becky said as they left. "Can you imagine that huge room filled with people who've had a bit too much champagne?"

"Glad I'm not paying for that extravaganza," Sam said. She pulled out her cell phone and noticed that she'd missed a call from Beau.

"Things are a little nuts here today but I'll pick you up at seven," he said in his recorded message. "I think you'll like the place where I made the reservations."

"Good—I love a man with a plan," she told Becky as they pulled away from the hotel.

Their next stop was at a private residence, one of the elaborate hilltop homes on a steep road above town; the place had been featured in *Architectural Digest* once, as she recalled. Sam negotiated the curves carefully while Becky kept an eye on the cake. The bride's mother dithered in and out of the huge great-room, directing the florist and caterer not to trip over the tangle of wires where the band was setting up, mainly getting in everyone's way. Finally, the bride herself, in curlers, came downstairs and showed them where to set the cake. She raved about the ruffled red heart on top of it and the sugar hearts that gave the piece the feel of an old fashioned quilt. Privately, Sam thought the country look was a bit of an incongruity in the glamorous house but it was never her place to argue with a willful bride or her mother.

"Whew! That makes me glad my mother didn't have a say in my plans," Sam said. She glanced at Becky, settling herself into the van. "It's okay. Really. We'll reschedule. Soon. Probably next week."

"Sure. I know."

Sam directed her attention to getting down the mountain. "Call the shop and see if there's anything else we need to do while we're out," Sam said, handing Becky her phone.

Jen must have answered. The short conversation went in the shorthand that two old friends would use. Becky laughed out loud as she hung up.

"Jen's got her hands full of men," she said, working hard not to howl. "Her exact words. I don't think she got the same mental picture I did."

"We better get back there. I knew the males of this town would wait until the last minute to get their Valentine gifts."

Two hours flew as cakes, cupcakes, cookies and chocolates raced out the door. Every time Sam thought they might turn over the Closed sign, some other harried guy would screech to a halt outside and they would find something to send home with him. Finally, they were down to one final square cake which Becky had decorated as a package—pink frosting with a red bow and a generic Happy Valentine's Day written in red gel.

"The next guy through this door will get lucky and the one right behind him better hope the flower shops aren't completely cleaned out." Sam said as she started to gather the credit card receipts from the cash drawer. "And he better hurry. I've got forty-two minutes to get home, clean up, dress elegantly, and put a little romance in my smile before Beau gets there to pick me up."

Luckily, she'd put a bottle of champagne in the fridge and had taken home one of Sweet's Sweets nicer little cakes yesterday. With the red dress she'd bought, originally for their honeymoon trip, she envisioned an evening that would start with an admiring stare from him, move through dinner to champagne and dessert, and end up in Beau's spacious bedroom. It was 6:54 when she slipped the dress over her head and stepped into the matching pumps.

At 7:15 she was sitting on her sofa, cursing the sheriff's department for keeping him late at work again. Okay, she thought, how late will he be? She plucked her cell phone from her black evening bag and speed dialed his number. His voice came across a little muffled, with a lot of background noise.

"Beau? What's going on? Are you tied up with—"

More noise. Laughter. Music.

"Here, baby, let me talk." Was that Felicia Black's voice?

"Samantha, come on over. The party's really warming up. I'm bringing out some of your chocolates for dessert pretty soon."

"What?" Sam's insides went cold. "Put Beau on this phone."

"Darlin'—"

"Do *not* try to sweet talk your way out of this, Beau Cardwell."

"Sam— Darlin'—"

She hung up and threw the phone across the room.

Chapter 24

The ridiculous shoes lay on the bathroom floor, one behind the toilet and the other with the red dress lying in a heap on top of it. Sam scrubbed away the makeup she'd worked so carefully to apply and reached for sweats she'd worn two days ago.

Rage flared through her. She couldn't decide where to direct it—at Beau or at Felicia—and the poor little Valentine cake had taken the brunt of it, now smashed to bits on her kitchen floor. The phone had rung, somewhat feebly, twice, but it had stayed quiet for the last ten minutes. Sam yanked a Henley shirt over her head, stalked past the mess on the kitchen floor and grabbed up her keys, put on a hoodie and stuffed the keys into the pocket.

Before she decimated the rest of her house or did something really stupid with that bottle of champagne, she better take a brisk walk—for about five miles or so. Once the dark and the cold had taken some of the fire out of her, she would have to clean up the kitchen and decide what to do.

The back door slammed a little harder than she'd intended. She jammed her hands into the pockets of her hoodie and stalked down the long driveway leading to Elmwood Lane. Before she'd made it halfway, though, a car raced off the road a skidded to a stop. Beau's Explorer.

She turned around, trying to think of another exit.

"Sam! Come on . . . don't do this." He left the driver's door open and came after her, his dress shoes slipping on the frosty gravel. "Darlin', please— We have to talk about this."

She spun on him. "What's to talk about? You were to be here at seven to pick me up for our special, secluded, Valentine's dinner. When I finally reach you, you're at a party—at your ex-girlfriend's house! I don't see where this discussion could possibly go."

His face crumpled. "Felicia didn't call you? Earlier?"

Sam's glare answered that question.

He was beginning to shiver in his good blue suit. "Could we go inside?"

Her first instinct was to pummel him, but something stopped her. She pulled out her key and marched toward the house while Beau stepped back to the Explorer and closed his door.

"Watch out for that spot," she said, pointing to the gobs of smashed cake in the middle of the kitchen.

She heard him mutter under his breath, "Uh-oh."

"Yeah, uh-oh. What on earth possessed you to think I wouldn't be mad that you stood me up in favor of *her*."

"Want to sit down—?" he stopped. "Ah, no. Okay." He stuck his hands awkwardly in his trouser pockets. "Felicia called me this evening. She told me that she had also called you, repeated the invitation to her party, and that you'd accepted."

"But—"

"She told me you were on your way, that I should just drive on over."

"And you believed her?"

He shrugged. "I heard party sounds in the background. I tried calling your cell, the bakery and here . . ."

"You didn't leave messages."

His mouth opened but Sam had turned toward the back door.

"We could still have dinner . . ."

She ignored the misery in his voice. "I seem to have lost my appetite. We've missed our reservation and there's no place outside of McDonald's where we'll be able to get in right now."

"Sam—"

"It's been a very long week, Beau. I think I just need to make it an early night." She held the back door open, closing it a little too firmly behind him.

After a long silent space, she heard his SUV start up. Gravel crunched as he backed out and drove away. Iris's garnet ring winked in the light and Sam pressed it to her lips. *Oh, Beau.*

The moment passed though. She stared at the ruined cake on the kitchen floor, then grabbed a roll of paper towels and set about cleaning it up. Her spirit felt weary.

* * *

When her eyes opened Wednesday morning Sam realized it was already daylight in the room. She'd not set her alarm the night before and her heart raced as she grasped that for the first time ever her shop should already be open and she wasn't there. Wandering into the living room she saw subtle signs that Kelly had come home last night and left already this morning. She found her cell phone on the kitchen table and dialed the bakery.

"Sam, it's okay," Jen said. "We'd made the plan weeks ago. You deserve a rest."

It hit Sam full force that the original plan was that she and Beau would be leaving for their honeymoon today. Her four employees already had their work schedules set up, an arrangement to keep the shop going without her. She mumbled something about coming in a little later, even though Jen assured her they had things well under control.

She felt numb as she showered and set the coffee maker to brew. The shock of discovering Beau at Felicia's house last night and the broken Valentine's Day date, on top of the emotional roller coaster of their postponed wedding, had settled into a painful ache in the center of her.

She dried her hair and stared at herself in the mirror. Every comment from last night's argument seemed to have etched another line into her face, every ugly thought about Beau and Felicia added a dozen gray hairs. She turned away from the medicine cabinet and pulled on her slouchiest set of sweats.

The television provided background noise, a blur of color and sound to offset the blank state of her mind. The phone rang several times but she couldn't summon the energy to get off the couch and answer it. Once, in the background, she heard Beau's voice leaving a message on the kitchen phone. She turned up the volume on the TV set and pulled a blanket over herself. At some point the light in the house dimmed, telling her it was late afternoon. She didn't particularly care.

* * *

By the next morning she'd decided that wallowing in misery was not her strong suit. She took a long shower and donned her baker's jacket and showed up at work. The girls were surprised to see her, but no one asked questions. She could only assume that Beau had called here yesterday, looking for her. She'd erased his messages from her machine at home and deleted the ones on her cell. It wasn't so much that she was avoiding him, she just didn't see much point in listening to excuses.

She baked cheesecakes and then made chocolate chip cookies for the after-school kids, even though Becky and Sandy could have easily handled those tasks. When Kelly came into the shop at noon, she approached Sam with a determined look in her eye.

"Mom, we need to have lunch." It was more an order than an invitation.

Sam couldn't even plead that she was swamped with work, because that clearly wasn't the case. With the extra two helpers and the absolute lack of custom orders, for once, her day loomed ahead as an empty bunch of hours.

"Okay, you are clearly a wreck," Kelly said, once they'd settled into a corner of a noisy little cantina that they both normally loved. "Beau says there was some terrible misunderstanding."

"Probably."

"*Mom*, what are you going to do about it? Just dump Beau, like that? I thought you really loved him."

Sam swallowed hard, covering her emotions while the server came and took their orders.

Kelly smiled brightly at the girl and watched her walk away. "He really loves you. When he called me yesterday he sounded absolutely miserable."

Sam picked up her fork and rubbed at its already-shiny surface with her thumb. Maybe a day was long enough to make certain that Beau had made his choice—Felicia or her.

"You're right, Kel. He's a good man and I don't mean to punish him. I'll talk to him today sometime." Maybe she should let him off the hook, at least consider the idea that Felicia, not Beau, was the cause of the problem.

Their enchiladas arrived just then and Kelly cut right into hers, apparently satisfied that she'd done her little mediation task satisfactorily. Sam gave herself over to the flavors of chicken and green chile and began to feel a sense of normalcy. She finished her lunch and excused herself to go to the ladies room, and when she came back she saw Kelly surreptitiously slip her hand into her jacket pocket. A second later, Sam's own cell phone rang.

"Gosh, what can I bet that this will be Beau?" she said with a smile at her daughter.

"Can we meet somewhere?" he asked before she had a chance to start the conversation.

They agreed that he would come by her house in thirty minutes.

"I have to get back to work," Kelly said. "Riki's got a full shop today."

Sam picked up the check and they walked outside to find that the sky had clouded over and a white mist filled the air. Kelly dashed for her car and Sam slid into her van. But before she started it her phone chimed again. She didn't immediately recognize the number on the readout.

"It's Jonathan Ernhart. I've got some DNA results."

Sam felt her mood take a dip. So soon? She'd hoped for a few more chances to see Marla and work her healing touch before this.

". . . what we expected," Jonathan was saying. "Our John Doe is Tito Fresques. I'm sorry."

"Will you be sending someone to inform Marla in person?"

"We already have. I've asked local law enforcement to pay a visit."

"Sheriff Cardwell, here in Taos?"

"Yes ma'am. I spoke with him about a minute ago. I've also notified the DEA. Given what we learned about his work for them, they need to know that Panther won't be coming back."

Sam thanked him and hung up. Condolence calls were one of any law enforcement man's least favorite duties, especially Beau's.

She quickly dialed Beau's cell and determined that he was on the way to her house.

"We need to talk about something. Other than us. Well, in addition to us," she said.

Chapter 25

Beau's cruiser was in her driveway when she pulled in. She faced him across the hood of it, imagining her own expression to be nearly as uncertain as his. Not letting go of the lock on her gaze, he crossed the front of the vehicle and walked over to her.

"I can't believe Felicia set us up that way," he said. "Telling me that you were on the way to her party."

Sam wanted to believe him.

"I tried to call you. When you didn't answer it seemed like proof that you were doing what she said." He looked so miserable that Sam felt the conflict dissipate.

"Beau, do you see why I was leery of her from the start? I told you she was after you. Now she's set this up so we would fight—"

He stepped toward her and put his arms around her,

pulling her against him in a tight little ball. His uniform smelled of aftershave with a faint undertone of coffee. Tiny droplets of the gathering mist cooled her hot skin.

"Baby, I'm so sorry that I believed a word she said."

"I know. Hey, let's get inside, out of the drizzle."

They walked into the kitchen, and Sam offered to make tea.

"Sorry, I better not. I've got an assignment and I'm not looking forward to it."

"Marla Fresques. I heard about the condolence visit."

"Damn, that's right. Tito Fresques's mother. I've been so swamped with other work that I'd forgotten about the case."

"Can I go with you?"

"You sure about that? These aren't really fun calls."

"I know. But I consider her a friend, and I'm thinking she might like to have someone nearby when she gets the news."

"It would be a big help to me," he admitted.

Sam excused herself to change out of her bakery clothes. Beau was right—this wouldn't be an enjoyable stopover. After putting on jeans and a warm sweater she picked up the wooden box. A few minutes with it on her lap, the familiar tingle of warmth in her hands, and she felt ready to go.

Beau smiled widely as she emerged from her bedroom. "Darlin', you look absolutely beautiful."

She heard that a lot after handling the box.

He pulled her toward him and when he touched her hand he laced his fingers through hers and drew her close for a kiss that sent quivers through her. The moment might have stretched into an afternoon, but Sam reminded him about Marla.

"We can take both of our vehicles," she suggested as they walked out the back door. "I think I'll need to stay with her awhile."

Marla's car sat alone in the driveway when they pulled up out front. Sam saw a curtain at the living room window move aside, and the door opened before they'd reached the porch.

Marla sensed their mission. Sam could see the mixture of anticipation, dread, hope, despair.

When Beau began his official line, "Ma'am, I'm sorry to inform you . . ." Marla crumpled.

"No, not my Tito," she whispered, both hands trembling as she raised them to her temples. Her chocolate eyes left Beau's face, traveled to Sam's, moved back again.

"Let's go inside and sit down," Sam suggested.

Beau followed, made sure that Marla was comfortably seated on the sofa and didn't have more questions for him, then he left. Sam knew that Marla probably had a million questions; she just hadn't yet thought how to verbalize them.

"Is Jolie at school?" Sam asked.

Marla gave a numb nod.

"I should wait with you until she comes home. I mean, I will if you want me to."

Sam glanced down at her hands, which were still pink from the effects of the wooden box. She reached over and took Marla's hands in hers. Warmth moved through her arms and into her friend. Sam saw a small rush of energy come to Marla.

"I need to let people know. Make some calls." Her gaze

darted around, looking for something, but Sam held fast to her hands. "Where's the phone? Where's my address book?"

"Give me a few minutes to warm your hands," Sam said. "It will help."

Marla submitted but she didn't relax. "Father Joe. I need to tell Father Joe."

"I'll get you the phone and the numbers in a minute," Sam said.

But when Sam let go of Marla's hands, fatigue immediately set in and her friend slumped against the back of the sofa.

"Here, let's cover you up and I'll find your things," Sam said, pulling a knitted afghan from the recliner chair across the room and draping it over Marla's lap and legs.

"I can't be lying around and resting," Marla protested. "There will be arrangements to make. I'll have to plan his funer—" Her voice broke.

"Marla, there are some things that the authorities have found out."

How much to tell? Sam couldn't decide what was best. Did a mother need to know that her son had done undercover work for drug enforcement? That he'd been murdered? That now his body would need to be exhumed and brought home? As she thought about it, Sam sat beside Marla and tried to work her healing touch once more, but the magic effects weren't working. The bad news and her own health problems were pulling Marla down, as surely as a rip tide pulls a person farther from the shore.

Sam took Marla's hands again and began the healing touch, running her hands up to the elbows and back, hoping to impart energy to the stricken woman. Then she began to speak. Only the basics, she decided. Tito had died two years ago, near Washington DC. It would probably be possible to bring his body back, give him a burial at home. There was no point in going into detail, no point in further upsetting her friend.

When the phone rang it was almost a relief. Sam patted Marla's arm and went into the kitchen to answer. It was Diane Milton, and it took only the briefest explanation before the neighbor insisted on coming right over. Sam put in a quick call to the number she found on a refrigerator magnet from St. Mark's and gave the short version of the story to Father Joe.

By the time she returned to the living room, Diane was coming through the front door. The neighbor crossed the room immediately to Marla and began reassurances that she would pick up Jolie from school. Sam remembered the twelve-year-old's wise look, her matter-of-fact approach to the DNA test, and knew Jolie would probably be able to accept the death much more stoically than her grandmother had.

Within minutes, other neighbors showed up—Joy, Deborah, and Jorge. They surrounded Marla, offering the kind of love that comes best from relatives and long-time friends. Sam realized that her own time could be better spent finding out more about Tito's last days and making sure law enforcement would search for his killer. She gave Marla's hand a last light touch and left.

Outside, the weather mirrored the mood in the Fresques home—dismal.

* * *

Without a better plan, Sam headed toward Sweet's Sweets. A government SUV sat out front and when she entered through the back door, Becky informed her that someone wanted to see her.

An agent of some kind, she knew from his clothing and posture when she saw him standing near the beverage bar. Probably in his forties. Blue suit, white shirt, striped tie, dishwater-blond hair, and gray eyes that scanned a room in continual sweeps. He turned toward her as soon as she entered the sales room.

Sam froze. She'd met this man.

"Ms Sweet? Rick Wells." He extended his hand and she saw the dawning of recognition in his expression. He covered quickly. "Jonathan Ernhart may have told you that I'd be calling?"

Now Sam remembered what had been nagging at her. The familiar sounding name . . . Ernhart's mention of an Agent Wells with the DEA.

"Can we talk somewhere?" His gray eyes darted toward the sales counter where Jen was helping two ladies.

The kitchen was no more private. "Let's walk," she suggested.

Outside, the clouds were growing thicker by the minute and a brisk breeze shook the bare-limbed branches overhead. Wells made small talk until they crossed the street and entered the slight shelter of the plaza.

"So. Your auditing position with Bellworth is past history and you misled me the other day? Or you're not an auditor at all."

"I'm DEA, have been since college. I worked with Tito Fresques, as his contact in Albuquerque during the time he worked at Bellworth. Other agents have similar positions to his and my auditor job is a cover, to provide a means for us to make contact. Jonathan told me that you've become close to Tito's mother and that you were assisting the local authorities in the search for him. Before it was confirmed that his body was located."

"That's right. But I don't know what I could tell you." Clearly, the government agencies had more information than she did.

"I wonder if Mrs. Fresques ever mentioned the name Javier Espinosa?"

Sam thought hard. "In what context? Was he a friend of Tito's?"

"More of a business contact. Espinosa works for one of the top kingpins in drug trafficking from Mexico. Tito traveled there quite a bit and had infiltrated the Diablo Rojo gang in Juarez."

"Espinosa doesn't seem like the kind of guy he would tell his mother about, does he?" Sam asked.

"Probably not. But we have reason to believe that his wife knew the name, and some of his co-workers at Bellworth were aware of it."

Sam stayed quiet, wondering why Tito would have mentioned the name of this drug runner. If he was any good at his DEA job that should have remained a secret.

"At this point, I think Mrs. Fresques is more concerned that her son's body be brought back here to Taos for a proper burial," Sam said. "I'd like to be able to tell her where he's been all these years, why he wasn't able to contact his family. She would appreciate that."

"We at DEA have a lot of missing gaps in that story, ourselves."

Sam looked at him but he didn't seem inclined to say

more. They had arrived at the shady side of the plaza and the breeze whipped alongside the buildings. Sam zipped her heavy coat closed against it but Wells, in his business suit, had no such protection. He began walking faster and Sam had a hard time keeping up with his long stride. When they reached the sidewalk in front of Sweet's Sweets, the agent turned toward his vehicle.

"Now that Tito's body has been positively identified," Sam said, "I guess the investigation will focus on finding his killer."

Wells seemed momentarily wary.

"Jonathan Ernhart told me he'd been murdered."

"I didn't realize he'd released that information."

"I haven't told Tito's mother," Sam said. "She's in very fragile health. She hasn't asked how he died, and it would probably be best to avoid telling her. At least not in detail."

"Certainly." He pulled the driver's door open.

She walked back into the bakery as he pulled away, her mind going in a dozen directions, puzzled at what exactly the DEA agent had hoped to learn by talking to her. Surely he didn't drive all the way up here from Albuquerque for chitchat. He was probably planning to stop by and see Marla. Was her warning not to upset the sick woman going to carry any weight with him?

She fished in the pocket of her slacks for her cell phone. A call to Marla's house got Diane Milton on the phone. She quickly explained that a former co-worker of Tito's might show up and it only took a small hint that his visit might upset Marla to put Diane in full mama-lion protective mode.

"I'll just tell him that she's resting and can't have company."

"That's probably best," Sam told her.

Feeling reassured that Marla wouldn't be unduly upset by the agent's visit, Sam shed her coat and surveyed her desk. With the crazy pace of the past few days, she'd let paperwork and receipts stack up. Now she spent some time organizing and filing, paying some bills, and planning for the coming week.

Jen had placed two new orders on the desk, birthday cakes. Sam set them aside until she could clear her head well enough to come up with original ideas for them. Her assistant had also left a sticky-note asking whether the handmade chocolates would become a regular feature.

Sam walked over to the shelf where she'd stashed the canister with Bobul's little spice packets, lifted it down and took it to her desk. The small bags appeared to be every bit as full as when he'd handed them to her, despite the fact that she'd taken from them regularly. More of the magic?

She quickly tucked the packets back into the metal container and set it aside. She would have to think about whether to make the delectable chocolates part of the everyday fare or to save them for holiday seasons. And, she would definitely have to work on revising her formulas, to curb their power.

She plucked the sticky note from her computer screen and headed toward the sales room.

"Jen, I think we'll hold—"

The bells on the front door tinkled and in stepped Felicia Black.

Chapter 26

Sam stopped in her tracks. It wouldn't be businesslike to say "What the hell are you doing here?" but she certainly felt like it.

"Samantha!" The brazen red-head lengthened her name so that it took about five minutes to utter. "I'm so sorry that you couldn't make it to the party."

"Really." *Is that why you invited my fiancé but not me? Is that why you lied to him, why you told people you were here in town to get him back? Is it why you sent him candy that you knew would cause him to be attracted to you?*

In the interest of not coming across as a completely insane maniac in front of her employee and the three other customers in the shop, Sam ground her teeth together. The nerve of this, this slut!

Felicia's gaze scanned the sales counter. "No more of

those chocolates? Too bad. They were yummy. I had two boxes of them for the party guests and I'll tell you, I think a few new romances began that night."

Like you hoped would happen with Beau?

She breezed over to the beverage bar, the silver fox coat flapping open to reveal a tight red dress that barely skimmed her thighs. Sam watched her pour a mug of coffee and doctor it heavily with low-fat creamer and fake sugar.

Jen met Sam's eyes, with a question. Sam edged behind the counter and whispered in her assistant's ear: "No chocolates for her, whatsoever. And charge her double for that coffee." Her wicked grin let Jen know that Sam wasn't kidding.

She'd turned toward the kitchen when Felicia raised her voice again. "Sam, dear. I'd love for you and I to have lunch sometime. We really should be friends."

Sam smiled. *When hell freezes over.* "Oh? I'd have thought you would be on your way by now. Doesn't New York need you or something?"

Felicia completely missed the sarcasm. "They do. But I've told my agent that I plan to take a few more weeks off. Next shoot is in Rio, but they're holding it until I'm ready."

Shooting seemed like the perfect way to deal with Felicia. Unfortunately, the other woman thought Sam's genuine smile was for another reason.

"So, then, lunch tomorrow?"

"I'm afraid I can't. Beau and I have other plans." Sam swept the curtain aside and stomped into the kitchen. Her heart was beating way too fast and her mind raced with all the should-have-saids that came to her after the fact.

She busied herself with the simple tasks of pre-mixing dry ingredients for tomorrow's breakfast pastries; the fact that she could grind away with a pastry blender as she cut shortening into flour and imagine performing the same action on Felicia's face was immensely satisfying.

When her phone rang a few minutes later and she saw the caller was Beau, she took it immediately.

"Just had a call from Felicia," he said. "She invited me to lunch and said you were coming."

"Sheesh, I can't believe that woman. She stopped by here awhile ago, flaunted her next modeling job and invited me to lunch too."

"You're not really going, are you?"

"Definitely not!" She stopped in mid-stride. "Not unless you are."

His laugh came through, loudly. "Not unless this weather gets even worse and you-know-where turns into an iceberg."

"That was *exactly* my thought." Sam brushed flour from the front of her jacket. "So, how are we going to get rid of her? Can't the sheriff run her out of town or something?"

"I think that only happened in the Western movies, darlin'. And I think the bad guy actually had to commit a crime."

"Hmm. Well, I may just have to work on that. I should be able to frame her for something."

"I have to officially pretend I never heard that."

"Maybe like any other old pest, we ignore it and it will just go away?" Even as she said it, Sam knew that simply ignoring Felicia was easier said than done.

She turned back to her bakery duties, deciding on a soccer-field theme for one of the birthday cakes; Jen had made a note that the girl was a sports player in school. The other cake was for a woman who loved gardening and she

pictured shaping the cake like a flowerpot and filling it with
a variety of spring blossoms, something to take her mind—
and the customer's—off the current cold-weather front.
She made a few sketches and looked around. Becky had
left for the day and Cathy was in the midst of washing up
the pans and bowls from the morning's projects so Sam got
Sandy started baking the layers.

"Once you put them into the oven, just set the timer. I
can take them out if you want to go on home," Sam told
her.

It was a nearly six when Sandy said goodbye and shortly
after, Jen brought the receipts from the register.

"Don't stay half the night," her assistant warned.
"You've put in too many late nights and early mornings
these last couple of months."

"I know. But I love the shop."

"Yes, but you'll wear yourself out." Jen looked at Sam
a little intently. "Are you sure you're okay? I mean, with
postponing the wedding and all?"

Sam nodded but wondered. Was she? Wasn't the sudden
appearance of Felicia Black bothering her more than it
should? A twinge of guilty conscience for spending more
time at the bakery than with her fiancé?

Jen was running through a short list, reassuring Sam that
she'd cleaned the display cases and tables and that the coffee
bar was set up for the morning, and Sam tried to bring her
attention back to the work at hand.

"As soon as that oven timer goes off, I'm going to set
those cakes to cool and I'll be out of here." She paused.
"What about you, Jen? You have plans with Michael
tonight?"

Her assistant shrugged. "Not til the weekend. I'm not

sure about that either. We'll see." She pulled on her coat and said she would leave the night lights burning when she left.

Sam heard voices out front and Kelly walked in as Jen walked out.

"I'm going home now," Kelly said. "Thought I'd see if you want me to pick up something for dinner."

"Dinner at home? It's been awhile."

Kelly smiled a little wistfully. "Yeah. It'll be nice though. So . . . I could grab a pork tenderloin and make a salad?"

Sam couldn't remember the last home-cooked meal she'd made; Kelly's suggestion sounded wonderful. She pulled some cash out of her wallet and sent her daughter on her way.

A glance at the oven timer told her the cakes had ten minutes to go. She leaned back in her chair. So much had changed in the last week. If all had gone according to plan, she and Beau would be married now and away on their honeymoon. Her crew would undoubtedly be running the bakery just fine. She'd hired Sandy and Cathy as extra help through the end of the month, and although she didn't really need them now it would be only fair to pay them for the agreed time.

Marla's condition had gotten worse, then better, and now possibly worse again. Her son had been located but it wasn't the happy homecoming Marla wanted. And what about Jolie? What would become of the girl? Sam realized that, along with solving the mystery of who killed Tito, it would be nice if she could help Marla locate someone who would adopt his daughter in the event Marla never got well. She envisioned the jolt, to both the child and the new parents, of bringing an almost-teen into a new home. It would not be an easy adjustment for anyone.

Could Sam possibly cure Marla's cancer by applying the healing touch from the wooden box? The results seemed so temporary. Her mood fell as she thought about it, but the beeping of the oven timer interrupted her thoughts.

With the cakes safely stowed in the fridge, Sam buttoned her coat and picked up her backpack. Out in the alley, the darkness seemed unusually deep and she noticed that the streetlight at the end was out.

As she fumbled through her pack for her keys a tiny sound near the van made the hair on her neck rise. She looked up and glimpsed motion, a shape. Her hand closed around the ring of keys, spreading them between her fingers.

A man moved swiftly toward her and Sam caught an impression of a bald head and a pattern—tattoos.

His voice came out low and dangerous. "Leave panther alone."

"What?" she squeaked.

But he kept moving and vanished into the shadows.

Chapter 27

Her heart raced as Sam debated for a fraction of a second. Try to chase him down—or run? The fight-or-flight choice zipped straight to the escape option. She punched the remote door opener on her van and scurried inside, locking the door behind her before she had a chance to think twice. She sat there in the dark for a full minute, watching.

No sign of movement in the alley. The man had disappeared.

For a second, she thought of calling Beau and reporting it but what would she say? Someone said something scary to me in the dark. He didn't touch me and he ran away but I couldn't tell you which way he went? Beau would feel obligated to file a report, which might be fine if there weren't hundreds of young men in this town with shaved heads and tattoos. She had absolutely nothing else by which to identify him. And Beau's department was way too busy with real cases—it wouldn't be right to add this little non-crime to their workload.

After a couple of minutes she let out her pent-up breath and started the van.

The kitchen was filled with the scent of warm meat and homeyness, reminiscent of her childhood days when her mother made real, actual Sunday dinners. Kelly stood at the stove, stirring gravy in a small saucepan.

"It's packaged, but it sounded good anyway," Kelly said, noticing Sam's glance toward the range. "And the tenderloin will be ready in five."

Sam dropped her pack near the back door and hung her coat on a hook.

"Mom? You okay? You look a little shaky."

"No, it's nothing. Just a crazy driver." There was no point in scaring her daughter. Later, when she felt a little more stable, she would caution Kelly not to park in the alley if she were leaving work after dark.

She pulled flatware from a drawer and set places at the kitchen table, then got plates from the cupboard. As they ate, Kelly chatted freely, telling Sam about another of the daily mishaps in the world of dog bathing and clipping at Puppy Chic. Sam laughed often enough to pass for attentive but her mind raced along in a dozen other directions.

What had the whispered voice in the dark said? Something about not disturbing the panther? No, that wasn't quite right. Leave panther alone. Where had she heard that term recently . . . there was something she wasn't quite remembering. She picked at her food.

Panther—a name for someone. Jonathan Ernhart

had used it. The catlike, stealthy name was . . . It was Tito Fresques's code name. She locked in on that. Yes, that was it. The code name Tito used in his DEA work. Funny, Rick Wells hadn't mentioned it. She'd heard it somewhere else.

She worked it around in her head as she put the dishes into the dishwasher. Kelly had taken a couple of cookies from the stash of day-old ones that Sam always brought from the bakery and had gone to the sofa, where raucous game show laughter filled the room.

Sam went into her room to change clothes, thrusting aside all thoughts of the encounter in the alley. More importantly, right now, was to check on Marla. As she emptied the pockets of her work slacks she opened her cell phone and dialed the Fresques home.

An unfamiliar voice answered.

"Oh yes, Samantha. This is Camille Gonzales. We met at Marla's party awhile back."

"I was there this morning when she got the news about Tito," Sam said. "How is she doing now?"

"She won't eat and she won't sleep," Camille said. "Neighbors have been bringing food all afternoon. All Marla wants to do is plan Tito's funeral."

"I guess it's understandable that she wants to finalize things, after his being missing for so many years." Her eyes strayed to the lumpy wooden box on her dresser.

"I suppose so." In the background Sam heard someone ask Camille a question and she told the person to look in the dining room.

"Look, I was thinking about dropping by for a few minutes," Sam said, instantly questioning herself. It had been a long day and she really didn't have a desire to go back out in the cold.

She eyed the box again. Perhaps there was something good she could do for her friend.

"Marla is tired, Sam," Camille said. "But none of us can seem to convince her to go to sleep, including Father Joe. So you might as well try."

"I'll be there in about thirty minutes." Sam ended the call and quickly donned jeans and a sweater.

As had become habitual, she held the box on her lap and wrapped her hands around the sides of it, letting the heat from the wood permeate her body. When she could no longer handle the intensity of it, she set it into a drawer and quickly bundled up in her coat.

"I'm going out to Marla Fresques's place," she called out to Kelly. "If I'm not back in two hours call the cops."

Kelly chuckled and went back to her TV show.

What possessed me to say that? Sam thought as she walked out the back door. When she caught herself studying the shadows and opting to drive her pickup truck instead of the bakery van, she realized that the tattooed guy was still on her mind.

The eerie ice-fog began to close in around her truck once more when she approached the tiny crossroads of Arroyo Seco. Sam slowed and found herself watching the sides of the road, half expecting to see the chocolatier, Bobul, appear out of nowhere; half dreading to see anyone else. She double-checked the locks on her doors, crept along, and finally broke out of the fog as she came to Marla's turnoff.

Two cars besides Marla's sat out front and Sam began to doubt her mission. Maybe it would be better to simply leave the woman alone, to let her grieve in private for awhile and eventually get some rest. The stimulation of constant company might be taking its toll on the woman's already fragile health. Sam parked the truck and walked toward the front door. She was already here. She would sit with Marla for a short while, try to impart whatever energy the box had given her, and then leave. *You can only do what you can,* she decided.

Camille answered the door. Her husband Jorge hovered near the kitchen door with a cup of coffee in his hand.

"Come in, Samantha. It's good to see you again."

Sam glanced into the living room where she saw Father Joe sitting in a chair he'd pulled up alongside the sofa where Marla sat. She looked animated in a tired way, gesturing with her hands, sitting up straight, but with a weariness that dragged at her features.

The priest patted Marla's arm and then stood up. Compared to this morning, Marla's energy level had definitely waned. She started to stand up when she noticed Sam, but it seemed like an effort.

"Don't get up for me," Sam said, crossing the room. She draped her coat over the back of the sofa and took the chair that still held warmth from the priest.

Marla's hand, in contrast, felt chilly.

"How are you doing?" Sam asked.

Marla nodded, her head wagging side to side a little. "*Bien, mas o menos.* I'm okay." Her smile faded at the corners and her eyes were heavy lidded.

"I hear that no one can convince you to get some sleep."

"Soon. I will rest soon enough."

Sam got the feeling she wasn't talking about going to sleep. "Let me warm your hands again."

Marla talked as Sam took her right hand, running her own warm fingers up and down the length of Marla's arm.

"I spoke for a long time with Father Joe," she said. "We decided on the funeral arrangements."

"That's good." Sam took a turn at the left arm.

"He will talk to the authorities and make them bring Tito home. Within a few days he thinks we can have a service here in Taos and put my boy to rest."

Sam concentrated on sending the radiant warmth down her own arms, through her hands, and into Marla.

"Are your feet and legs also cold?" she asked her friend.

At Marla's nod, Sam suggested that she put her feet up on the sofa and let Sam massage them. She glanced toward the other visitors but Camille seemed occupied seeing the priest out the door and Jorge had disappeared into the kitchen. She applied the warm touch to Marla's feet, running her fingers upward to the knee, back to the arches. One leg and then the other. Energy ran through her fingertips and Marla's color seemed to improve almost immediately.

The knitted afghan lay over the back of the sofa and Sam retrieved it and tucked it around Marla's lap.

"Stay warm," she said. "And try to get some sleep soon. I think you'll feel better in the morning."

Marla settled a pillow under her head and leaned into it. "I will. Thank you, Sam." Although her coloring was better, the tiredness remained in the lines of her face.

Sam stood, a wave of lightheadedness washing over her.

She held her balance against the chair for a second until the dizziness passed. Camille stared at her, but with some concentration Sam walked away, picked up her coat and said her goodbyes to the group. The outdoor chill felt good, bracing her as she willed energy into her legs and walked to her truck.

Chapter 28

The drive home felt like it took forever. She seriously thought about pulling off the road at Beau's place; she knew he would welcome her. But there was something more appealing about settling into her own bed at the moment. No conversation, no intimacy, just the temptation to walk into her bedroom and totally, completely, crash.

She kept her eyes on the road and forced them to stay open. She'd never experienced such a complete letdown after transferring energy to someone else. Perhaps Marla's cancer was too formidable a challenge for Sam's abilities. As she'd told Zoë, a terminal disease was a whole different thing than a pulled muscle.

She nearly missed the turn onto her own street.

"I'm too tired for this," she said out loud, talking herself into staying awake two more minutes. "I can't keep—"

She hit the brakes hard, a fraction of a second before

the truck would have run into her van in the driveway.

"Okay, Sam, slow and careful. Just get inside and get into bed." She coached herself through each step of locking the truck, opening her back door, walking through the kitchen.

Television noises came from the living room.

"That you, Mom?" Kelly called out.

Sam sent a feeble wave toward her daughter. "Going right to bed," she mumbled. But Kelly's attention had already wandered back to the screen.

Inside her room, Sam's backpack fell to the floor and her coat landed across the bed. She barely remembered pulling back the comforter before everything went black.

* * *

Sam startled awake to unaccustomed bright sunlight in her room. She still wore her same jeans and sweater and had pulled the comforter over herself at some point.

Marla Fresques. Memories of driving out to Marla's house, trying to heal her, coming home completely exhausted, falling into bed. She groaned and rolled over. From somewhere in the room a muffled tune played. Her cell phone.

She sat up and patted the bedcovers until she located her coat and fished around in the pockets for the phone.

"Sam? Everything okay?"

She assured Jen she'd merely overslept.

"We got a little worried when you weren't here first thing. But it's fine. Sandy and Cathy got all the muffins and scones made. Becky is decorating cupcakes. It's been a little slower than normal up front."

Sam thanked Jen and told her she would be there in

plenty of time to finish the two birthday cakes for pickup later in the day. Then she dialed Marla's number, which was answered by Diane.

"She's hanging in there," Diane said. "I think she finally slept some last night. Father Joe just called to say that the funeral home has Tito's body, and of course Marla's first reaction was that she wanted to go see him. They pointed out that wouldn't be possible."

Thank goodness. Sam didn't even want to think what a murder victim from two years ago would look like.

"Let me know if there's any change in Marla's condition," she told Diane.

"Realistically, she should be back in the hospital." The neighbor's voice came through quietly. "But she won't go. There's no debating this until after Tito's funeral."

Sam glanced at the readout as she ended the call. After eight o'clock. She pulled herself out of bed and took a long, hot shower complete with shampoo and lots of conditioner. In the kitchen she stared into the fridge and decided to go all out with eggs and toast for breakfast. A pastry at the shop just wasn't going to give the energy boost she so desperately needed this morning. For good measure she rummaged through a cabinet and came up with a multi-vitamin and a few vitamin C chewables.

By nine she was on her way to the bakery, wondering if she could entirely chalk up the lag in energy to her visit with Marla last night. She walked in to find that the girls actually had everything well under control, and Jen showed a decent sales amount on the register.

Sam pulled the layers for the two birthday cakes and began assembling them. She put Becky to work icing and smoothing the quarter-sheet for the soccer girl, while Sam lost herself in the sculpting of small figures of the players and soccer balls for the green field. With a miniature goal net and some other details, the piece came together quickly.

The flowerpot cake was a little more challenging. Becky began creating sugar flowers and hanging them from a raised rack to chill in the fridge, while Sam took a stack of round layers and carved at them until the flowerpot shape emerged.

"Let's dirty-ice this one and get it back in the fridge," she told Becky. "I'll do the fondant and assembly after lunch. The customer isn't planning to be here until around three."

When she took a short break and headed for the coffee pot at eleven, she felt surprisingly better.

"I don't know what happened to my energy this past day or so," she commented to Jen when they were alone in the sales room. "Glad it's coming back, though."

"You push pretty hard, Sam. Gotta give yourself a break now and then."

Yeah, us old gals, she thought. But she didn't say anything. Her phone rang, down in her pocket, at that moment.

"Hey, darlin'. How about lunch? Stop by my office in an hour or so and we can go from there?"

It felt like it had been awhile since she and Beau had any private time for themselves, and although restaurant lunches were rarely quiet, it would be something. She told him she would get there as close to noon as possible.

When she walked into Beau's office, a man stood inside, talking animatedly with Beau.

"Hey, Sam, come on in, you've met Jonathan."

His smile was warm when he turned to face her and she could tell that the two old buddies were enjoying catching up.

"Mind if Jon joins us for lunch?" Beau asked.

She couldn't very well refuse. Besides, she had a few questions for the FBI man.

"I had a visit from Rick Wells," she said as they settled at a table at the Taoseño. "I guess the two of you are working the Tito Fresques case together."

Jonathan raised one shoulder. "Off and on." He lowered his voice. "Sometimes our agencies work certain operations together. Rick grew up in Arizona and has connections to the informants we're using against the Mexican cartels. We take the evidence they gather and work to build the case."

He got quiet when their waitress approached. Sam didn't speak again until the woman had taken their orders and walked away.

"I haven't told Tito's mother anything about his role in all this and I didn't think it was a good idea for Mr. Wells to spring that information on her either," Sam said. "I hope you aren't going to upset her."

"Seeing Mrs. Fresques was part of the purpose for my trip north," Jonathan said. "But Beau tells me the lady is in poor health and maybe it's not a good idea to be too frank with her."

"I wouldn't. I really don't think she knows a thing about Tito's undercover work."

Ernhart's eyes scanned the room constantly.

"Are we . . . Is it not good to talk about this here?" she asked, lowering her voice.

"It would be best to wait," he said.

Their plates arrived just then, and the agent picked up his hamburger. Before they'd gotten halfway through their meal, Beau's radio squawked.

"Sorry, looks like I need to get back to the office. Since

you all rode over here with me, I guess that means we're all leaving." He signaled the waitress and asked for three carry-out boxes.

While Beau placed a call with his office door shut, a file open in front of him, Sam and Jonathan carried their lunches to the interrogation room.

"So, now that we're in a secure place, can you tell me more about Tito Fresques's involvement with the DEA?" she asked.

"I'm just now learning a lot of it myself," Jonathan admitted as he picked up his half-finished burger. "Tito apparently did some undercover work in the Navy. From the start, the electrician training was a cover. He got out, DEA recruited him, got Bellworth to hire him. He was fluent in Spanish, blended well, knew how to handle himself in covert operations."

"And his family never had a clue about this?"

"Few do. Even if a guy can readily admit to his wife that he works for one of these agencies, there is *never* any work discussed at home. The job at Bellworth provided Tito with what he needed—a way to fit into a middle class neighborhood, a way to let his family see a paycheck from a legitimate source."

"You said there's new information now?" Sam picked up a French fry that had already lost its crisp.

"Well, finding his body changed everything. Wells told me they were pretty sure something had happened to him, but assumed it was back then, when he first disappeared. Now that we know he was on the run for eight years . . . well, our two agencies are piecing it together."

"Have you come up with what started the whole chain of events—why he vanished that weekend in August all those years ago?"

"There's either a mole within the agency, somebody who gave him up to the bad guys, or there's a bad guy out there who pinpointed him. I'm working on that."

Sam abandoned her tepid meal. "A strange thing happened to me last night," she said. "I haven't even told Beau about this."

She recounted the encounter in the alley, the man who practically raced by her, dropping the name Panther as he went.

"And you say this was the same day Rick Wells talked to you?"

It was. Sam had not put the two events together.

Ernhart got quiet for a minute or two, but when Sam tried to push for more information he stayed silent.

"There's still the other situation," she said. "Tito's mother is dying—cancer. The doctors are surprised she's lasted this long already. When she goes, it leaves Tito's young daughter Jolie all alone."

"That's tough. Maybe the grandmother has made provisions, named someone in her will?"

"I don't think so. I asked once. It seemed that she'd not yet made a will, a superstition that taking care of paperwork would hasten her death. She didn't want to die until she knew Tito was coming home."

"And now he is."

Sadly, that was true.

"Let me ask again," Sam said. "See what I can find out. Meanwhile, if there's anything at all in his employment records, the name of anyone that might have been close enough to take this on, could you . . .?"

"I'll let you know."

Sam closed the lid on the takeout box and looked around for a trash can but there wasn't one in the interrogation room. She picked up the remains of Ernhart's lunch as well, and opened the door to the squad room.

Beau's new deputy, Waters, nearly bumped into her. "Oh, you startled me!"

"Sorry." He stared at the carpet.

"Did you need something?" Sam asked.

"No, just looking for the sheriff." He shuffled toward the closed door to Beau's office.

Sam watched him walk away. Strange guy.

Chapter 29

Sam tossed away the lunch containers and saw that Beau's door was still closed. Waters had vanished into some other part of the building. She pecked at Beau's window with her fingernail and gave him a tiny wave. No point in waiting around his office; she still had a complex cake to finish this afternoon.

Back at the bakery, she tinted fondant to the exact color of terra cotta, rolled it and fitted it to the sides of the cake layers, eyeing the flower pot shape critically. When she finally had it to her liking, she sprinkled crushed chocolate cookies over the top to represent dirt, then looked over the assortment of flowers Becky had worked on all morning.

Brilliant yellow daffodils, red tulips, pink and white stargazer lilies, pansies with bright purple and gold faces . . . she began arranging them as if they were fresh flowers.

"Did you make some extra greenery?" she asked Becky. "I think this needs a little something more."

Her assistant pulled a tray from the fridge. "I thought about that. How about these? I did some broad leaves and a few that are more delicate."

"Oh, those ferns are nice." Sam picked them up by their wooden-pick stems and placed them among the colorful blossoms.

"Sam?" Jen stuck her head through the opening in the curtain. "It's almost three and I think I saw the customer for that flower—oh, wow . . . that is gorgeous!"

"Think she'll like it?"

"She's going to be blown away."

Sam placed a few loose petals on the board at the base of the flowerpot. "Okay, let's take it out there. Grab one of those deep boxes."

The cake didn't quite fit into the box and Sam cautioned the customer not to try closing the lid on it. "It will ride fine in your car if you don't take any sudden turns."

"Ms Sweet, it's absolutely a dream," the lady gushed. "Mother is going to love it!"

Sam carried the cake out to the woman's car and assured that it was firmly resting on the back seat. When she turned back to the shop she spotted another car pulling into one of her parking slots.

Felicia Black got out of her silver Lexus and gave her bright hair a toss.

"Sam, dear, so great to catch you here."

Uh-huh. And just what is so great about it? Sam crossed her arms.

"I just had a marvelous idea," Felicia said, oblivious to the frosty reception. "Some friends and I tried a new restaurant the other night—Cuarto del Oro—and I'd love to take you and Beau there for dinner this weekend. Tomorrow night?"

"Felicia, that's not—"

"Oh, Beau's available. I already asked him. He said he'd love to."

Yeah, right. The new Gold Room was very high-toned according to rumor. Sam didn't believe for one second that Beau would agree to go there. "I'll check that with him, Felicia. Let me get back to you."

Obviously, the woman wasn't going to take a simple 'no' for an answer. It would be better if she and Beau put together a firm refusal and delivered it together. Sam turned back to the bakery, saying she had work to do, but Felicia didn't go away. She followed Sam through the door.

"I need to get back to work—"

But Felicia had turned her charms on Jen, exclaiming over something in the display case. Sam escaped to the kitchen and flopped down onto her desk chair. How could she get rid of this pest, once and for all? She tapped her toe, her mind going in a hundred directions. When she heard the front door bells tinkle, she peered out through the curtain. The Lexus was backing out.

She dialed Beau's cell. "Did Felicia just invite you to dinner at some new restaurant?"

"Well, yeah, both of us. She breezed in awhile ago and acted like it would be such a fun evening, the three of us having a fancy meal. Her treat, of course."

"Same here. She said you'd already agreed to it."

"Not me." She could envision him backing away as he said it.

"Good thing we're checking with each other on these

wild claims of hers. I guess she somehow thinks we never talk." She picked up a paper clip and bent it with her fingertips. "I've heard of the place. White table cloths, a guitarist strolling around playing requests, way too many knives and forks and glasses."

"You don't actually want to go, do you?"

"Absolutely not." She suppressed the temptation to blame him for the ongoing contact. The fault lie completely with Felicia. "I'll handle it. And if she tries to tell you I accepted, do *not* believe her."

He chuckled as they ended the call. But Sam wasn't in quite such a cheery mood. Her gaze traveled around the kitchen, as she tried to think of a way to put a stop to this nonsense. She spotted the canister with Bobul's special spices on the top shelf above the stove. Two could play at this game. She quickly called the restaurant and left some instructions, then dialed the number Felicia had given her and left a message to meet at Cuarto del Oro at eight o'clock the following evening.

An hour later she'd mixed up a small batch of truffle filling and as she dipped the small orbs in deep, dark chocolate she finalized her plan. While the coating set, she located a classy paperboard box covered in luminous red foil. The perfect size for the six special chocolates. On a thick cream velum card she printed the words ASK THE GUITARIST TO PLAY "LOVE ME TENDER." I'LL BE LISTENING FOR IT. She found a length of gold ribbon.

One by one, the employees left for the evening. Sam took out her smallest decorating tips and piped tiny designs on the truffles—one with two hearts overlapping, a miniature nosegay on another—whatever romantic designs popped into her head at the moment. She placed the six beautiful pieces into the box, set the red foil lid on top, tied an elegant bow with the gold ribbon, and inserted the small envelope under it.

She closed up the bakery and drove to Cuarto del Oro.

"Yes, madam," a pointy-nosed maitre 'd said, with a downward glance at her baker's jacket.

She stepped in close. "One of your regular patrons is planning a special surprise for tomorrow evening. The reservation is under the name Felicia Black. When the lady arrives, please seat her at a table for two and be sure this box is at her place. Tell her the gentleman will be only a few minutes late but he insists that she open the card and the box immediately."

The man gave her a long look.

"At Sweet's Sweets we make pastries and wedding cakes for some of the most influential people in this town. I can send a lot of business your way if I get positive reports from this particular couple."

His manner changed quickly and he placed the small red box under the podium. "I shall keep this safe, madam, and deliver it as instructed."

Sam walked out to her van and sat there for a minute, thinking that another visit to Marla might be a good idea. She could run home first and try for some more of the healing power from the wooden box. A smaller dose, she promised herself. It wouldn't be good to repeat yesterday's complete energy drain. She quickly phoned Beau and cautioned him not to speak to Felicia if she were to call.

"I've got a plan in place that I hope will send her off in a new direction," Sam said, ignoring his questions.

Luckily, he got a radio call from dispatch and had to sign off quickly.

She arrived at Marla's house about an hour later, after stopping for a chicken sandwich and grabbing the wooden box. It occurred to her that the power might work better if Marla held the box herself.

Camille answered the door and showed Sam to Marla's bedroom.

"Hey, Marla," Sam said.

It was the first time she'd seen the woman take to her bed, other than the time she'd been sent to the hospital, and once again her condition seemed to have deteriorated. Sam glanced around and saw that Camille had left them alone.

"I have something I'd like to try," Sam said, pulling the box from under her coat. "It's . . . well, I'm not sure exactly. But it seems to give me energy. I thought it might do the same for you."

She placed the box on Marla's abdomen and her friend reached out to touch it.

"It's funny, isn't it?" Marla said. "Kind of ugly, but kind of pretty too?"

Sam smiled. "Try rubbing your hands over the surface of it."

Marla complied but Sam saw no reaction—either from the box or the woman. After two or three minutes, Marla shrugged.

"Is it supposed to do something?"

"I guess it won't. I'd hoped it would make your hands warm, make you feel energetic."

"How would it do that?"

Sam shrugged and picked up the box. "Never mind. It was just a thought."

Immediately when she held the box close to her own body, Sam felt the warmth start to flow. When Bertha

Martinez had given her the box she'd said Sam was meant to have it. It must be true. She sat on the edge of the bed and held the box for a little while, then clasped Marla's hand.

"Your hands feel warm," Marla said, closing her eyes. "That's nice."

But there was only a small rush of energy, and no obvious signs of healing. She watched Marla drift into a light sleep. When Sam stood up Marla awoke.

"Marla, there's something I wanted to talk to you about. It's Jolie."

Marla's eyes grew bright at the mention of her granddaughter but her smile was filled with sadness.

"This is hard, I know . . . Marla have you made out a will? Without one, you know the State will decide who gets to raise Jolie. It will probably be a complete stranger."

A tear slipped from the corner of Marla's eye and landed on the pale blue pillowcase. "I didn't talk to Diane's lawyer that day. I really thought Tito would come back."

"Are there no other relatives? Someone Jolie would feel comfortable with?"

Marla shook her head. "I have cousins in California. But Jolie has never met them. They would be strangers to her."

"Have you talked with your friends? Maybe a neighbor would be willing—"

"I can't ask that of them. Most of them are older, not able to take on a child. The only neighbor with children is Diane. I know she would keep Jolie for awhile. But they don't have the space for another child, or the money."

Sam thought hard, but couldn't come up with an alternative. "Let me do some checking. Maybe Beau will have some ideas."

She pulled the blanket over Marla's shoulders and asked

whether she wanted the bedside lamp on. As she switched it off and left the room with the box tucked into her coat once more, she saw Jolie standing in the doorway.

"I'm not going to live in California. I won't like it there," the girl insisted.

Sam pulled the bedroom door shut and nodded toward the living room. "It wouldn't be easy, but you might need to be open to new ideas. California has beaches and palm trees—"

Jolie stared hard at Sam. "Don't you think I already know what it's like to have my life turned upside down?" Her voice was quiet, not belligerent. The calm tone hit Sam harder than a tantrum would have.

"Oh, sweetie, you're so brave," Sam said. She reached out to put her arm around Jolie's shoulders but the girl turned toward her bedroom. Sam followed. "I promised your grandmother that I would try to find an answer to this. Will you give us that chance?"

The dark eyes welled. The girl nodded. Then she walked into her room and closed the door.

Camille came out of the kitchen, drying her hands on a towel, and Sam blinked back her own emotions.

"I need to go home," the neighbor said. "They've been doing all right alone here at night, but the time will come soon . . ."

"I know."

"Tito's funeral is scheduled for tomorrow afternoon. I think Marla is hanging on for that. She knows they probably wouldn't let her out of the hospital for it, and she's determined to go."

"I'm so sorry," Sam said, regretting that the box's powers had not worked.

"We all are," said Camille. "I wish . . . but the doctor isn't . . ." She pressed her lips together and shook her head.

Sam squeezed her hand and told her she would be at the funeral tomorrow. She walked out into the dark front yard and let out a sigh that became a shudder, which turned into a sob.

She started her van and drove slowly down the dirt road toward the highway. She'd passed through Arroyo Seco and made the turn onto 522 by the time the emotion abated. The highway was dark in all directions but within a mile after she'd turned onto it, a large vehicle came up behind her, blinding her with bright lights in her mirrors. She slowed to allow it to pass, but it stayed. The lights came closer, until she felt sure the truck was within inches of her bumper.

She sped up. It sped up.

Chapter 30

She slowed again. The large vehicle tailed her relentlessly. "What the hell are you *doing?*" she shouted. Some stupid drunk. She didn't dare take her hands off the wheel to dial 911 or call Beau. She sped up again, doing over sixty, then realized that there was a curve in the road ahead. She slowed for it and felt the nudge of the guy's bumper against hers. She gripped the wheel, praying not to go into a skid, her eyes riveted on the northbound traffic facing her.

Then all at once he backed off slightly, whipped into oncoming traffic, corrected, and zoomed off into the distance. Sam caught only the briefest glimpse of the boxy dark shape as she straightened her wheel and got her van back under control.

At the first wide spot she pulled over, the trembling in her arms traveling throughout her body. Her hands raked through her hair and she let out a shaky sigh. On the passenger seat the wooden box throbbed with a soft glow. She reached for it.

"What is it?" she whispered.

The glow sent a calming energy through her limbs so she kept holding it. Traffic streamed past. "What just happened there?"

What am I doing, talking to a box? Do I expect it to answer?

She stared ahead at the highway and the flow of traffic. That vehicle had been nowhere in sight when she pulled onto the pavement back there. And then suddenly it was right on her tail. Had he been waiting? Purposely targeting *her?*

She debated calling Beau for an escort home, but that seemed silly. It was a drunk driver—had to be. She set the box back on the passenger seat and put the van in gear. Watching for a good, wide berth she pulled back onto the road and caught herself watching for dark SUVs the rest of the way home.

Kelly's car was in the drive and lights at the windows reassured her. She scanned the yard and then chided herself for being so jumpy. Inside, the television played canned laughter from a sitcom.

"Some guy called for you earlier, Mom," Kelly said over her shoulder when Sam walked in. "He said he had some kind of information . . . I don't know."

Sam spotted the note on the kitchen table. Jonathan Ernhart. No number.

"He didn't say to call him back," Kelly explained when Sam showed her the note.

Sam left the note and went to her closet to choose

something appropriate for Tito's funeral tomorrow. Flipping through the hangers she came across the dress she'd worn for Iris's service. In January, it had been far too cold for a dress and it wasn't a whole lot warmer yet. She pulled down a pair of black slacks and matching jacket. At the graveside, she would have to add a winter coat and she wished she owned a dressier one.

She hung the garments on the closet doorknob and felt the familiar fatigue of the end of a long day. She washed her face and brushed her teeth in a stupor and crawled under the heavy comforter, falling asleep in moments.

A black grill with headlights came out of the dark, reeling down upon her, sending Sam diving for the side of the road. She looked around, confusion reigning as one side of the road seemed to be out in the country, the other side part of a six-lane freeway. Vehicles came at her and she tried to run but her legs wouldn't work. The muscles were frozen. She pressed herself against a concrete barrier and squeezed her eyes shut, waiting to die.

She awoke spread-eagled on her bed, her hands gripping at the sheet beneath her. Her eyes were tightly closed, her breathing coming hard and fast.

When her eyes popped open she realized it had been a nightmare.

Country road or high-paced expressway. The message became clear. Tonight, it was the same SUV that had nearly run her off the freeway in Albuquerque a week ago. She closed her eyes and worked to bring back the picture. Scraps of detail emerged. A white license plate that started with the letters PDX. A male driver, muscled arms. Strings of blue designs on the arms. Tattoos. But that didn't make sense.

The SUVs both had darkened windows and she'd not seen the drivers. Tattoos belonged to the scary man in the alley and the guy in the red car who'd almost hit her several days ago. But the more she tried to concentrate on details, the more she lost clarity and the picture faded.

Sam sat up in bed and hugged the warm covers to her. She'd gone to Albuquerque to ask questions of the supposed other woman in Tito's life, Lisa Tombo. No one unconnected with Tito should have known Sam was in town. At the time of the freeway incident she'd chalked it up to a crazy driver. Again, tonight, she'd chalked up the near-miss to someone drunk or nuts. How likely was that? Very.

How likely that both vehicles had similar plate numbers? Miniscule.

Names went through her head: Lisa Tombo, Javier Espinosa, Harry Cole, Bill Champion. Not to mention the two government men, both of whom seemed overly secretive.

Had Lisa Tombo or one of Tito's other co-workers called someone, told them Sam was asking questions? Why would they do that? To warn Sam away from the case?

She rubbed at her temples and got out of bed, putting on her robe and heading for the kitchen. The clock said it was barely past midnight but she knew sleep was a long way off now. She heated milk and made hot chocolate.

* * *

By four a.m. Sam felt as if she'd only slept a couple of hours and she decided to get a head start at the bakery. When her employees began to arrive at six, she'd already baked three cinnamon coffee cakes, scones in four flavors, an assortment of cookies and there were three dozen muffins in the oven.

"I love coming to work here?" Sandy said, sniffing the air. "The smell is so wonderful?"

Cathy rolled her eyes. Sam got the feeling that of the two temporary hires, Cathy would be the one happiest to leave the job and her somewhat-irritating co-worker behind. Sandy would probably continue her strangely obsequious behaviors, but it would be somewhere else after today. Sam let them know that she would write their final paychecks before she left for the Fresques funeral at one o'clock.

While her employees stayed busy, keeping the oven filled and the customers happy, Sam checked her orders for the coming week and organized her workload. This afternoon and evening would be tough, being with a dying woman who was laying her only son to rest.

She stacked her small sheaf of order forms neatly and set them in the basket at the corner of the desk. It only took a few minutes to write the paychecks for Sandy and Cathy before she turned to the rack of chocolate cupcakes that awaited her attention. Piping thick buttercream frosting onto them and experimenting with various sprinkles and other decorator touches occupied her hands but not her mind.

The close call last night on the highway seemed to cap it for her—the pain of watching Marla's condition worsen, the knowledge that Sam had not been able to find the missing son in time, the sight of that young girl who would soon have no remaining family, and her own ambivalent feelings about her cancelled wedding plans. Her chest constricted and Sam took a deep breath, shelving the thoughts once again. Sunday was her only day off and she felt herself holding the entire week's emotional tide at bay, waiting for the one day when she could let herself release it all.

Meanwhile, there was nothing so pressing at the bakery that she couldn't spare a little time away. It was only ten o'clock. She shed her baker's jacket, put on her winter coat and went out the back door to her van. Beau had involved her in this case. She would damn well stick with it now.

Chapter 31

She arrived at the Sheriff's Department to find Jonathan Ernhart and Rick Wells there when she walked into Beau's office. They appeared to be in that chit-chat phase of the meeting, before getting down to business.

"Samantha, darlin', come on in." Beau waved her through the open door.

Ernhart greeted her, but when Beau pulled up a chair for her the two agents didn't say anything. Two deputies were working at desks in the squad room, but only Denny Waters had momentarily looked up before turning back to his paperwork.

"Sam has been in on this case, even before we officially reopened it," Beau explained. "She's talked to several of Tito Fresques's old co-workers and might be able to contribute something today."

Wells nodded, although Sam remembered both men's earlier hesitancy at sharing information. They took seats around Beau's desk. Beau leaned back in his chair as Wells began speaking.

"You both know that Tito's job at Bellworth in Albuquerque was merely a cover. He'd been with Drug Enforcement since he got out of the Navy, and DEA regularly sent him into Mexico where he had infiltrated one of the cartels."

Beau nodded.

"That particular gang had strong ties in northern New Mexico, even here in Taos. Of particular interest to us was a man named Javier Espinosa. You're familiar with him?"

"The name has come up. Locally, he's one of those with a mile long record of minor offenses—possession mainly—gang ties. Every town has 'em. What's his connection to Fresques?"

"Tito had gathered hard evidence of Espinosa's connections with Mexico, details about supply routes, names of underlings who moved the bulk of the stuff around. We're talking cocaine by the truckloads and marijuana in the tons. Taos is ideally suited because we're on the back roads leading to Colorado and from there they can cover all the Rocky Mountain states and channel the stuff to either the Midwest or the west coast without traveling the major interstate highways.

"Things were heating up. Tito assured me that he had enough evidence to put away Espinosa, plus at least two dozen others here in the States, and to grab some of the Mexican leaders as well. The raids were being set up, warrants would be issued as soon as Tito sent us his report.

He vanished before it was ever received."

"But DEA knew he had evidence. You couldn't go ahead and make the arrests?" Sam asked.

Jonathan spoke up. "The law doesn't work that way. A judge isn't going to issue warrants without cause and even though we knew what we had, we needed the proof— spelled out. We could have pulled in most of these guys on suspicion and we might have gotten enough information out of them to put a few of them away. But the ones at the top, especially the Mexicans, they hide behind so many layers—we'd never have gotten them without the whole chain of evidence."

"So . . ." Beau said, "rather than take the chance of spooking them, you wanted to wait."

"Exactly." Jonathan leaned forward in his chair and lowered his voice. "We also had reason to believe that we had a mole inside one of the agencies. Every time we got close to one of these higher-up dealers something would jinx the deal. He'd leave the state or he'd have an airtight alibi. After it happened several times, it was more than coincidence."

Beau let out a low whistle.

"Tito was the only person on my team that I felt a hundred percent sure about," Wells said. "We'd worked together for a lot of years. He was just one of those genuine guys, you know. The type that you know is being straight with you."

"And you had no idea who this mole was," Sam said.

"Still don't know for sure. After Tito disappeared I watched everyone like a hawk. I looked for anybody who acted like they knew what really happened to him, anyone who seemed relieved that he was gone . . . that sort of thing. No hints at all. Whoever did it was good."

"*If* they did," Beau reminded. "Tito may have left voluntarily and no one else was responsible at all."

"I believe he did leave voluntarily. But there was a reason. And there had to be a damn strong reason for him to stay out of touch all those years. I think he wasn't sure who the mole was, so he felt like he couldn't trust anyone. Maybe not even me. Otherwise he would have found some way to contact me and get me the evidence he'd gathered."

"Makes sense," Beau said. He'd picked up a pen and made a few notes. Now he tapped the pen restlessly against the pages in the folder.

Sam excused herself to go to the bathroom, mulling the information as she walked down the hall. Deputy Waters was coming out of the men's room wafting an air of hand soap, rolling his sleeves down as he walked and he nearly ran into her.

"Oh, sorry Ms Sweet. Didn't see you there," he mumbled.

The man was like a fly, an irritating distraction that she wanted to swat out of the way. But she didn't say so. Maybe she'd not given herself a chance to learn whether he actually had a personality.

"Nice art," she said, with a nod toward the colorful marks on his arms.

"Uh, thanks." He seemed more weasel-like than ever as he slunk back toward his desk.

Okay, be that way, she thought as she pushed her way into the women's bathroom. By the time she got back to Beau's office it looked like the three men were wrapping up their meeting. Ernhart stood near the door with his overcoat on and Wells had wandered into the squad room. Beau closed the Fresques file.

"Do we have time for lunch somewhere?" Beau asked as they watched the two federal agents walk away.

Sam checked the clock on the wall. "If it's a very quick one. I obviously have to get home and change into something more appropriate for the funeral." She looked up into his ocean-blue eyes. "I'm really not looking forward to this."

"I know."

"It's been devastating for Marla, this news, on top of her own health problems."

They ended up taking both of their vehicles, eating a quick burger at McDonald's and then heading their separate ways, with a plan to meet at the funeral home at a quarter to one.

* * *

The service was small and typical. Doleful music that brought tears before a word was spoken, a closed casket with an American flag draped over it, a large portrait photograph of a smiling Tito with a dated haircut. The congregation consisted of Marla's neighbors whom Sam had already met and a scattering of younger people.

Marla looked like a ghost. Diane Milton's husband wheeled her chair up the aisle and parked it beside the frontmost pew. During the ride, Marla's eyes never strayed from the silver box at the front of the room. Jolie, in a burgundy dress and matching coat, sat next to her grandmother. The other neighbors took seats nearby, a little cluster of comfort.

At least Sam hoped so, for Marla's sake.

Sam and Beau, feeling out of their ordinary milieu in dressy clothing, had taken seats near the rear of the group and she found herself gripping his hand. Jonathan Ernhart and Rick Wells arrived at the same time, just as the organist struck her final chords.

The priest, mercifully, kept his message short and Sam was thankful that Marla had opted for the memorial format, rather than a full-blown Catholic mass. The older woman was clearly losing energy as the minutes ticked slowly by. At the end of the formal part, the priest announced that a graveside service would take place, but in light of the cold weather it would be very short. Then Jorge and Camille stood and announced that everyone was invited to Marla's where they had prepared a meal to share.

Sam chided herself for not thinking ahead and baking a special cake. As the mourners filed to the front, stopping to hug Marla and Jolie, she thought quickly. She could pop by the bakery and assemble a nice tray of cookies. She whispered as much to Beau, suggesting that she could meet him later, but he offered to drive her.

They arrived at the cemetery in time to hear the closing prayer. The small crowd was already beginning to disperse, Diane and her husband helping Marla and Jolie into their roomy Honda SUV. Sam noted that neither of the government men were there—they must have needed to return to Albuquerque. A few figures that she didn't remember from the service stood off to one side—three men in casual black clothing, with shaved heads and visible tattoos. The encounter in the alley sprang to mind. The guy in the middle could be the one. She wasn't sure.

She reached out to get Beau's attention, but he had

moved a few feet away and was speaking to one of the young couples they'd seen at the funeral home. When Sam turned her attention back to the three rough-looking men, they had already moved to the cemetery gate, toward the parking area behind a stand of evergreens.

"Sam, I'd like you to meet Jimmy McMichael and his wife, Callie. Jimmy was a good friend of Tito's," Beau said.

Sam didn't recognize the name but she registered a clean-cut Anglo man in his thirties, inexpensive blue suit and patterned tie, short sandy hair, a straight nose and tiny gold stud in his right earlobe. His wife wore a navy blue dress of thin fabric that was inadequate for the weather and she shivered visibly in her cardigan jacket. They both greeted Sam with warm smiles.

"We won't be able to go out to Mrs. Fresques's house," Jimmy said, running a finger around the collar of the fitted shirt. "Work. You know how that is. But I've got something for her, Tito's mom. It's a box of things Tito gave me that morning. The day he left."

"You saw him that day?" Beau asked with a sharper edge than usual.

"Well, yeah. He stopped by my place. I remember I was working on my car. Had a gorgeous little Mustang back then." His wife gave him a quick smile.

"What did Tito say that day? Did he seem worried or anything?"

Callie McMichael was clearly freezing and she nudged her husband.

"Let's walk toward the car. I can get her out of this wind and I'll give you the box of stuff." They headed as a group toward the parked cars.

"The conversation that day?" Beau reminded.

"Oh yeah, well, not much that I remember. He had this carton with him, just a box of stuff. Said I should see that his mom got it if anything ever happened to him. I held onto it all this time. Kinda forgot about it, really. It was in our garage and I did some cleaning about six months ago and came across it. Meant to take it over there before now, but things just got busy."

He opened the passenger door and Callie gratefully got inside and closed the door behind her.

"If you don't mind taking it to Mrs. Fresques . . ." He unlocked the trunk and raised the lid, then reached for the box. It was a cardboard carton about twelve inches square. The top was taped down with clear packing tape and the single word TITO was printed in marker on one end. He held it out and Sam took it.

"Do you remember anything else about that day?" Beau asked. "Tito's exact words, anything he might have mentioned about his plans?"

"Not really, man. Oh, he said he might try to come by to watch the game with me the next day, but then he didn't come. I figured he'd just gotten busy with family."

"But he seemed worried for his safety? Did he say that?"

"Sort of. Something like 'if anything happens to me and I don't come back' . . . you know, words kind of like that."

Chapter 32

Jimmy was starting to look a little cold, himself. Beau thanked him for the box and asked Jimmy to call his office if he thought of anything else. They watched the younger couple back out of their parking spot as Sam and Beau walked to his cruiser.

"Do you think he'll come up with any new information later?" Sam asked as she fastened her seatbelt.

"Hard to say. But I definitely think we need to check out this box before we give it to Marla. If it contains personal mementos, that's one thing. But if that were the case why wouldn't he have just left it at her house?"

"Exactly," Sam said, picking at the edge of the tape with a fingernail.

"Here." Beau handed her a pocketknife and she slit the cellophane.

She raised the cardboard flaps and lifted out a sheet of crumpled newspaper. The page was dated the week Tito disappeared. Her fingers trembled a little as she picked up the topmost item. It was a folded sheet of lined paper. *Dearest Mama, If you are reading this . . .*

Sam looked up. "I'm not sure I should read this. It's private."

Beau held his hand out and she placed the page in it.

He quickly scanned the handwritten lines. "I don't see anything about his work or his feeling threatened. It's a goodbye." He folded the page again and set it aside. "What else is in there?"

Sam picked out a rubber-banded packet of envelopes. Bank statements. Through the glassine windows she could see that they were solely in Tito's name. She pulled one out, unfolded it and scanned to the bottom of the page. The savings account balance was a little over a thousand dollars. The second one showed several CDs, to be automatically reinvested. Ten years ago they had totaled about ten thousand dollars, back in the time when interest rates were considerably higher than present day. She handed each statement to Beau as she pulled out the next one.

"Looks like he'd squirreled away nearly fifty thousand dollars," Beau said.

"Do you think it was legitimate money?" Sam asked.

"I do. For one thing, there are tons of rules about cash transactions with banks nowadays. And, I doubt he would have opened accounts under his real name if he were dealing with stolen money. Plus, it's not a large enough amount to take that kind of risk against the cartel."

"How do you mean?"

"If a guy decides to cross the bad guys, he'll do it for a

lot more than this. This whole box would be full of hundred dollar bills, or there'd be a roomful of them somewhere."

Sam stared down into the box. "I don't see any cash at all."

"He probably just wanted Tricia and Jolie to have a little nest egg, maybe a college fund."

"I still don't see why he didn't just hand this directly to them." Sam pulled out a small box, like something jewelry might come in. When she opened it, she discovered a military medal and a key.

"Purple Heart." Beau said, stroking the medal with his finger. "I'm surprised no one's mentioned this. But then again, maybe he never made a big deal out of it."

"There's only one more thing," Sam said. She held up a yellow plastic floppy disk. "I'm thinking his mother is not meant to be the beneficiary of this." Across the front of the disk, written in black marker, were the words: *Get this to the authorities.*

Beau took the disk and turned it over but there were no other notations. "What authorities do you think he meant? Jonathan told us that Tito had reason not to trust many people in his own agency."

"Well, you're the sheriff of this county," she said. "That makes you qualified on some level, don't you think?"

She could see common sense fighting with the bureaucracy that governed Beau's daily work life.

"You can't very well know who you should give it to until you know what it says," she pointed out. "Besides, who can read one of these old floppies anymore? Hint—my computer at home has that drive."

He looked up at her and chuckled. "Okay, you've made a good case. Shall we?"

It took Sam about three seconds while Beau started the cruiser and put it in gear to decide that it would be okay to show up late for the gathering at Marla's house.

"Hit the lights, would you?" she said.

Getting through town went so much faster with benefit of an official vehicle, she thought as they zoomed through intersections and past lines of cars that pulled over for them. In under five minutes they were walking through her kitchen, heading for the computer desk in the corner of the living room. She set the cardboard box on the desk and pulled out the floppy disk.

"This thing may be old but I knew there was a reason I never fully upgraded." She pressed the power button and warned Beau that it might take a few minutes.

"Hey, it's not any slower than the stuff the county gives us." He held out the disk and she inserted it into the drive.

When the directory came up it appeared to contain only one file, a very small Word document. "This can't be much," Sam said as she opened it.

On the screen appeared two terse sentences:

Find someone you can trust in law enforcement. Have them go to 1800 Front Street NE in Albuquerque and retrieve the items in Box 99.

Sam and Beau stared at each other, each with the same *huh?* look on their faces.

"Okay," he said finally. "Tito obviously didn't know who to trust or he would have named someone. The only Feds I know are Jonathan and Rick."

Sam stared at the screen. "Tito reported to Rick Wells and yet he didn't entrust him with this. I know—that was then and this is now, but should we maybe check this out before getting anyone in the agency involved?"

"How are—?" Beau's eyes traveled to the carton beside the monitor. "That key!"

Sam grabbed up the small box with the Purple Heart in it. The key with it could belong to nearly anything and she hadn't thought to question it earlier. It made sense that Tito would put the disk and the key close to each other but not so close that it was obvious they went together. She took the key out and returned the medal to the box with the other personal items.

"I'm thinking we need to make a quick trip to Albuquerque," she said. "Would it be a horrible breach of ethics if we got there the same way we just now got here?"

Beau groaned at her sneaky little grin. "Well, we're dealing with information that got a man killed, and it involves some pretty high levels of the federal government."

"And it would be a lot quicker. We could be there and back before dinner."

He rolled his eyes at that suggestion but didn't argue.

"Let me call out to Marla's house real quick." While Beau locked the back door, she dialed the number and told Diane Milton that something had come up and that she would stop by with something for Marla in the morning.

"That's fine, Sam," Diane said. "She's awfully tired right now anyway. It's been a hard day."

Never in her life had Sam experienced the thrill of making the long highway drive in such record time, but she took a deep breath and braced herself. A few times she squeezed her eyes tightly shut. It was mid-afternoon when they hit the edge of the big city and Beau took full advantage of his lights and siren to cut through the clog of early rush hour. Fighting a queasy feeling in her stomach, Sam pushed the buttons to program the address into his GPS and to study the little map that came up.

He cut the emergency gear when they got to the correct street, and Sam picked up the brass key as they approached the mail drop location. It was one of those places where you could rent a box for years at a stretch with no questions asked and no one clearing the box and stamping "Return to Sender" on your stuff. The perfect place to send things that you didn't want anyone else to touch. They walked inside together and it took only a minute to find Box 99 and unlock it.

"Good thing he rented the largest box," Beau said as he pulled open the door. The cubbyhole was stuffed full. As he pulled out handfuls of envelopes, Sam cradled them in her arms. When the metal compartment was completely empty, they carried everything out to the cruiser.

"Let's just make sure there isn't some kind of 'more mail at the counter' type of notice in here before we leave," Beau suggested.

Sam handed over half of the unruly stack and they began straightening and organizing. Some of the envelopes were a bit ragged and dirty, some felt thin as if they were nearly empty while others were fat little packets. All were addressed in masculine writing, the return address was the same as the delivery address, the one where they sat right now, and the postmarks coincided with the ones she remembered from Marla's greeting cards.

"Looks like this is all of it," Beau said, handing his portion back to her.

"So, now what?" Sam said. "I still don't think you want to turn Tito's secret information over to just anyone. We really need to go through all of it and find out what it says before we'll know who to trust."

"There's at least a day's worth of reading here."

She nodded. There went her Sunday but she wasn't about to drop her interest in the case at this point.

"I don't really feel like staying over in the city, finding a hotel or whatever. Do you?" he asked.

"Nah. I can't handle these clothes much longer either. So . . . home, James?"

He backed out and joined the flow of traffic. As the evening rush became more oppressive he succumbed to the temptation and switched the strobes on again. They arrived back in Taos, as Sam had predicted, in time for dinner.

She'd called the bakery and made sure Jen had things under control. Another call to Kelly let her daughter know that she was heading to Beau's for the night. They picked up a bucket of chicken, retrieved her truck from the lot at the funeral home, and headed for his place.

Once she'd changed into flannel pajamas and they'd each polished off a couple pieces of chicken, Beau brought out his pocket knife and began slitting open the envelopes. Sam automatically began sorting the mail by postmark date and she soon had four neat stacks of well-ordered mail.

Beau started with the first envelope, which had been mailed about a week after Tito's disappearance.

"Listen to this," he said. "Quote: 'Can't believe it. Close call. Espinosa knows something, not sure how he found out. He nearly had me in Taos. Now I don't dare contact anyone. The only thing I can think to do is start documenting. Got this mailbox, will send evidence as I get it. This way, if I'm dead someday, eventually someone will come across my findings. I've rented the box for a year. Will renew it if necessary. I listed my mother as the contact person but I don't want her involved."

"What does that mean?" Sam asked.

"Probably had to fill out some kind of rental contract and since he didn't have a home address once he skipped out, the company would send the remaining mail to Marla if the contract wasn't renewed and there was anything left in the box. I don't know. That's my guess."

"Hmm . . . probably so."

"As long as Tito renewed the box, the mail could just continue to pile up. I could verify by questioning the manager there, but my guess is that at some point Tito realized this would be a long-term thing and he just paid the rent for five-years or so—maybe longer."

"It would explain why no one ever cleared out the box even though the mail stopped coming."

Beau picked up the next envelope in sequence, but Sam found herself getting impatient. Some of the later ones were bigger. They had to contain more information. One was a padded mailer, the kind with bubble wrap on the inside. Like a kid at Christmas she couldn't stand waiting for it.

She reached for it and ripped it open by the little tab. Inside was a scuffed leather-bound book, no wider than an index card. The covers were well worn and the pages were held closed by a rubber band, which broke and flew across the table when she touched it, hitting Beau in the chest.

The pages of the small book contained Tito's tight handwriting.

"Whoo—we may have just hit the jackpot," Sam said.

Chapter 33

Sam turned to the first page. The same handwriting filled it but nothing made sense. The letters and numbers formed some kind of code. She flipped through the entire book but it was all the same.

"That thing looks like it's been through the wringer," Beau said, eying the small notebook.

"Or hidden in someone's dirty sock for a long time," Sam said. "But what can we do with it? Look, it's coded."

"Let's keep going. Maybe the rest of the letters will help explain."

Sam hated to admit it, but he was right. Without the code key, the little book would do them no good. She sighed and reached for the next envelope in the chronological stack.

The letters kept them going until well past midnight, each reading and sharing new information as it came out.

Eventually, though, they were both struggling to keep their eyes open and when they finally fell into bed somewhere around two they didn't even have the energy to do more than cuddle into a ball in the center of the king-size bed.

When Beau's alarm went off at five, he groaned and rolled over, but Sam found herself alert with that kind of adrenaline exhaustion that could keep a person going who was way past tired. She tucked the covers close to him and made her way in the pitch-blackness to the bathroom where she borrowed his robe off the back of the door and snuggled into it.

Downstairs, she reheated some coffee they'd brewed the previous evening and stared at the nearly-finished pile of Tito's letters. They'd learned that during some of the years Tito was gone he'd actually lived among the cartel in Mexico and continued to gather evidence, but since the dangerous men were with him 24/7 he couldn't contact anyone. He would occasionally mail these handwritten pages he'd clandestinely created whenever he was able to cross back into the States, at the same time he sent the cards to his family. It must have been awful, living in fear for his life, keeping the little leather journal hidden somewhere on his person, praying that he wouldn't be discovered, knowing that if they figured out what he was doing they would murder him without a second thought.

His trips back to his homeland were rarely unaccompanied. He skipped around when he could but could never check in with his DEA contacts, not knowing who would help him and who would rat him out to the cartel. And he could never see his family; the risk was far too great to them. He'd somehow found out, more than a year after the fact, that his wife had died. Sam cried openly when she read the letter where he detailed that. But since there was nothing he could do about her death, and knowing that Jolie was safe with her grandmother, he'd stayed silent and in hiding.

Mainly, he gathered evidence in hopes that when the day came, he could present a strong enough case to take the entire gang out at once. Including those bad apples within the Agency who'd threatened his very existence.

Now, Sam tucked her feet up onto the sofa and held the warm coffee mug with both hands, tempted to get into the final few letters that they hadn't finished but thinking she should wait for Beau. One cup of coffee later, she felt too jittery and impatient to wait. She reached for the top letter in the stack.

Two lines into it she felt an electric jolt.

The proof is documented in my notebook, he'd written. *I don't dare spell out the code here. Anyone finding this would know where I am and who I'm working with. So I'm going to write it out and mail it in a series of short messages.*

What followed were a few lines of his cleverly constructed code—partly letters and numbers, with a few math symbols and small cryptic designs thrown in. It was almost like stenography in places, where one little curlicue represented an entire word; at other times numbers meant letters and vice versa. The letter in her hand covered less than a third of the alphabet. Sam dropped it and grabbed for the next letter.

It, too, covered a few letters of the alphabet plus a few whole-word translations. She flattened that page, as well, and opened the rest of the envelopes. Spread over ten separate communications, Tito's special code was revealed. He'd invented symbols to represent places. Special codes for dates and times. An ingenious plan to avoid the most common repetitions that allowed code-breakers to solve puzzles easily.

She picked up the small leather book and flipped it open again. It would probably take weeks to decipher it all, word for word. But when it was done, she had no doubt that the evidence therein was complete and thorough. From the key sheets, she found symbols for names, and two of them jumped out at her: Rick Wells and Javier Espinosa.

At a glance, she could tell that those two names featured heavily in the book of secrets, often together.

She and Beau truly had discovered the bonanza.

Thin shafts of sunlight showed through the barren tree branches outside, casting faint shadows across the pasture. In the still air she heard the horses whinny softly. It must be after seven.

She picked up the letters with the code and the little leather-bound book and dashed up the stairs.

"Beau, wake up! I've discovered the answer!"

He moaned and she felt badly about waking him. He'd put in such long days recently. But when he saw the letters in her hand his eyes came fully open.

"I haven't translated any of the book yet," she said, "but in this code . . ." She shuffled through them. "Rick Wells is the mole inside the DEA. Tito says the coded messages in the book give all the evidence."

Beau rubbed at his eyes and then squinted at the letter she held out to him.

"I'll bet that Tito's messages get more explicit toward the end of the book. Can I try it?"

He nodded. "I'm going to take a quick shower. Is there any coffee?"

"I'll have it ready when you get downstairs."

She dashed back to the kitchen, excited over the find, and dumped the old coffee to start a new pot. At the dining table she spread out the ten letters which revealed Tito's code. He'd purposely not put them in any alphabetical sequence, so it was slow going. Sam figured there was no real need for her to translate the whole book—the authorities would do that anyway. She turned to the final page, wanting to know Tito's thoughts as he neared the end of his investigation.

The date on the last page corresponded to the postmark on the envelope from which the small book had come. One letter at a time she figured it out and wrote it down.

When Beau came downstairs ten minutes later, smelling like fresh soap and shave cream, she pointed to the page.

"This is what I have so far. We need to get Jonathan Ernhart in on this," she said.

"He's not involved?" Beau asked.

"Look through the code sheets. There are symbols for Rick Wells, for Javier Espinosa, for a bunch of other names. Nothing for Ernhart. If Tito didn't make a code for his name, I'm thinking he's not mentioned in the book. Therefore, not involved in whatever was going on."

"Makes sense," he said as he walked into the kitchen and poured coffee into his mug.

"Beau, there's something else. In his final letter, the one that was mailed about two years ago, Tito spells it out. He thinks Wells might kill him. He says, quote, 'Rick Wells and a few others in Washington are in this up to their necks. I have to go to DC and find out. To pinpoint them I'll have to come out of hiding, and that's going to be dangerous. Details are in the book. Wish me luck.' "

"Well, we have to tell someone. This is more than my office can deal with. Your idea of calling Jonathan Ernhart is a good one." He set a fresh mug of coffee on the table beside her.

While Sam reorganized the letters, Beau made the call. She heard him say something about meeting at his office in thirty minutes.

"I thought he went back to Albuquerque yesterday," she said.

"Nope. He stayed at a hotel here. Something about Javier Espinosa. I didn't ask a whole lot at this point because I'll see him pretty soon." He caught the look on her face. "*We'll* see him pretty soon."

The squad room was empty when they arrived, although Sam could hear voices from the other end of the building where the two holding cells were. Ernhart arrived first and was waiting near the front desk. Beau offered coffee, which they all declined, and then showed the FBI man into his office. He closed the door firmly, Sam laid the stack of Tito's correspondence on the desk and they took seats.

Beau laid it all out for Ernhart: the computer disk, the mail drop, the years' worth of documentation Tito Fresques had accumulated.

"Sam actually came to the parts where Tito revealed his coded system for keeping evidence," he said, holding up the small leather book.

When Jonathan looked at her Sam met his gaze. "I'm sorry to say that he names Rick Wells as the mole inside the DEA."

Ernhart shook his head and stood up. "I'd like to say that I don't believe it, Beau. But there have been a few recent signs."

He paced the length of Beau's small office.

"Little things he said about Tito when we began this investigation. A couple of comments about Javier Espinosa." He rubbed at his temple. "I just didn't put it all together."

"The book has a lot of references to Espinosa, too," Sam said. "It will take awhile to translate the whole thing, but I spotted the code mark for his name."

"The bureau has code-breakers we can put on it. With several people working it, we can probably decipher it pretty quickly." He stopped in mid-pace. "We'll have to move on this pretty fast, I think. Rick has been acting jumpy lately. Yesterday at the funeral, I couldn't figure out what was eating at him."

An image materialized to Sam. "He drives a black Suburban, doesn't he?"

Ernhart nodded.

"I've had two really close calls in traffic in the past week, once in Albuquerque and again on the road north of Taos. Both involved a big dark SUV."

Beau stared at her.

"Sorry I didn't mention it. You've had a lot on your mind."

He gave her a look that basically meant *we'll talk about this later*.

"Rick travels back and forth between Washington and Albuquerque. But this week he's been in New Mexico," Jonathan said, starting to pace again.

"So, what now?" Beau asked. "We need a plan."

Jonathan flopped back into his chair and blew out a long breath. "First, we pull all the names we can get from this book. There will have to be warrants. It would be a mistake to arrest one of the suspects and not get them all. Timing is going to be crucial, to be sure no one is able to phone or text a warning to the others."

Beau nodded. "Absolutely. How soon?"

Ernhart looked at his watch, drummed his fingers on the desk. "It's Sunday. That's going to make it a little trickier to get enough people on the job of decoding the book."

"Look, I've spent a little time with this," Sam said. "Even though it would take awhile to decode the entire book, word for word, I noticed that Tito created special symbols for most of the names of people. That's how I spotted Wells and Espinosa on those final pages. So, what if you looked only for those names at first? Wouldn't that be reasonable enough suspicion to bring them in?"

Ernhart nodded again, and Beau seemed eager. "Worth a little of our time, I'd say."

They tossed ideas around and amid the legal jargon, with talk of warrants and probable cause, Sam felt her eyelids growing heavy. The three hours sleep weren't holding her very well.

When Jonathan took the letters out to the squad room to make copies, she turned to Beau.

"Looks like you boys don't need me for this part. I think I'll go on home and try for some rest."

Nestled into her bed, Sam was soon dead to the world, but when she awoke it was suddenly and completely. Faint sounds came from the living room, the drone of the TV. She gathered some fresh clothing and took a long, hot shower. Fluffing her hair, she padded into the kitchen to find her daughter staring into the refrigerator.

"Just thinking about dinner," Kelly said.

"Geez, what time is it anyway?" Sam looked at the clock. After five. She'd slept away eight hours in dreamless oblivion.

"Is it okay if I just make mac and cheese?" Kelly asked.

She smiled at her daughter, the kid who would never quite grow up. In fact, it actually sounded good, some old-fashioned comfort food. "Do enough for two."

"Mommy?" Kelly said as they sat on the sofa with bowls in hand. The reversion to childhood might as well be complete. "You know what I'd really love to have with this?"

Sam stared over the top of her spoon.

"Some of your brownies . . . the ones with chocolate buttercream and nuts . . ."

Sam looked at her, trying to convey *If you think I'm starting to bake at this point on Sunday evening, think again.* But what came out was, "Dark ganache frosting, no nuts, and you've got it." She'd remembered that there was an extra half-pan of them in the fridge at the bakery.

"I'll do dishes . . ."

"Okay, I'll go get the dessert." Sam gathered their bowls and set them in the kitchen sink on the way out.

She pulled her Silverado pickup into the alley. The street light was still out and she located her key by the bakery's porch light, which she'd begun leaving on. The brownies were in the fridge, protected from drying out by a foil cover and she picked up the entire pan.

When she locked the back door and turned around, a man stood beside her truck.

Chapter 34

S am let out a small yelp and nearly dropped the pan.

"Hello, Ms Sweet."

"Deputy Waters? What are you doing here?" *Did Beau send him over?*

He wore black jeans and T-shirt and a black jacket with the sleeves pushed up. The porch light showed that his normally neat hair hung limply across his forehead and he held a nightstick, rhythmically slapping it against the palm of his left hand. A circular tattoo on his forearm flexed with each swing of the stick.

"I saw your truck. Thought the sheriff might be here with you," he said. He seemed agitated. His eyes darted up and down the alley. Sam's gaze followed. She didn't see another vehicle.

"No, I haven't seen him since this morning," Sam said.

She'd locked the door already, and her mind zipped through the possibilities. Her keys were in her coat pocket, her cell phone at home. All help was out of reach. "Did you try calling him?"

"He's not at the office." Waters stepped forward. "I heard that a bunch of arrests went down this afternoon."

Sam kept her expression neutral. "He's probably busy with that, then." She walked down the two steps to the surface of the alley. "You could call his cell phone."

His face screwed up in a scowl. "I'm not gonna handle this on the phone," he said. "He's got a friend of mine. I can't ignore that."

What? You're an officer of the law. Why would you side against your boss?

But what she said was, "Really? Who's your friend?" As she talked she moved subtly, keeping her distance from the crazy deputy and his nightstick, trying to get closer to her truck without being obvious about it. Beau and Jonathan must have worked all afternoon, setting up the arrests in Taos and Albuquerque quickly.

"Javier. We go way back, to school."

For the first time, Sam saw the hard edge to the deputy, the tough punk he might have been, or wanted to be.

"Why did you choose law enforcement, Denny?"

"What do you mean?"

"With friends like Javier it just doesn't seem like something you'd be interested in, you know."

"I *always* wanted to do this!" he shouted. "Tito and Jimmy and those guys. I wanted them to be *my* friends."

Sam froze in place. His outburst startled her. *Go carefully here. This guy is unbalanced.* "You all knew each other in school?"

"Yeah. Me and Jimmy and Tito. Javier, even. He was in the group for awhile."

She saw the history of these guys unfolding. Young kids, elementary school, all buddies. By high school there'd been some rifts, a little fighting. Javier and some of the others would start getting caught up in gangs and drugs. Tito and Jimmy went the straight path—did their military service, stayed on the right side of the law. And there was Denny Waters, stuck in the middle, not really fitting with either group. And instead of leaving his small hometown for an education and a new start somewhere else he hung around, resenting the others' successes. Never quite a bad guy, but never really reaching the echelons of the good guys either.

"So, I'm curious about your tattoo," Sam said, tilting her head toward his arm.

He lowered the nightstick and held out the arm with the emblem. The second his attention went to the inked piece of art, Sam swung the baking pan toward his head. The edge of it caught him squarely in the temple and he staggered back a few steps, dropping the nightstick. She ran for her truck, fumbling in her pocket for the keyfob opener.

She pressed the button and reached for the door handle at the same time. Waters had recovered and was circling the back of the pickup. She yanked the door open, dove inside and groped for the lock, finding it just as he got his hand on the handle. She scrambled across the center console and thrust the key into the ignition. His nightstick came up, ready to bash her window. Sam landed in her seat, cranked the key and the truck roared to life. She jammed it in gear and screeched away, leaving the deputy staggering.

Her heartbeat had slowed a little by the time she got home. She blew out a shaky breath and dashed inside. She had to let Beau know about this.

"About time," Kelly called out from the living room. "I'm dying for those brownies."

"Well, there's been a little problem with that." Sam heard the tremor in her own voice as she picked up the phone to call Beau.

"Mom? You okay?" Kelly peeked around the edge of the wall.

Sam nodded. "Beau. I'm glad I found you. Denny Waters just threatened me."

"*What?*" Kelly and Beau said it at the same time, a stereo moment in Sam's ears.

"At the bakery. Five minutes ago. I don't know where he is now, but you need to get him off the streets. The guy is unbalanced." She knew that she sounded like a shrew, demanding of him that way, but the words came anyway.

"Darlin', where are you now?" When she told him, he said, "Calm down. I have to wind down something here but I can be there in fifteen minutes. Lock yourselves in and I'll deal with this."

Kelly was staring at her from the living room doorway, but Sam shook her head. "I'll have to repeat it all for Beau anyway. You can hear the story then." She turned on the tap and filled a glass with water.

An hour later she'd recounted the incident, along with everything Waters had told her about his ties with both Tito and Espinosa. Beau made some calls, got his other deputies who'd been called in along with a group of State Police officers to make the earlier arrests, and told them to find Waters and bring him in.

"I'll need for you to make a statement at the office," he told Sam. "Either tonight or in the morning."

"I'll come now," she said. "It will be fresher in my mind, plus I doubt I'll sleep. Repetition will help get it out of my system."

She turned to Kelly. "Keep the doors locked, in case he comes here looking for me."

Kelly's eyes went wide.

"Maybe you better go somewhere else. Zoë's house maybe? Or Jen's?"

But Beau's radio squawked just then and one of the deputies said he had Waters in custody.

"I'll be fine here," Kelly said. She looked comfy in her flannel pajamas, unwilling to get dressed and go elsewhere.

"Keep the doors locked," Beau said. "We're pretty sure we just caught everyone involved in this thing, but just in case."

You didn't know Waters was involved, Sam thought. "I'd rather you went to Jen's," she told Kelly.

With a little huff but no argument, Kelly called her friend and changed clothes. They left the house in a little procession, with Beau tailing in his cruiser to be sure they got to their destinations.

* * *

Sam's statement went quickly—she'd run through every harrowing second in her mind at least a dozen times already. While she talked in Beau's office with deputy Joe Gonzales, Beau was in the squad room with Denny Waters cuffed to a bench.

"I need to see if you can pick out the man who threatened you outside your shop," Joe said. "I've got a lineup ready in the interrogation room."

"I'm ready," she said. Anything to get this wrapped up. Four men stood side-by-side and she stared at them through the two-way glass. "Three of them were at the cemetery after Tito's funeral. The first one, on the left, he's the guy from the alley. Can they turn sideways?"

When they did, she recognized the row of tattoos up his neck, the profile which had flashed past her in the red low-rider on that other occasion. "Is that Espinosa?"

Joe nodded. "Thanks, Sam. You're free to go."

"I'd like to wait for Beau, if that's okay." Joe ushered her back into Beau's office where she found herself impatiently wanting to talk to him, to find out all that had happened during the afternoon.

Two hours dragged by, during which Javier Espinosa was taken away by the State Police, and when Beau came in Sam thought he looked tired.

"I can't believe Denny's connections with Espinosa didn't come up on his background check," Beau said.

He'd dismissed Joe Gonzales, and Waters was sitting in a holding cell now. Beau sat at his desk where Sam had occupied herself by doodling sketches of the symbols she remembered from Tito's code book.

"Espinosa's unsavory past has been known to us for a long time, but it was all petty stuff," he said. "He'd do a little time, get out, start over. One of those guys who's always going to be in the system. At least now, with Tito's evidence, I think we have a strong enough connection now to put him away forever. The more we question these guys, plus with the evidence from Tito, we think Rick Wells actually pulled the trigger. He knew Tito was on to him. He was beginning to panic, knew he would lose his job. Figured a random shooting in a DC park would just be chalked up as normal and would get lost in the mountains of such cases they have out there."

"It nearly did," Sam pointed out.

"Of course, Wells will lawyer up and we may never know the whole truth, although Tito's book is already revealing the depth of Wells's involvement—bribes, corruption, private deals with the cartel. Plenty of motive for him to kill Tito."

"Denny Waters told me that the local guys were all friends when they were kids—he and Javier and Tito and Jimmy McMichael. I got the feeling he was jealous that all the others formed solid friendships and left him on the outside."

"It's true. We found that they were all within a year or two of each other in school. We know that Waters was the one who tipped Espinosa that Tito was in town the weekend he disappeared. Of course, Rick Wells knew that Tito had made a lot of connections between the cartels in Mexico and the gangs in northern New Mexico. Once Tito had confirmed Espinosa and the Taos connection, Rick Wells knew it was a matter of time before his own involvement with kickbacks and bribes would come to light. That activity went way back, from the years when Wells started with the Border Patrol and then went into DEA in Arizona. He'd long ago figured out that taking money to pave the way for these guys was a lot more profitable and less dangerous than actually touching the drugs or cash shipments himself."

Beau tapped a pencil against the desk blotter, his brows pulled together hard in the middle.

"Don't beat yourself up over this, Beau," Sam said.

"A background check will reveal a lot, but not everything. Denny's connections to his childhood friends could have gotten by anyone."

He leaned forward and lowered his voice. "It's just that sometimes I feel so *new* at this. Like I'm really out of the whole loop of connections and political savvy in this town."

"You are new at it. But look at what your predecessor's record was like. He had all the connections and political savvy in the world. And it corrupted him." She met his gaze. "Stay new and fresh and open to all the possibilities. It's better than falling into the system and becoming hardened to it."

"I guess."

She stood up and walked around to his side of the desk. "It's late and I'm fading fast. I'll talk to you tomorrow?"

She kissed him on top of the head and walked out to her truck. The parking area around the county offices was well lit, but Sam didn't entirely relax until she'd made it home and locked everything up tight.

Chapter 35

Sam rushed through Monday morning's baking, getting everything started so Becky could take over when she came in at eight. Last night's session at Beau's office had gone on too late to call Marla, and she didn't dare wake her early this morning, but Sam was anxious about her friend and worried that she'd not touched base as promised on Sunday.

Once she had the first batch of breakfast items out in the displays, Sam sat at her desk and dialed Marla's number. When there was no answer, Sam looked up Diane Milton's number.

"Marla is back in the hospital," the neighbor said. "I'm afraid it doesn't look good."

Sam's heart sank.

"The past week was a lot for her to handle," Diane went

on. "She collapsed shortly after everyone left on Saturday afternoon. We called the ambulance. I'm so sorry that I didn't think to call you right then."

It didn't matter. What was done, was done. "I'll go by to see her now," Sam said.

Something told her not to wait. She gave Jen and Becky some quick assignments and left her baker's jacket on its hook.

Marla looked more ghostlike than ever, her hair lying lank and wispy against her skull, her skin showing the pallor of death. Sam gulped and pasted on a smile.

"Hey, Marla," she said softly. "I'm sorry I didn't come by sooner."

"Sam. I'm so happy to see you." Her voice came out thin, reedy. "I have news."

Sam sat in the visitor's chair and took Marla's chilly hand. She had the fleeting thought that she should have tried, one more time, to bring some of the box's magic with her.

"Those young people, the ones with the daughter Jolie's age?"

Sam nodded.

"They've asked if Jolie might come live with them. They would raise her and even adopt her if I agree. I didn't know what to think."

Sam pictured Jimmy and Callie McMichael, who seemed so stable and happy. "Tito thought a lot of Jimmy. He trusted Jimmy with some very important things." She started on the story, telling Marla about Tito's bank accounts and giving the gist of his DEA work. "Tito wanted to get some really bad people put away. He was a real patriot."

Marla's gaze traveled past Sam, to the doorway of the room. "Hi, baby," she said.

Sam turned to see that Jolie was standing in the doorway with Jimmy and Callie McMichael. They greeted Sam. Jolie walked to her grandmother's bedside and ran her hand down the length of the blanket, tucking it closer to Marla's emaciated legs.

"Jolie spent the night with Taylor," Jimmy said. "We've been talking about the idea of—"

"Marla told me. What does Jolie think of it?"

"I'm standing right here," the girl said.

"I'm sorry. That was rude of me not to ask you directly. So, what do you think?"

"I never really knew Taylor all that much. But I think we could get along."

Jolie looked at her grandmother, seeing far more, Sam realized, than any of the rest of them did. She'd lived with this woman nearly her entire life. She surely remembered Marla as a vibrant, healthy woman who'd seen her through the loss of both parents, had taken her to her first day of school, who'd watched her grow from toddler to adolescent. Who would not be there for her teen years, her college days or to witness her marriage and children. Sam swallowed hard against the lump in her throat.

"I think it's a good idea," Jolie said.

Marla's smile was sad to see—the combination of wistfulness, relief and pain. "I do too," she said.

Jimmy and Callie wore warm smiles. Suddenly, to Sam, this seemed like exactly the right answer.

Jimmy cleared his throat. "We brought papers. I hope you don't mind that we asked our attorney to write them up— It just seemed like maybe we should . . . do this soon."

Sam edged to the far wall while Jimmy read the words aloud to Marla.

"I want to add one thing," the older woman said when he'd finished. "Tito left some money. It should be used for Jolie, for her schooling and such. Is it okay if I write that on here?"

Callie pressed the buttons to raise the bed and wheeled the portable table into position. Marla accepted a pen and worked laboriously for several minutes to write out what she wanted to say. Callie found two nurses to act as witnesses. At the end, Marla signed the line Jimmy indicated to her and the witnesses added their signatures. When it was all finished, she slumped back into the nest of pillows.

"Jolie, come here. Come talk to grandma for a minute."

Sam had the sudden, unshakable knowledge that this was goodbye. She motioned to the McMichaels's and the three of them stepped out of the room. Four or five minutes passed before Jolie came out to the hallway.

"She wants to see you, Ms Sweet."

Sam looked at Jimmy and Callie. A silent message passed between them, something Sam couldn't even voice. A prayer of sorts, to care for the little girl. The two adults took Jolie's hands.

When Sam walked into Marla's room again, her friend had stopped breathing. She blinked her stinging eyes and sent out a little prayer that Marla rest peacefully.

Chapter 36

Five days after her son's funeral, Marla Fresques's casket was lowered into the ground beside him. Tight green clusters—the first of the spring crocus—poked through the bare earth. Sam and Beau stood among the small group of friends and neighbors. Jimmy and Callie McMichael stood with their two daughters, Taylor and Jolie.

Beau squeezed her hand. "Take a minute, if you want to," he whispered as the priest finished the final prayer.

As if the others understood, everyone else moved aside as Sam approached Jolie.

"They were wonderful people," Sam said, "your parents and your grandmother. You'll always remember them that way, won't you?"

"I knew this day was coming," Jolie said matter-of-factly. "For a long time she was sicker than she wanted to let on. My grandmother believed Dad would come back, but I knew it would end this way."

"Really?"

"I never knew what good friends my dad and Mr. McMichael were, but we've talked a lot in the past couple of days. They care for me. I can appreciate what they are doing for me. I can handle it. "

Sam believed her. This adolescent girl had endured more than many adults.

"I've got plans, Ms Sweet. I'll keep up my grades in school and I'll get into a good college. I'll be an engineer, maybe design big buildings. Something fabulous like they have in Dubai."

Sam's throat closed when she tried to respond. Jolie reached out and took her hand.

"Really. Don't worry about me."

Sam squeezed her hand and smiled. "You are truly someone special. You'll be a strong woman one day. What am I saying? You're strong right now. Stay in touch, okay?"

She watched Jolie walk back to her new family and the four of them get into their car. Beau appeared at her side.

Across the way, Iris's headstone caught Sam's attention and they moved toward it.

"Three funerals in less than two months," she said. "It's been a rough winter, hasn't it?"

He nodded and put a strong arm around her shoulders. "You okay?" he asked.

"I tried to save them, Beau. I tried so hard and it didn't work." She blurted out the whole truth, the ways in which the magic box had empowered her, energized her to accomplish so much with her business, and how it was the box's power that allowed her to see things, which in the past had helped solve his cases. "It nearly wiped me out, honey, trying to give that healing energy to Marla last week. I wanted to do more but . . ."

If he had questions, he saved them. He simply pulled her close and wrapped her in his reassuring warmth.

They walked out of the cemetery together. He took her to his house and to his bedroom, where they spent the afternoon forgetting the last few days.

Late afternoon light cast stripes on the log walls, turning them golden, when Sam awoke from the luxury of their post-coital nap. She stared at Beau, asleep with the innocence of a little boy—his head on the pillow and the light sparkling off the curls that were forming as his hair grew out from its last haircut. This could be her life—forever.

She slipped from under the sheet and took a quick shower, wrapping herself in her own robe this time. Downstairs, she made a cup of tea and stood at the windows that faced the wide pasture beyond. Both dogs lay on the wooden deck, flat on their sides, at ease with the world. So much had happened in recent months, since the day she'd met this wonderful man.

The sun went behind the trees at the western edge of the land and she felt him beside her. He smelled of piñon soap and his damp hair brushed her cheek when he bent to kiss her neck.

"I still want that 'to have and to hold' part," he murmured in her ear.

She turned to look him in the eye. "What about Felicia? Will she be back?"

He chuckled. "I heard an interesting rumor a couple days ago."

She tilted her head.

"One of the duty officers was gabbing on the phone with a friend who dated this guitar player, a guy who plays romantic songs in restaurants around town. Well, the story is that the guitar player dumped his regular girlfriend, fell madly in love with a striking redhead, and that they'd eloped to Vegas."

"Felicia?" Sam gave a silent mental cheer. She'd forgotten about her delivery of the extra-strength special chocolates to the restaurant.

His grin widened and he nodded. "She's gone—I hope forever."

Then a wave of uncertainty. "Beau, I love you. I just wish I knew what other surprises lurk out there."

"Samantha, I hope there are always surprises. I don't want us to ever get tired of each other, to become so predictable that we're bored together."

She started to open her mouth, but he held up a hand.

"I love you. I will always love you. Just know that." His gentle hands squeezed her shoulders before he turned to go into the kitchen.

She stepped out to the back deck. The dogs raced past her to get inside for their dinner and she pulled the robe more tightly across her chest. The evening was chilly but she felt a tiny hint of warmth in the air. Maybe spring really would come a little early this year.

Discover all these books by Connie Shelton

Connie Shelton is the #1 bestselling author of more than two dozen books, both fiction and non-fiction. Her Charlie Parker mysteries and the newer Samantha Sweet series are both set in her home state of New Mexico. She and her husband, guitarist Dan Shelton, live in New Mexico with their two dogs.

Follow Connie on Facebook and Twitter
Sign up for Connie's free email mystery newsletter at
www.connieshelton.com

Contact by email: connie@connieshelton.com